MOUNT SUBASIO

A LEGEND OF ASSISI

PRISCILLA CALDERINI

Published by Gulvin Publishing and printed by
Witley Press Ltd., Hunstanton, PE36 6AD in 2014
Reprinted in 2016

ISBN:978-0-9931566-0-1

First published and printed in 1985 by Malvern Publishing
Company Limited

First published in eBook format in 2014

INTRODUCTION

In Gina's home there is a picture, a panoramic view of Assisi; of ancient city walls, bell towers, pink and sandy yellow roof tops, the pink and white stone of old houses, churches, convents and monasteries, the narrow slits between the buildings are the medieval streets that open out into piazzas. There is the fortress-like structure of the Basilica of San Francesco down on the left and the real castle at the top of the city, a little detached from the line of the upper houses. All is in perspective against the background of Mount Subasio. But in the foreground of the picture, disproportionately large, slightly to one side and on a different plain, looking in on the city like an outsider, an observer, there is a profile self portrait of Peter, the artist. The painting is signed and dated 1939.

Immediately after Anna died, the family decided that Gina should have the painting as it was she who had volunteered to take in the baby, Francesca. Years and years later, when Francesca returned to that house, she recognized the picture with the man she had been told was her father.

This is primarily Peter's story, as he painted it— himself, Assisi and Mount Subasio. But beyond the limitations of the frame there is the Europe of 1938-39 and Assisi is made up of people and Mount Subasio is a wide open space on top of the world.

* * *

In Assisi there is a legend that the Saracens hid a piece of magnetic black stone in the People's Tower of the Piazza Comune when the tower was being built. It was a stone to hold the city's inhabitants spiritually close by it for ever, including those who wanted to leave and those who, like Franco, actually did so. Certainly Gina, Clair, Anna, Fausto and Peppe could never have survived far from the sound of the tolling of the tower bell. Their families for centuries had lived in the same houses, prayed in the same churches. The buildings of Assisi belonged to these people; the people belonged to the buildings. All their family births, marriages and deaths had taken place here within sound of that bell and generations of ancestral bones had accumulated in the little cemetery just outside the city walls.

But according to the legend, the Saracens' black stone also attracted from afar, madmen, saints and sinners. Whether mad or not, it was certain that throughout the centuries, others besides pilgrims came to worship, to do penance and ask for help at the tomb of St. Francis. There were always less pious visitors as well; people whose lives were in a void, who had no anchorage of domestic complacency, like the abandoned French woman looking for a substitute for her husband and Paolo needing a wife. Some people had no idea what they were searching for at all. Peter was looking for himself, though he didn't really know it to begin with, but for him the attraction was different. The magnet was only partially in the city of Assisi. An even stronger force was pulling him above and beyond, to the very top of Mount Subasio. He was just twenty two years old when he first felt that force, compelling him to cross the valley from Perugia, compelling him to climb the mountain.

PART I

CHAPTER 1

Peter had not planned to come to Italy at all. When he found himself there, his will, his conscience led him to no immediate destination. He spent Christmas in Rome, completely alone but not lonely. He saw so much art, felt so much history. He was there just long enough to begin to appreciate through his senses all that he had only learnt through books in the past. Roaming through the Forum, climbing the Palatine and Capitoline hills he could almost see the primitive huts of those early village settlers, the building of the first temples, wood and rough cut stone being replaced by cement mix, brick and polished marble, styles changing from the crude to the classically simple and then to the over decorated. As he could almost see, so he could almost hear the political orators outside the Senate House trying to persuade the crowds that they, and they alone, were the people that counted and the crowds preferring the Colosseum, shouting for more fierce, hungry animals and more gladiators to replace those that had already been killed. He could almost see, almost hear the city's birth, full magnificence and slow decline. He could almost smell the burning and destruction and decay when the protective walls could no longer keep out the invaders. For centuries no more unity, no more glory, all power divided amongst the quarrelling nobles. Just once in a while there came a Pope strong enough to dominate instead of being dominated, who was determined, to try at least, to make of the Rock of St. Peter an Imperial Throne.

Through the streets of Rome, through the centuries, Peter reached the Renaissance and discovered the sculpture of Michelangelo, not flat book reproductions but the original works in all their dimensions. These were for him the real attraction of Rome, more than anything else, because he was more artist than historian. When nobody was watching, Peter had to touch the soft, gentle Pietà. He had to feel through his fingers the young virgin mother with her dead son across her lap, that marble that had been polished and polished to the texture of skin. But in front of Michelangelo's live, all wise, all powerful Moses, Peter kept his hands to his sides. This statue held too much authority to allow anything so intimate as touching.

Out in the streets again he sensed the city's shallow decline, shallow rise so that the atmosphere of the present Rome was heavy with a sense of power that had none of the enlightenment of the Renaissance. The voice of Mussolini was a throw back, right back, an imitation Roman Emperor, shouting from a radio in a bar and suddenly, unexpectedly, round a corner he met a group of his black shirt thugs.

In the New Year, Peter travelled north to Florence and again it was Michelangelo's sculpture that attracted him. He walked round and round the statue of David, a virgin youth about to become a man, on the threshold of experience, a youth still innocent enough to believe that with nothing more than a sling he must be able to kill the great Goliath of iniquity. Innocent enough to believe that Right and Wrong were distinct opposing forces and that Right must surely win. The prisoners, struggling to free themselves from the marble that still gripped them were like the Spanish peasants he had known but never visualised out of the context of their history, apart from their heritage of feudal and religious submission and military regimes.

Peter had never tried sculpture himself. He was only just beginning to understand what art was all about. He visited the Uffizi Gallery and all the museums and all the churches until he had seen too much. He felt stifled by art and then he went and stood for hours on the Ponte Vecchio, watching the Arno river flow beneath, washing away the winter rains. He remembered his mother's books of poetry lying around the house in Barcelona, open where she had been reading and where Shelley had said, "If winter comes, can spring be far behind?" But he had seen the beginning of the Civil War in Spain. He knew. Even though the seasonal winter might be coming to an end there was a different type of cycle. The period of desolation had only just begun.

When he was a child, his mother had made him have piano lessons and his teacher had said he had great potential and ought to become a concert pianist. Then in England his uncle had insisted he could and should become an excellent horseman. In his school reports after one term he was a potential cricketer, after another a budding mathematician and then he had the makings of a Wimbledon tennis champion. Maybe it was all true. The development of any potential was only a question of Will and Talent and Opportunity working together. His father had made him go to Oxford and he had chosen to study history but the only potential he had ever really wanted to develop was that of his art. Now was the time when he could be doing so. If he had the time. If only he could find his sense of direction and could decide what his own style should be.

In the pensione where he was staying, he was told. "If you are so interested in history, in Italy's art, if you are an artist yourself, you must go to Assisi to the Basilica of San Francesco and then, perhaps, you'll understand how it was possible for the Renaissance to develop. You'll find your inspiration there."

Peter knew, without looking on a map, that to go to Assisi he would have to pass through Perugia. He had been putting off going there ever since he had landed in Naples. He did not want to deliver his letter of introduction to any domineering old Contessa, nor be obliged to give her his sketch of the Spanish peasant girl and her baby.

For four more months, until the warmer weather came, he stayed on in Florence and then in May, early one morning, he caught the train to Perugia. He checked into a pensione not very different from the one he had been staying in before, left his few belongings and began walking to get the feel of this new city, new to him but actually centuries older than Florence, perhaps as old or older than Rome itself. He went up to the central piazza, to the fountain and then down, circling the lower girdle until he came out into the open space in front of the University for Foreign Students and looked up at the massive wall and the vast North Entrance to the ancient city that the Etruscans had built more than a century before Christ. He looked up at the huge blocks of stone built one on top of the other without any cement between them and at the great rounded arch with the sculptured shields, the symbols of war and of defence.

He had read a guide book of the region of Umbria on his way down in the train. Who were the Etruscans? What were their origins? Were they native to Italy? Had some of them come overland or by sea from Lydia, from somewhere near Troy and before or after Helen? Or were they part of one of those great mythological nations from even farther away in the East? Had aristocrats and slaves lived here or a population of bourgeois merchants, independent farmers in the countryside around? How much of their decorative art came second hand from the Greeks? How much of their engineering knowledge did they pass on to the Romans?

He could enrol right now in this University for Foreign Students, not to learn the Italian language for he was already speaking that without too much difficulty, but to attend the lectures on Italian culture and history and listen to the theories of the Etruscologists. He could try to do a course at the Accademy of Belle Arti. But No.

The Etruscans believed in Destiny. It could sometimes be postponed but it would get you in the end whether individual, city or nation.

Peter began climbing the steps that would lead him to the highest part of Perugia above the Etruscan arch itself. He reached the top. There were houses up here too, and piazzas. The Etruscan wall was the supporting foundation of the higher level. And below? He turned to look beneath him at the roof tops. The streets were dark clefts. It was almost impossible to see the windows of the houses, the lives within were enclosed as though in boxes with irregular tiled lids on them. The lives of the humans were hidden but up here, all around him, swooping and screeching down over those roof tops were swallows. No, not swallows, for these had no white breasts. They were swifts, dominating the air, squadrons of screeching, menacing black shirt Fascists such as he had seen in Rome when he had come round that corner too quickly near Piazza Venezia after one of Mussolini's speeches.

He had seen no political demonstrations whilst he was in Florence, and he had not been in Perugia long enough to feel any atmosphere. If he had never seen a fascist uniform, he would never have made a comparison between birds in search of food for their nestlings and any kind of menace.

He looked beyond the roof tops, closed his ears to the noise of the swifts and then it was that he saw Assisi. From this distance it was just a triangle of grey stone on the far side of the valley on the lower slopes of Mount Subasio. It must be Assisi. It was in the right direction. He had read about it too in his guide book, the birth place of St. Francis, the lover of animals. There was the famous Basilica built in his honour that they had told him in Florence he must go to see. He could go tomorrow or the next day, after he had been to visit the Contessa for there was nothing else he had to do. The swifts were still screaming in spite of his concentration on Assisi. St. Francis would have humbled them and have sent them away to sing his messages of peace throughout the world.

That distant patch of grey stone was more than a suggestion. Rome and Florence, the Renaissance artists, he had known why he had wanted to see these. He had no idea that the mountain existed or why he should feel compelled to go there. He went on gazing for a while and then, as though hypnotized, he walked down the steps he had previously climbed to this vantage point. He did not go towards the centre of Perugia nor towards the pensione where he had left his belongings. He looked for no sign posts marked Assisi. He took the first road that seemed to lead in the right direction, then left it and cut across country. He forded a shallow river not knowing it was the upper reaches of the Tiber that ran on down from here through Rome. He continued along a lane, past a peasant farmer whose bare feet were as horny as the hooves of the white oxen he was leading. A woman crouching in the rough grass between olive trees looked up as he passed. Then she went back to her searching for just those particular weeds that could be eaten as salad, which she cut out by the roots with a knife and collected into her apron. He never deviated from the right direction but passed through a yard with children scattering and geese chasing him. He went on walking. He had no idea how long it took him to get to Assisi but when he reached the city he walked straight past the Basilica and on up through the Piazza Comune, past the People's Tower and the pagan temple of Minerva, via San Rufino, past the Cathedral, beyond the outer walls of the city, up the mountain itself.

It was already dark and there were shadows and rustlings amongst the pines until he came out above the tree line. There was no more steep climbing for he had reached a great rolling plain on top of the world. There was no bracken or heather here to entangle his feet as there had been on the Longmynd, only short grass and a few thistles.

He spent the rest of the night lying on his back with his arms behind his head, staring at the sky. He was too cold and too hungry to sleep, he had eaten nothing since early morning. He had no extra covering with him, but that night it did not matter. He thought of the farm at the foot of the Longmynd in Shropshire, of school, Oxford, the house in Barcelona, of Rome and Florence. He had never been at home in any of these places but now he knew, here on the top of Mount Subasio, he belonged.

CHAPTER 2

The first Italian Peter had learnt had been words describing food. The Italians talked about it all the time, in the train, in the streets, in the shops, of what they had eaten yesterday and of what they hoped to eat tomorrow. Only the need for food brought Peter down off Mount Subasio the next day and, when he realised how little money he had left to buy it, made him send a cable to his bank in Oxford. Then his conscience made him send a cable to his Aunt Sarah in Shropshire telling her to forward his address, care of the post office in Assisi, to his parents in Barcelona. From Italy it was possible to communicate with England still but not with Republican Spain.

He returned to Perugia to collect his haversack and blanket and whilst there his conscience made him decide to pay his debt, and fulfil his promise to visit Old Tagliatelle's mother, the Contessa.

She lived in a great eighteenth century palace house with blackened wooden doors that led into a vast, bare, high-ceiling entrance hall. When it was all one home, there must have been carpets and tapestries and statues. He climbed the wide, crumbling stone staircase to the apartments above. The Contessa had kept only the top floor for herself. He rang and a woman he thought at first was a servant answered. He pushed Old Tagliatelle's letter and the rolled up sketch into her hand, mumbled an explanation she could not have heard properly and turned, wanting to run down the stairs and away.

"You're the English boy. You've got to see my mother, she's been waiting and waiting for you."

He had to follow the woman down a long, polished marble corridor. The walls on either side were covered with portraits in gold frames. A diamond sparkling chandelier reflected an incredibly brilliant daylight from the open windows at the end.

"Wait." The woman went into a room on the right. "Mamma, he's here." She spoke into the darkness. All Peter could see of the room from where he was standing were the shadows of furniture. He walked down to the end of the corridor. Across the roof tops of Perugia, across the valley, he could see Assisi and Mount Subasio. He had to get back there.

When he was called into the Contessa's room the shutters had been partially opened, enough to let in light but no view. Her world was restricted to her possessions. All the surfaces of antique tables, bookcases, desks, stools, the piano, were covered with precious little nick nacks and ornaments. There were hundreds of books, a pile of them on the floor by her side, but she could not have been reading in the darkness. She was sitting in an arm chair, dressed completely in black, her white hair beautifully combed, perfectly in order, as though she had been posing to have her own portrait painted, ready to join those of her dead ancestors out in the corridor.

"So you are the potentially great artist?" She held out her hand. Perhaps she expected him to kiss it. He took it for a moment and then she waved him to sit down opposite her. "What do you usually drink at this time of the day? Coffee? Cognac?"

"Nothing, really, thank you."

"Battista, go and get two coffees. Bring the bottle of cognac as well. Bring a cup of coffee for yourself if you want one."

Peter saw Battista's face clearly as she turned to leave the room; it was exactly like Old Tagliatelle's, her movement too. Old Tagliatelle had not seemed like a soldier at all but a funny little hypochondriac intellectual spinster. Perhaps he and his sister were twins.

The conversation began formally. The Contessa spoke English perfectly, almost without an accent. "My son wrote to me about you. We were expecting you before this."

"I'm sorry, I should have come before."

"It doesn't matter. The letter you've just brought has nothing in it different from the one we already received. My family have always been great admirers of the British. Maybe my son told you? I used to take the children to England for at least a month every year. We used to love London and the theatre. I am probably the only Italian living today who will admit that Shakespeare was a greater writer than Dante. I have the complete works of Shakespeare. I read them and re-read them. Do you like the theatre?"

"Sometimes. I haven't had much opportunity to go in England."

"I understand you met my son in some village in Spain."

Battista returned with a silver tray and her mother made her put it down and pour Peter a tiny cup of black coffee.

11

"What about a lacing of cognac, the way my son used to like it? It's the greatest pick me up in the world. I'm going to have it that way myself."

He was handed the small porcelain cup, almost too delicate to hold, with too little in it to sip slowly. If only his mother could see him now, sitting on the edge of his chair being polite!

"Yes, I met your son in Spain. It was rather a strange encounter."

"In his letter he said you had great potential as an artist, an exceptional talent."

"He was very complimentary, but I still have a lot to learn."

"Of course. If you are any good you'll go on learning for the rest of your life. He saved your life, didn't he?"

"In a way. He gave me the alternative of being shot as a spy or coming to Italy to study art."

"I like that. That sounds just like him. He wanted me to help you. But he didn't know how much things have changed here. Our friends, the people I used to know, to whom I could have introduced you have either left the country or they are in prison or confinement somewhere; or they are very quietly trying to carry on their ordinary lives without being noticed, certainly not wanting to appear to know too many foreigners from countries that disapprove of our government's actions."

"Please, I never wanted to go to formal classes. Your son told me, the whole of Italy is a school of art."

"And he was right. You're intelligent. Don't be afraid to copy the old Masters until you have understood their techniques and can choose from their styles as much as you wish to assimilate into your own. All great artists are humble enough to learn from the past."

"Have you looked at my sketch?"

"Not yet. Battista will take the cups away and then hold it up for me. Please go and open the shutters a little more."

He waited in silence for her verdict. It was crazy. But nothing was rational, nothing impossible. When the wounded had been put ashore in Naples, he had found himself free, a tourist who could travel to any place he liked, look down on the world from the top of Mount Subasio. Now he found himself here like an artist of the Renaissance introduced to a new patron. Only this patron had lost her Court and wouldn't be able to help him in any way at all.

"Is this all you've got to show me?"

"It's all I've brought with me. Your son wanted me to give it to you as a present from himself."

"He always did have a good eye. Of course he was right about you. Battista, I want this framed. It is the most traditional and yet the most modern, the most beautiful Madonna and Child I've ever seen, at least from any artist who has not yet established a name for himself. I want to have it in my bedroom, over the bed." Her voice had changed. "He always knew what I liked. He was a good boy really."

Now that there was more light from the window Peter could see her face, her eyes and all those black mourning clothes. He had to ask. "Have you heard from your son recently?"

"You didn't know then? Naturally. Who could have told you?"

Battista motioned to Peter from behind her mother's chair.

"The day after we received his letter telling us you'd be coming, we received the official communication. We were told he and his boys died like heroes."

"I'm sorry. I'm so sorry." Peter stood up. He didn't know what else to say. "I'm so sorry."

"He died doing what he thought was his duty."

"Of course."

The Contessa held out her hand to him. "I know what the British think about Italy, about our going into Ethiopia and intervening in Spain; but there is something you ought to know. When Mussolini first came to power many of us believed he was what our country needed. We didn't approve of his methods always but he brought discipline. He started reforms that the country needed. Do you remember, Battista? The trains began to run on time, the post office became efficient, people were working, children were going to school." She was squeezing Peter's hand, not realizing how hard. "It is only now that some of us are beginning to understand the disaster that he's leading us to. Who knows how long you'll be allowed to stay in this country or how much time you have? Don't waste this opportunity, for my son's sake." She released his hand.

Battista showed him to the door. "Come back and see her. Please come back and see her."

He meant to, very soon, but he did not; at least not until it was too late. Once his money came through he travelled again, back to Rome and Florence. He discovered Urbino and the painting of Piero della Francesca and that led him to Arezzo. He knew he should go on to Sansepolcro to see

Piero's Resurrection but he did not immediately. He kept postponing the occasion as he kept postponing his return visit to the Contessa. The magnetism of Mount Subasio was too strong for him.

He was becoming more and more a vagabond. When he was in any of the cities he still slept under a roof but he was careless of his appearance and preferred to shun people and their conventions. He never reached Venice. Every few days, after a week at the most, he returned to Assisi and climbed up above the town to sleep out in the open on top of Mount Subasio.

CHAPTER 3

The weather held fine until mid August, and then there was the first big storm of the year. Great clouds came rolling down off Mount Subasio, black, swirling, rumbling. They touched the castle, smothered and obliterated it and then moved on down to the Basilica of San Francesco and almost reached San Pietro before a wind from the valley drove them back up the mountain. The clouds retreated, shooting lightning, getting denser, gathering force. The wind from the valley was the forerunner of two other storms, one that came down from Perugia, one up from Spoleto and the direction of Rome. These were not opposing forces but allies. The two masses of cloud seethed into each other, turning, swirling, moving hugely and heavily towards Mount Subasio. But the clouds that had previously retreated up the mountain had become more compact and were ready now, more furious in tone than those of the valley and they returned, tumbling, not rumbling but roaring back over the upper city wall, the castle, Via Capobove, Via Santa Rosa, the Roman temple of Minerva and the Piazza Comune. The two storms met and burst each other apart right there over the centre of the city. Peter was sheltering in the porch of the temple of Minerva at the time.

The storm was nothing unusual for Assisi. Through all the city's history of attacks by enemy soldiers and internal bloody feuds, when wolves were waiting beneath the walls for the bodies, when there were earthquakes and plague, the noise of those battles overhead in the sky had been more violent and dramatic than anything that was happening on earth. The storms must have had something to do with the lie of the mountains whose clefts and valleys caused contrasting air currents. Or maybe it was that black stone in the Peoples' Tower attracting the electricity in the atmosphere.

This time, as so often in the past, it was all over quickly. The air was cleared and Peter moved out from his shelter and down towards the lower part of town. Suddenly, between the houses, he could see for miles across the valley. Then, while the streets were still running with red brown, muddy water the colour of blood, the sun came out and there was a rainbow stretching from Subasio right across to the far distant mountains.

Paolo arrived in Assisi just after the storm. He saw the rainbow and thought it was a good omen for himself. He had come with a purpose. He had a suitcase in his hand and a raincoat over his arm. His shoes were too thin and too well polished. He stepped fastidiously across the wet cobbles, his feet slipping into the rivulets that ran between them,splashing up his trouser legs. He intended staying for the whole two weeks of his annual leave. He calculated that in that time he could see and choose a girl and make the necessary enquiries about her. He would approach her parents before leaving again for Rome.

He walked under the arch of San Pietro, up Via Fontebella. There were one or two tourist shops in the little ground floor basements beneath the houses. The embroidered blouses and tableclothes and scarves had been hastily gathered in before the storm and now were being hung out again. On either side of the entrances the shelves of ceramics and wrought iron and polished copper and bronze dripped still.

He stopped to handle a tray of rosaries. Casually he looked into the shop itself. It was very dark compared to the brilliant sunshine outside but he could dimly make out the figure of a girl sitting behind a counter in the back. His search for a wife had begun from the moment he stepped off the coach. He could not afford to neglect any opportunity of looking into a girl's face.

He entered the shop holding a rosary in his hand.

The girl looked up and he felt a sudden shock; his legs felt as though they could not support him and that he would fall to his knees. His eyes became accustomed to the dim light and confirmed that he was looking at a girl as beautiful as the Madonna herself. He held out his cupped hands with the rosary in them.

The girl put the embroidery she had been working on on top of the counter and came round to him.

"Do you want to know how much that costs?" she said. He nodded.

She moved her embroidery so that she could open the glass-topped counter. "We have better ones. Look. The prices are all marked on them."

"No, no. This is quite good enough." He dug into his pocket for small change.

"What about some other little presents, a blouse for your wife or . . .?"

"No, no. No, no. I only wanted this." He handed her the money.

"Shall I wrap it for you?"

"No, no. There's no need." He hesitated, looking at her. She was like a Raphael Madonna, that reproduction his mother had hung above his bed when he was a child, that was still there, calm, unemotional, perfect, that his mother had said would protect him from all evil. There was no ring on this girl's finger. He smiled, his whole face smiled, but not his eyes.

He left the shop and stood outside, accustoming himself to the sunlight. He turned and took his bearings in the street, almost opposite a grocery shop, a little lower than the Hotel Giotto. He did not want to forget this place. He fingered the rosary in his pocket. It would be his first present to her. He would give it to her before he left Assisi, as a momento of their first meeting. If his enquiries proved that she was as good as she was beautiful then he need look no further. God had guided his thoughts to Assisi, his footsteps up this very street, his eyes into this very shop with no time wasted.

He peered into the dimness and saw her, once again seated, her head bent over her embroidery.

Whilst this meeting took place, farther up Via Fontebella, Peter was sitting perched on the edge of the fountain from which the street derived its name. He was painting. He was wearing torn trousers, a ragged check shirt and sandals that had their straps broken and were tied up with string. He was unshaven and his hair was too long. Mussolini would never have approved of his appearance. There was a crowd of children milling round him, peering at his painting, giggling.

Two refined English lady tourists came down the street towards him. They too were tempted to go closer; they too had to satisfy their curiosity. They pretended to glance quickly, casually. Horrified and embarrassed, they remained fixed for a moment then moved a little away but not out of earshot. They wanted him to know of their disapproval.

"Oh dear, even here—this terrible modern Socialist youth—this uncouth generation."

"It's creeping in everywhere—it's creeping in on us."

"But it can't have got Assisi yet."

"I'd thought we were safe here but did you see what he was painting?"

"Those children, naked, with haloes on their heads and forked tails, their little you-know-whats were pulled back between their legs into forked tails."

"They were ordinary children, properly clothed, from decent homes. If their parents could see how he's depicting them."

"Botticelli painted naked children."

"Round and pink and innocent."

"But this young man is giving them haloes and then pulling out their—oh dear—long and vicious forked tails."

"A scandal, a blasphemy. He can't be an Italian. If he's English, I'll die of shame."

Peter overheard and looked up and shouted. "He's English alright. Please die. I need a couple of coffins in a corner."

"Oh really, oh really." The two ladies hurried on and he put them in his painting, bare, black, shrivelled breasts showing through ragged nun's robes, their faces and heads, centuries old skeletons, skin and bone, hair and teeth.

The children were silent and staring.

He balanced up the picture with three live, fat monks in the opposite corner.

There were not only children watching now but other tourists and local men who had come up quietly around him, fascinated.

He looked up and saw them smiling. With his brush he suddenly daubed a huge cross in the centre of his painting.

"Isn't that what you wanted?" he said.

He stood and rolled up his painting, still wet, and shoved it under his arm together with the board it had been pinned on. He picked up the haversack with the rolled blanket tied to it, that he had rested on the edge of the fountain, and heaved it all onto his back. Then he pushed his way through the crowd that had gathered. Some of the children tried to follow him but he shoo-ed them away. The men shook their heads.

"Crazy, crazy."

"But what a brush."

"He can paint. He's got style. I'm no artist but I can recognize a true one."

"Anybody could recognize him as that."

"He can paint alright. He's great. Could be as great as Giotto."

"Nonsense. It's the line."

"The way he puts his ideas together, opposites, impossibles."

"Modern."

"Rubbish."

"No. It's true."

"He's powerful."

"Capturing a spirit."

"What spirit?"

Peter sniffed his way up a street, round a corner and found what he was looking for. In England you followed your nose for fish and chips; in Spain it was chips without the fish; in Italy it was pizza. He bought himself a whole tray. He made them wrap the pizza in newspaper after the brown paper to stop the oil and tomato from oozing out. Then he shoved it up under his arm against his painting, and laden, but not staggering because he was a strong young man, he stalked off, climbing through the upper streets of Assisi towards the mountain.

Peter and Paolo never met though they nearly did that day. Clair was to be the only link between them.

CHAPTER 4

A group of local boys sat outside the cafe opposite the temple of Minerva in the Piazza Comune. They were good looking, virile, young men toughened from working as stone cutters in the quarries or climbing over roof tops and rubble as builders.

It was late evening, too hot and too early for bed. There was nothing to do but watch the people passing in the Piazza.

The food shops were selling their last cheeses, slices of salami, sardines and then closing for the brief night. Heavy metal shutters, like garage doors were being pulled down, clanging in the silences.

Clair came up from Via Fontebella and crossed the Piazza, going home.

"She must be the most beautiful girl in Assisi this year."

"And the stupidest."

"Do you remember when we were in elementary school together we used to kiss her just to hear her squeal?"

"She was fat then."

"She'll run to fat again. Like her mother."

"But just at the moment she's beautiful. You can't deny she's beautiful."

"And she hasn't got a fiancé. How old is she?"

"She must be the same age as ourselves. She must be twenty at least."

"I thought you were interested in her once. She wouldn't even speak to you."

"Nor to the fishmonger or that school teacher from Santa Maria or Enzo the policeman."

"She'll end up in a convent."

"Last year she had these one day dates up on the path towards the castle behind her mother's house. She still squealed if anyone tried to kiss her."

"How do you know?"

"When he can't get a girl himself, he gets his thrills by proxy. He's a peeping Tom like Fausto."

"Sh! Fausto's at the next table."

"It's not true anyway."

"How do you know she squealed then?"

"I bet she did."

"She'd never dare go up towards the castle alone with a man. The only place I've ever seen her walking with a boy is out along the main road beyond Santa Chiara."

"We know what she's like, but have you seen how the tourists can't stop staring at her?"

"Maybe she'll marry some foreigner. They don't all try to kiss a girl straight off."

"Who told you?"

"They don't. The Anglo Saxon ones don't. They're better educated."

"That's what you think."

"They'd give up before ever they got started. She wouldn't even let one hold her hand. And she can't talk."

"What can you say in a foreign language?"

"The essential words."

"And if the foreign boy could speak Italian fluently he still wouldn't get anywhere with her because she's so stupid."

"She can read and write."

"You mean she learnt at school. But she's probably forgotten by now. If you told her England, America and Australia were islands on the moon, she'd believe you. She's never been out of Assisi without her mother, never been farther than Perugia in her life."

"So where have you been?"

"Nowhere yet but I'm going."

"Where? Ethiopia. You're too late. Spain?"

"You don't have to go out into the world to know it nowadays. It's coming in on you all the time."

"It hasn't got into Assisi yet."

"Oh yes it has. Just listen to the radio and the music and the marching and the shouting."

"It hasn't touched our glorious, cretinous cousin Clair yet."

"Talking about foreigners, did you see that artist again today?"

"With the broken sandals and torn trousers and long hair?"

"Assisi always attracts the craziest characters."

"This one isn't so crazy."

"My uncle says he's been asking in the post office if there were letters for him from England or Spain."

"He speaks Spanish when he can't find the right words in Italian."

"But he's English."

"He was last seen heading up towards Mount Subasio to meditate with a roll of pornography and a couple of kilos of pizza."

"Pornography?"

"Art."

"All that pizza."

"He's no dispeptic saint."

CHAPTER 5

Clair climbed the hundred and fifty steps from the Piazza Comune up to the corner of Via Capobove and then turned right past the little fountain into Via Santa Rosa. There were another twenty five steps from street level up to the inner door of her home. The key was in the door.

She paused on the last step, a little out of breath. Her mother had been waiting for her footsteps and came and opened the door.

"What were you standing there for? Why didn't you come straight in?"

"I was just going to come in. I was resting for a moment."

"Why? Aren't you feeling well?"

"I'm alright. Only tired."

"What have you to feel tired about? You sit still all day, don't you? Never mind, don't just stand there. Come in. What do you want for supper?"

"I'm not hungry."

"You must eat. You'll lose your looks. You're pale tonight. What's happened?"

"I told you. I'm tired."

"You can't afford to lose your looks. You've still got to find a husband. What'll happen to you when I'm dead and gone if you're not married? I shan't last for ever, you know. What are you going to eat then?"

"Some salad and a piece of cheese, if I must."

"I've made some minestrone soup specially for you."

"Alright."

Her mother was out of breath just from slopping around the kitchen in her heelless slippers. She was enormous. She looked worried. She sat opposite Clair and stared at her daughter whilst she ate.

"You haven't got anybody, have you? There isn't some young man who's courting you that I know nothing about?"

Clair shook her head.

"You'd tell me if there was somebody, wouldn't you?"

"Of course. I've always told you, haven't I?"

Her mother went to the stove. "Do you want a camomile tea? You'd better and then go to bed."

Clair opened the door onto the tiny patio outside the kitchen. She stood looking up at the mountain, at the patch of deep, dense sky, at the stars. There was a slight breeze, refreshing after the thunderous heaviness of the day. It was a romantic night. A night to be up at the castle with a good, gentle prince, whose hands remained by his sides, whose lips smiled whilst he told her, not children's fables but grown-up stories of the world beyond Assisi, a world of the imagination, rich and beautiful that could never, should never, be visited.

"Come inside. You'll catch a chill," her mother called.

Clair sighed and closed the door.

"I went to the doctor's today," her mother said. "I didn't want to tell you till you'd eaten but it's serious this time. I've got blood pressure."

"You knew that already."

"But it's gone up. It's going up all the time. He says I've got to stop work and I can't eat this and I can't eat that. If I don't take care, I'll explode. That's what he said—I'd just blow up."

"He told you to go on a diet before. Has he given you any medicines?"

"He gave me a mass of bits of paper I've got to take to the chemist. If I don't work what's going to become of us?"

"I'm earning. You've got your pension."

"A lot that's bringing in, isn't it? And when winter comes and you don't go down to the shop any more?"

"I'll do dressmaking like I did last year."

"I can't even do embroidery. My eyes aren't good enough any more. The doctor says that's the blood pressure too."

"What did he say you could eat?"

"Nothing, almost nothing at all. No spaghettis or bread or potatoes or fats. I can eat all the meat and fish and cheese I want, he says. What does he think a beefsteak costs—and fish? I can eat cooked greens and lettuce."

"You like that."

"Not all the time. We'll end up like a couple of rabbits living on greens and lettuce."

"There are people worse off than you," Clair said.

"Who, for instance?"

"There's Giuseppe down at San Pietro, Rosanna's husband, the one that drives the taxi, you know, the brother-in- law of Gina and Maria and Franco."

"He hasn't got blood pressure."

"No, but he's got stomach ulcers so bad the doctor says he has to eat raw snails on an empty stomach every morning for forty days."

"I know all about that. Fausto's going to collect them for him from the mountain so they'll be fresh and lively."

"You mean it's true they slither around inside, leaving all that slime for two hours before they die?"

"Why shouldn't it be true. He didn't need to go to any doctor to be told—everybody knows about snails. And they don't cost anything, do they? Blood pressure's far more serious."

"It's not that bad."

"Isn't it? You don't know what it means being a widow, not having a son to lean on, being responsible for a daughter like you. Life's just trial and tribulation, pain and sorrow, nothing else. If you'd get married I could die in peace but I can't even do that yet."

"Mother, let's go to bed. Tomorrow get the medicines and start taking them. You'll feel better then."

"I shan't. The only thing that'll make me feel better is knowing you've got a steady young man who wants to marry you. If you don't hurry up you'll lose your looks like I keep telling you. You'll get fat like me and then nobody'll want you."

CHAPTER 6

Peter rolled himself out of his sleeping blanket and sat with his arms around his knees. It was dawn.

"Dong a dong. Dong a dong." For a moment he thought he could hear a church bell ringing for early Mass from way down in the valley, in Assisi. Then he saw a flock of sheep coming over the ridge towards him. "Dong a dong. Dong a dong." The leaders had bells round their necks.

He watched them approaching, nibbling their way towards him.

Church bells, sheep bells, staring people, these blank, woolly masticating faces. God was in man or God was outside man or God didn't exist at all. No that was last night's thought. Now it was too early in the morning—on an empty stomach.

It was cold. He rolled back into his blanket and closed his eyes. The sheep came closer, crowding around him, breathing over him. He sat up suddenly. "OOHHa." The sheep, startled, jumped back, those in front shoving against those that were still pushing from behind. He lay down but again the pressure from the back of the flock pushed the leaders closer, closer around him, almost treading on his face.

"OOHHa." He sat up, pulled his arms free of the blanket and flung them wide. The closest sheep tried to flee, those behind still pressed forward.

"Curiosity. It's brought man from the stone age, leading him to the moon, setting him aiming at the stars. It's the same bloody instinct as yours, dear brothers."

He lay down and covered his face with his arms but they wouldn't give him peace, closer and closer, breathing, nuzzling.

If he lay still long enough they'd get tired of an inanimate object—or would they trample him to death first because he smelt of human sweat?

The sheep suddenly scattered in all directions as a huge white dog bounded onto him and began licking his face. And then an old shepherd came along and prodded him with a heavy stick.

"Oh, what the hell's going on here?"

"You're not dead then?"

"Do I look as though I'm dead?"

"You looked like a corpse, yes. How was I to know you weren't one?"

"Well, I'm not, yet."

"Good morning to you then." The shepherd had none of the curiosity of his flock. He was not part of the mankind that was aiming at the stars. He was an individual on a mountain top. He walked off, following his sheep.

The dog licked Peter's face again and then raced after the shepherd. It chivied the sheep, interrupting their nibbling, keeping them moving. "Dong a dong. Dong a dong." The bells grew fainter.

When they were out of sight, Peter sat up. "God, I'm hungry," he said out aloud. He had finished the pizza the evening before. He pulled his haversack closer and unrolled his painting of the previous day. It was smeared through being rolled wet and there was a patch of oil and tomato on it. But that did not matter. He would do it again. And again and again, and again, if necessary. He knew technically he was learning, getting better every day. He had the ability to become as much a Master in this century as any of those who had worked down in the Basilica— Cimabue, Giotto, Simone Martini, Lorenzetti. But he lacked their inspiration, their certain knowledge of God, Christ, Mary Virgin and Saint Francis. Because of this belief they had become the concentrated channel of Creation, the revival of life after the Dark Ages. The Renaissance artists had been more worldly but he was not one of them either. For even in the Renaissance there was the sense of man going forward with optimism, with energy and competition in the creative arts. He did not believe in anything at all. He still did not know what his own style really was. How could you create if you did not know what to believe or who you were? He had been born into the wrong century. One that was leading towards a Dark Ages, not coming out of one.

Yet the Crucifix he had daubed in that painting down in Assisi was right there. It tied together, gave sense to the fat monks and devilish children and withered foreign females. Assisi was not of this century. It had opted out of the world way back before the Renaissance; wound a Holy cocoon around itself, gone to sleep. There were as many monks and nuns in the city as people wearing ordinary clothes. Everywhere you went you could see Crucifixes. You absorbed them. They remained printed on your eyeballs when you closed your eyes. Of Christ crucified and St. Francis and the little tabernacles on the street corners with the pictures of the Madonna that the women venerated, putting fresh flowers in front of them, blowing kisses to them every time they passed, as they must have been doing for centuries. Almost every day there was a blue or pink ribbon on some door because a boy or a girl had been born in that house. Almost every day on the walls where any news was plastered another black outlined death notice appeared of some worthy citizen who had dedicated his or her life to work and family. Life continued in Assisi but it never progressed. What then did he hope to find in Assisi—only the technique? Was that why he had not stayed down there, why he was on Mount Subasio searching for his style, searching for himself?

Peter jumped up and turned to face the sunrise. It was no longer a pale light spread across the horizon but a red glowing concentrated ball, radiating warmth. He spread out his arms, absorbing its warmth, re-awakening his whole body.

"God! Why does man have to be so hungry? Surely there must be somewhere closer than Assisi where I can find food." There was nobody to hear him. He had started talking aloud to himself. He picked up all his belongings and set off towards the ridge over which the shepherd and his flock had disappeared.

CHAPTER 7

Early in the morning, Fausto, the hunchback cripple, was the only lay person up at the Hermitage to receive Mass. He went on purpose at that hour because he knew nobody would be watching with pity or disgust as he opened his mouth of rotten teeth and stinking breath and the priest placed the Host on his tongue. He always kept his eyes tight shut as he walked to his place at the back of the little chapel and only when the wafer had completely melted did he open them. Then he had to get out fast onto the mountainside because God in Christ made flesh, condensed, imprisoned in that tiny morsel could remain down there inside him amongst the dormant worms for such a short while—God's true place was in the light of dawn on the mountain top.

Fausto collected Giuseppe's snails in the evenings. This morning, after Mass he was going to search for mushrooms.

He progressed up the mountain, using a stick, half hobbling, half hopping, moving incredibly fast. He was grotesque, like a figure from Dante's Inferno. One side of his body was strong and as virile as Peter, the artist's; the other sprouted a hump like a half formed angel's wing with no waist beneath it but a hip that stuck out at right angles and a leg that seemed too small and shrivelled to support an eight year old child. His body had all the bones distorted as though the spirit inside the cage had clutched at the bars of the ribs, dislocating shoulders and hips in an effort to get out at birth, when the spirit was strong and the bones were soft.

But his mother had known how to save his body, pressing his face against her breasts, pinching his mouth open, shoving in her nipples, forcing him to suck—for a whole year. And then feeding him on bread and olive oil and garlic—panchotta which she boiled for hours and hours very slowly over a low heat.

All his childhood his breath had smelt of garlic. He had burped and farted garlic and he never showed signs of worms as other children did. The doctor said garlic did not kill worms but it anaesthetized them. Fausto knew, while other children had defecated theirs and got clean of them, he would have his inside him, lying semi-dormant for the rest of his life. That low down pain and movement that bothered him so much as an adult was not always sex; sometimes it was those worms waking up, just enough to try to escape.

But not this morning, so soon after Mass. He had gone up to the altar as he so often did, not believing, and when he had opened his eyes the sun was stronger outside and his lips were smiling because some of its rays were within him. He started humming before he was out of the chapel. Racing up the mountain he forgot his deformities and all about his stinking body. He was singing. He was free.

He carried an old canvas bag to put the mushrooms in. He knew every patch where they might be found; patches where the grass was damper, greener, thicker, that most people would never see.

Before beginning his search he stopped to rest. He was near the top of the mountain and looking down he could see Assisi and the valley beyond Perugia and the mountains in the distance and almost, almost, he could see further than the geography right into the history of this land.

The rising sun was glinting on Lago Trasimeno more than forty kilometers away. Trasimeno, where the Roman soldiers had been massacred by Hannibal's army. Those who had not died by the sword had fallen back into the water, weighed down by their armour, disappearing for ever beneath the surface, to give life to the treacherous reeds that clung around swimmers' legs and to the fish and give a strange taste to the water.

It was said St. Francis had spent forty days of Lent fasting like Christ in the wilderness on the island in the centre of the lake.

Much closer, the sun was shining on the low hills that Francis had walked across on his way to Gubbio right up under the ridge of the Apennines. Fausto could almost see the pampered rich man's son, barefoot, naked except for a peasant's sacking tunic. On that journey Francis had tamed the wolf or the brigand, whichever it was, that had been terrifying the inhabitants of Gubbio. In those early days people were still saying that Francis had gone crazy, and did not care that already he had known how to reason with criminals, and talk to and make friends with animals.

Fausto had a way with animals too, especially with birds. In the cellar which opened onto the street below his house, where he did his wood carving, he kept canaries and abandoned fledglings and wounded creatures that the dogs had failed to discover in the shooting season.

Fausto moved the grass beneath him with his stick, going down on his knees, searching for the mushrooms.

He found them. Not pretty, pink, artificial little buttons but of all shapes and sizes, yellow, brown, ugly, dirty white, distorted as his own body. They were not poisonous, they were quite safe. The women of Assisi were not afraid to use them, instead of meat in a spaghetti sauce, or fried or roasted over an open fire where their flavour was heightened by wood smoke.

He worked his way over the ridges of Mount Subasio in the same direction that the shepherd and his flock had taken; in the same direction as Peter.

He came across them outside the shelter near the old crater called Mortaro, that people thought was an extinct volcano. The shepherds themselves had called it Mortaro because it was like a mortar without the pestle. The sheep were all clustered into one of two wire pens that led into each other. The ground beneath them was trodden free of grass, leaving only earth and dust. The shepherd was preparing to milk them.

"You could come and give a hand and get them moving," the shepherd called to Fausto. "I've nobody to help today, the wife's gone to her mother to see the kids and the dog alone's no good."

Fausto hobbled through the small opening which connected the two pens beside which the shepherd was already sitting on his three-legged stool, his buckets beside him.

Fausto passed round behind the sheep to the far side of the pen and then, using his stick, accompanied by the dog barking and worrying at their heels, he began to chivy the sheep towards the narrow opening. As the first one was shoved through by the pressure of those behind, the shepherd dropped a forked stick like the handle of a giant catapult over its neck. With his free hand he squeezed the few drops of milk out of its teats and then released it into the second pen. He did the same with the next and the next and the next. The young rams and the ewes with the flat empty udders missed the forked stick and got slapped through with a heavy hand on their backsides.

Peter had been watching, his arms around his knees. Now he searched in his haversack and took out a sketching block. he worked quickly, like a cartoonist, not doing one but a dozen sketches. He drew Fausto distinct with hump and stick and shortened leg; then the flock, a mass of rounded sausage bodies on narrow legs; then individuals, all the same and all different like humans in a crowd; then the dog, the shepherd and his forked stick and jets of milk squirting into a bucket.

Time passed. The sun rose higher, hotter. The crickets all across the mountain grew louder in their leg scraping chatter and the larks soared up and up, until invisible, only faintly adding their highest notes to the orchestra of insect sounds on earth.

Peter left the detailed work close by and focused on the winding white road up a mountain over thirty kilometers away. There was no snow on the peaks of the Apennines now but there would be in winter.

It took over two hours to milk the sheep. When they were finished, Peter stood up and stretched and yawned. He left his sketches on the ground and sauntered over to the pens.

"Could I buy some of that milk? Maybe you've got bread too?"

The shepherd shrugged. "You wouldn't like the milk. It's not like cow's milk."

"Good God. Do you live on air up here? Just now I could drink anything, eat a whole roast sheep if you've got one."

The shepherd shrugged again. "There's cheese. There's always cheese. It's fresh from yesterday's milking. A bite of bread and there's wine."

Fausto winked and nodded to Peter. Together they helped the shepherd carry his buckets and stool up to the shelter. The sheep were left in the second pen guarded by the dog. It was dark and dreary inside the shelter so they took the food out into the sunshine. Fausto had a knife that he had used for digging the mushrooms out of the ground. He wiped it on his trousers and then used it to cut the bread. He handed a hunk to Peter; the bowl of cheese was between them.

"I'm Fausto," he said. "And you're the artist."

"My name's Peter."

"Pleased to meet you."

They shook hands over the bowl of cheese.

"Help yourself. It's difficult to eat. It's too mushy. You'll just have to scoop it onto your bread with your hands. Don't be afraid, it's good."

The shepherd did not sit down. He took a swig from the bottle of wine and then handed it to Fausto. "Put it inside with the bowl when you've finished." He left them without saying goodbye. He had bread in his pocket. He went back to his sheep, let them out of the pen and followed them, grazing their way out of sight over the ridges of the mountain.

"He doesn't like strangers," Fausto said. "You'd think the whole of Subasio belongs to him. He knows me. We can sit in silence sometimes but I come from the valley too. He must bed down with his wife in that hut or under a bush occasionally, they've got four kids. But they don't tag around after him. They're kept out of the way with the grandmother. He's happiest alone with his sheep and his dog."

They finished the cheese and rinsed their hands with the dregs of the wine and then wiped them dry on the grass. Fausto picked up the empty bowl and bottle and took them back to the shelter. Then he returned and squatted down beside Peter who was studying the sketches he had done earlier.

"Can I see?' Peter handed them to him.

"Well?"

Fausto put the one of himself face down on the grass. "They were talking about you in the Piazza last night."

"And?"

"Can I see the one you did yesterday, the one they were talking about?"

Fausto looked at the painting closely, then stood up and held it at arms length. "It's not finished. What are you going to put in that last corner?"

"Maybe the sheep; the shepherd; you; I don't know yet."

Fausto opened up his bag and shook out the mushrooms. "Ugly enough? Copy them. They're a perfect subject for you. Use them to frame your painting of dead nuns, bloated monks, disgusting children. And the misshapen dwarf. Of course I belong there. The sheep would be far too innocent and beautiful."

"Why don't you sit down instead of standing there in judgement over me."

"I'm not staying."

41

"Please."

Fausto sighed, dropped his stick and let himself down onto the grass beside Peter again. "Why did you have to put a Cross in the middle of all that—that blasphemy?"

"Crucifixion was always ugly, wasn't it? Intended for criminals. Only religious hypocricy made something pretty of it and reproduced it in gold and jewelled ornaments."

They sat in silence for a while.

"I'm an artist too," Fausto said. "But not like you. I carve little wooden replicas of the Byzantine crucifix in the Basilica of Santa Chiara, the one that St. Francis believed spoke to him. I go and sit outside the different churches and do sketches of them and sign them and sell them to the tourists. And I never know if they are bought because they are really worth something or only out of pity for me. Assisi is full of artists, some local, some just holidaymakers. We're all just copying what we see, for better or worse. Just copyists. You're different. It's as we were saying in the Piazza last night."

"What were you saying in the Piazza last night?"

"Just that you were different. Someone said you were able to reproduce the spirit within the outline, whatever that might mean. Anyway you're young. You've not been disillusioned yet. Maybe you'll never get like the rest of us. Maybe you'll succeed."

The sun was getting hotter. They moved back farther into the shadow of the shepherd's refuge. The larks soared higher and higher. Peter watched one that had swooped down close by and then rose singing and was still singing, still beating its wings, no bigger than a gnat, until it was too high to be seen or heard at all.

"What makes you think I've still got illusions?"

"You're young, strong. You haven't had to live with a body like mine, have you? You come here on holiday . . ."

Peter shook his head. "Before I came to Italy I was in Spain."

"Fighting? Which side? You were injured or you ran away?"

"Not exactly."

"I'm sorry. It's not my business."

Peter said. "Look at this mountain, listen to the birds, smell the perfume. What is it? Broom? Even so late, now in August, all the mountain is perfumed. Yellow broom and the pine trees in the heat."

"You should see what it's like up here in the spring— wild narcissus and primroses and violets, crocuses, forget-me-nots, wild orchids. You can't walk without treading over flowers. It's all rather late, May usually. On Ascension Day people come up here from Assisi and all the local villages, even old grandmothers on any old donkey or cart that has wheels. We make crosses and wreathes and decorate long poles with the narcissus and then a priest celebrates Mass and then we have picnics. There's so much space nobody feels crowded. Sometimes we have games and competitions. There's a greasy pole erected with hams and salamis hanging from the top. One year I got the lot. You wouldn't think I could climb a greasy pole, would you? After that time people started saying my mother must have had an affair with a monkey escaped from a zoo. I couldn't race up from the bottom of Mortaro though. You've seen how steep the sides are?" Fausto began laughing.

"What is it?"

"Remembering the old days and you talking about perfume. Years and years ago, when I was a kid, I used to come up here with my friends to beg bread and cheese like we did today. We were always hungry and this old shepherd's father always used to make him give us something. But once, even though we were hungry we couldn't resist throwing the cheese at each other. One of the boys flicked just a little splodge and then we all grabbed handfuls. It was a really stinking fight. There was a drought that year and there was no water for us to wash ourselves clean when it was all over. We rolled in the grass and the smell just got worse and worse, sourer and sourer. You should have heard our mothers when we got home. All the next morning round the public fonte, they were scrubbing and their voices got higher and shriller and angrier because the smell wouldn't come out. The others threw the clothes away but my mother couldn't afford to. She wouldn't feed me until I'd been to confession. She made me wear the same clothes when I went so that the priest would recognize my sins. I could see him behind the grill holding his nose when he gave me absolution. I told my mother so afterwards and she wanted to send me back again for blasphemy."

Peter laughed. Fausto laughed with him. "You don't mind my staying here and talking to you?"

"Why should I?"

"Someone like you, I don't know. If you're sure I'm not disturbing you. St. Francis used to come up this mountain when he was searching for his sense of direction. He came up here to meditate too. The monks always say he lived in a cave. You must have seen the chapel and monastery of the Hermitage that was built over the cave

44

where they say he lived. But he wasn't that crazy. Maybe he slept there when it rained but why should he hide in the dark of a cave when he could have had all this open mountain to himself?"

Peter shook his head.

"Even before St. Francis there were men who came up to the top of Subasio to meditate, early Christian hermits, holy men. They couldn't all have been crazy."

"And, before them, probably pagans as well. Fausto, you're very wise."

Fausto stood up. "I don't understand anything at all. I don't even know who you are. I only know you're different like we were saying in the Piazza last night. But it's not only because you're a good artist. It's something more than that. I'm going down into Assisi now. You're not coming?"

"Not yet."

"Don't. Not until you're ready to. I can bring you food, anything you need up here."

Peter laughed. "I can take care of myself."

"You can't live on cheese alone. The shepherd hasn't always got bread to spare. But there are villages closer than Assisi, Armenzano over the ridge, San Giovanni, Collepino. You can always get wine and bread and salami."

Peter watched Fausto hobble out of sight. When he could no longer see him, he began sketching again, the deformities, the grotesque movements, the expressions of his face. He didn't realize then that it wasn't only his body that was distorted. Fausto was already seeing Peter as a potential Saint, some kind of a Saviour with himself as the first follower, the first disciple.

The next day Peter walked down into Armenzano on the opposite side of the mountain. He had no difficulty in buying the food that he needed, the farmers' wives made bread for their families enough for a week. There could always be a loaf to spare.

That evening, returning again towards the western slopes, Peter stopped to watch the sunset. The sky was inflamed as though the world beyond the horizon were already on fire. He wanted to forget that world. And yet sooner or later he would have to know. He would have to go down into Assisi to ask at the post office if there were any letters for him, and go into a bar, listen to the radio, or at least buy a newspaper. The world beyond the horizon was the one that he had grown up in, the one where his mother and father were still living. He did not know, then, that what was happening much closer, in Assisi itself, since Paolo's arrival, was going to make as much difference to his own future as anything that was happening in that world beyond the horizon.

CHAPTER 8

On his very first night in Assisi, even in this Holy Place, Paolo had been having erotic dreams again. He remembered them distinctly when he woke in the morning, pleasurable and disgraceful. He jumped out of bed and dressed quickly. He had to go to confession before receiving Mass. It was becoming increasingly difficult. The Grace of God did not last long enough—and to think he'd once intended to become a priest!

He went into the Basilica of Santa Chiara. After confession and receiving absolution, he said the Hail Maries and Our Fathers of his penance, counting the beads on the rosary he had bought from his girl. Such a petty act of contrition. In five minutes he had finished and was ready to have the Host dissolve on his tongue, melting away his sin.

Once again cleansed, he went down into the crypt to stare for a long time at the body of Santa Chiara laid out in her simple nun's habit for all to see. Her face was as black as the cloth that covered her, showing seven centuries of death, but the bone structure was still fine. She must have been a beautiful woman, who had yet, for all her physical attractions, had the strength to resist temptation and set an example of virginity to the world.

Paolo had to see his girl again. She must talk to him and tell him something about herself. Then he would check to see that it was true. She must be, should continue to be, as pure as Santa Chiara herself until their wedding night. Then they would sacrifice her virginity together. When they had finished, they would rise and kneel by the bed and pray, that their act would bear fruit and that they would thus form a rightious, God-fearing family. There would be no need to keep running to confession once he was married.

There were two English women trying to buy something from his girl when he arrived down at the shop in Via Fontebella. They pretended not to understand the price she was indicating on one of the hand embroidered blouses. She crossed the street within a few feet of him without looking at him, rang the bell of the house opposite and when the door opened called up the inner stairs. "Signora Genevieve." An older woman, the proprietress, came out, spoke a little English, gave a slight reduction and the tourists were satisfied, paid and went away chatting.

Paolo was alone with his girl. Now she looked at him. "Can I help you?"

"Don't you recognize me? I was here after the storm, yesterday."

"Oh yes. I remember now. You bought a rosary, I think."

He took it hurriedly out of his pocket. "I want you to have it. I want it to be my first present to you. You'll accept it, won't you?"

"I don't know. I . . ."

"I'll buy another exactly like it for myself." He took her hand and folded the rosary into it and closed her fingers over it.

She blushed and lowered her eyes and slipped her hand out of his grasp.

"What is your name?"

"Clair."

"Like the Saint?"

"Almost. It's a form of Chiara."

"You're as beautiful as she must have been. I hope you're as good."

Clair moved away from him behind the counter. "Did you say you wanted to buy something else?"

"Today I came to see you."

"The Signora Genevieve doesn't like me speaking to people unless I'm trying to sell."

''Show me the rosaries then. I want one exactly like yours."

The proprietress looked in through the doorway. "All right, now, Clair? No more problems?"

"No. I'm alright." She put the tray of rosaries hurriedly down on the counter and picked up one of the most expensive ones.

"I said exactly like yours."

"I'm sorry. I wasn't thinking."

He picked up the one he wanted and handed it to her.

"Shall I put it in a box?"

"There's no need."

"Just paper?"

He didn't answer. She raised here eyes. He was staring at her strangely.

"Kiss it," he said.

"I don't understand."

"I want you to kiss it. I want you to kiss the rosary."

"Why?"

"Don't be foolish. Why do people kiss rosaries? If you are as good as you are beautiful, if you are as good as Santa Chiara, kiss that rosary. Bless it for me."

He held out his hand. He was trembling. Clair glanced towards the doorway. There was nobody passing to observe them. She put the rosary quickly to her lips. He snatched it from her and hid it away in his pocket.

"My name's Paolo, Paolo. I must leave you to do your work now." He gave a strange little laugh. "Don't forget me. You must recognize me at once the next time I come into the shop. What time do you close in the evening?"

"Half past nine, sometimes ten o'clock."

"That's too late for a respectable girl to be out alone. I'll come back at half past nine, that's what I'll do. You'll let me accompany you home, as far as the street where you live, won't you?"

"I don't know . . ."

"Yes, of course. Until tonight. I'll see you. God bless you."

He left so quickly that Clair did not realize until he had gone that he had not paid for the second rosary. She retreated into the back of the shop and sat down behind the counter. After a while she went to her purse and took out a lira and put it in the takings drawer. If she went on getting the money wrong, she would lose her job and then she would have to stay at home, shut in the house all day with her mother. Then her mother would tell her how stupid she was and tell everybody in the street the same.

CHAPTER 9

After he had left Clair, Paolo walked on down Via Fontebella and then up into Via Frate Elia until he found what he was looking for, a barber's shop. If there was any gossip about his girl then it was here that he might expect to find out about it. He went in.

There were no other customers. He sat down smiling at himself in the mirror. He could combine his investigations with the one luxury he allowed himself. The barber began soaping and shaving him—a wealth of foam and long clean strokes of the razor. Paolo relaxed, closed his eyes and sighed. Being patted, served and pampered was so different from scratching away at his own chin. There was plenty of time. He must not appear to be in too much of a hurry for the gossip. What he wanted to know about Clair must appear as part of the general conversation. There was no harm in beginning by spreading a little information about his own importance.

"You know, this is my first holiday since I entered the service of the post office. I get two weeks paid holiday a year, taken care of when I'm ill and a pension when I'm old so that I don't have to save every lira I earn. What would you give to have a job like mine?"

The barber smiled. "I own this shop. Nobody gives me orders."

"But what happens if you get ill? What happens when you're old?"

"Why should I get ill? My father worked till the day he handed over the shop to me. He kept me when I was a kid, now I keep him. Why shouldn't I have a son to do the same for me?" The barber's smile reflected off the glass mirror. "Just a second, please."

Paolo had to hold his next question until the razor had slicked down beneath his nose and around his mouth. But then—"Tell me about the people of Assisi," he said. "Are they honest?"

"Have you any reason to doubt their honesty?"

"No, no, of course not. What about the girls, the ones who work in the hotels and shops?"

"What about the girls?"

"I mean, are they respectable?"

"Why shouldn't they be?"

"Of course you have no political problems. I mean in a place like Assisi you couldn't have any Communists?"

"Why not?"

"Do you mean you have Communists, in Assisi, the home of St. Francis who was the most Christ-like man that ever lived, here in the heart of the Franciscan Order?"

"I have a friend who's convinced Marx got his ideas from Francis."

"You don't believe that? People couldn't be so ignorant."

"Why couldn't he have been the first? Communist, I mean. He was the opposite of his father and from all accounts his father would have made a very good Fascist."

"In Rome they're saying Francis is going to be made Patron Saint of Italy very soon. Is that true?"

"That's what people are saying. You know as much as we do."

"Mussolini, the Duce, would never allow that if he knew people were saying Francis was a Communist."

"Not everybody's saying that. What about your hair now?"

"Yes, yes, after that journey yesterday. It was so hot and so dusty. Washed only, not trimmed, I had a cut last week. Tell me more about the girls, those that work. Aren't their parents worried when they return home so late, after dark? There's one very beautiful . . ."

And then they were interrupted. A man, a rough, clumsily moving creature in working clothes, burst in and flung his arms around the barber's shoulders and kissed him on both cheeks. "Peppe, so you've done it. Congratulations, so you've done it at last!" He stood there laughing.

The barber pushed him towards a chair. "Sit down, let me finish."

"I can't stop. I'm working." The man sat down. Then another man came in, and another, and soon there was a crowd around Peppe, the barber, patting him on the back. The serene, polite, atmosphere was polluted by the hoarseness of their laughter and the roughness of their voices and the crudeness of the dialect and bad language. Paolo had lost control of the conversation and had to listen to all the gossip that did not interest him and he knew he was not to hear what he wanted to know.

"God of Pigs, you took your time."

"Where the hell did you find the courage? It's not that you had to? That she's?"

"Mario keep your mouth clean. Peppe keeps this place holy like a church."

"From doctors and lawyers and blasphemers, please God, protect us."

The perfume of cleanliness, soap, cologne, lavender, brilliantine, was overlaid by the odour of human sweat. These men had had their Saturday night baths only two days ago. They'd been sleek, polished gentlemen all day Sunday. But in August, in this heat, when the body oozed even at night, after only a few hours of physical work, when two or three were gathered together in a confined space, this smell of good, honest virility, that would go on accumulating and not be washed away for another five days, was already overpowering.

Peppe laughed with his friends, so different from them in his white overall, so aware of his customer's disapproval. He finished shampooing but he could not turn the little man out into the street with his hair wet. The men who had come to see Peppe, who should have been working and were not, used this stranger as an excuse for explaining, and reminiscing, knowing he was listening, even though they were ignoring him. Paolo sat there trapped beneath his hair net whilst the barber wafted a blow dryer round his head and the men bounced their conversation off him and back again like a ball against a wall.

"So it's true? You're going to have lunch with Maria's family on Sunday?"

"There's Maria's mother telling everybody down in the vegetable market now."

"Ah but you're such a handsome, good boy," she's saying. And "nothing's certain these days. They might want barbers in the army, and then you'd disappear into deepest darkest Africa and never be heard of again!"

"Like Agnes's son."

"Or die a hero in Spain."

"It'll be closer to home next time. She wants you to fix the date for next summer, did you know that?"

"It's not the army she's afraid of. For years she's been afraid you might get caught by one of those rich, foreign women. You might have had to marry one and go off and live in America,"

"She shouldn't say things like that. If anybody's going to get trapped and taken off to America it's her own Franco."

"He's crazy. He boasts he doesn't worry about any precautions, doesn't even try to withdraw."

"He gets all excited, he doesn't know how."

"He gives and gets his full pleasure, he says, with any woman who'll have him, even the forty-year-old married ones."

"That old witch he's been trailing around these past few weeks . . ."

"Is French."

"I tried picking her up myself before I'd seen her face properly. She got angry, tried to hit me, said she didn't want any of that. She was staying in a convent. She was looking for God."

"And she found him in Franco?"

"Our Peppe's such a faithful dog."

"The only one of us who could afford to go to the house of Tolerance in Foligno every Saturday."

"Twice a week if he wanted."

"And he doesn't even understand our trying to get it free from the foreign women."

"He's saving it all up for his Maria."

"Now he's officially engaged! In no time at all he'll be a husband. Hey, you know, by this time next year he could already be on his way to being a father!"

"How many are you going to have, Peppe my boy?"

"Three, four, five, six? The slow starters are always the ones who have the most."

"Look what Salvatore's doing to poor little Gina."

"She's not been without a paunch since she got married."

"Stop it," Peppe said.

"Seriously, you'd better get started straight away. They won't take you for the army if you're the head of a family."

"When are we going to celebrate?"

"Tonight?"

"Tomorrow night?"

"Let Peppe decide."

"What are we going to eat?"

"Sausages."

"What about a goose?"

"Peppe, your mother can make a pizza like she did the last time, can't she?"

"Where?"

"Up at the Hermitage like last time."

"There's no problem about cooking then."

"Who's going to pay?"

"Three and a half lira each and Peppe pays the extra."

"Are we going to ask Fausto? He always comes, doesn't he?"

Peppe removed the hair net from his customer. "A little brilliantine? Lavender, cologne perfume?" He unwound the sheeting and Paolo stood up, looking at himself in the mirror. Peppe smoothed and brushed across his shoulders. "Enjoy your stay in Assisi. If you want to come back, I assure you my friends won't be here next time. We never see each other normally during working hours. It's just . . .I've been courting the same girl for ten years, you understand . . ."

"Look at the time!"

"Mary pig! God of pigs!"

"See you in the Piazza tonight!"

"In the Piazza!"

The men pushed each other out through the door and Paolo paid Peppe exactly the one lira he asked, the same price as his rosary, and then left without commenting, without smiling, without congratulating.

Alone, Peppe cleaned up, rinsing out his lather bowl, stropping his razors, laying out everything ready for use again. There had been something unpleasant about that little customer. He had insinuated that the local girls were not respectable, and why was he asking about people's politics? Maybe Salvatore should be warned he was asking about Communists. Perhaps he was some kind of investigator. But no. He was too insignificant. All he probably wanted was a girl for the night and he had not got round to asking where he could get one.

As he polished the mirror, Peppe could see the reflection of the green and white tiles of the floor stretching back like a miniature piazza. It appeared that there were twice the number of instruments and chairs and the shop itself was doubled in size. He went to the door and stood looking out into the street.

Why should he worry because one little stranger did not smile or wish him well? Everybody who had been born and bred in Assisi would be congratulating him in the next few days. They were the only people he cared about. He had never felt so happy, so wealthy, so pleased with life and himself.

There was going to be a big wedding in the Basilica of San Francesco on Sunday. He had got to go down to the Hotel Windsor Savoia before he opened up his shop to shave six of the guests, foreigners, French or Belgian or something. It was becoming fashionable for people to come, not only from the big Italian cities but even from other countries, to get married at the tomb of St. Francis. The last time he had gone to shave foreigners in the hotel where they were staying, he had received more in tips than in three days ordinary takings in the shop.

His father had done well to buy this old basement before the reconciliation between Church and State, when this lower part of town was no better off than the upper part.

For centuries, after Francis' death, it was the lower part of town that had prospered, with the pilgrims coming to the Basilica, never taking their money up as far as the Piazza Comune or the Cathedral. Then, at the end of the last century the priests and monks had lost their rights and, for a short while, it made no difference in which part of town you lived or had your business. That was when his father had bought the basement. Now, if Francis really was going to be made Patron Saint of all Italy, the area near the Basilica was going to become richer than it had ever been before.

Franco had been right to insist that he should not keep Maria waiting any longer. He could afford to get married now. He would not have to deprive his parents or his sister of anything. He had already saved up almost enough for the bedroom furniture they wanted—a wardrobe and a dressing table, the bed and two lockers, all to match, and a piece of carpet when you put your feet out in the morning instead of the cold stone floor. When Maria came into the house and became part of his family, his old bedroom would be completely renewed and be as good as any he had seen in the hotels. It was going to cost him three hundred and fifty lira, perhaps more, but with the help of St. Francis he would have nothing more to worry about. He was going to be better off than any miserable little post office worker with a pension.

CHAPTER 10

Paolo walked up towards the centre of Assisi. It was good to be out in the fresh air after being shut up in that barber's shop listening to those stinking provincials and their picnics. Of course, labourers had known, since ancient Rome, that washing the whole body more than once a week was physically debilitating. The barber really should not have allowed them into his shop in that condition. Poor, unsophisticated country folk who did not know what was going on in the rest of Italy. It was such a very low level of life. They did not even have a repertoire of swear words but just kept on repeating the same blasphemy. The greatest pleasures they could think up for themselves in their spare time were fornication and food. Eating and drinking themselves silly up in the mountains. His own way of life was vastly superior, work in a trusted position, clean, requiring intelligence. His own way of spending his free time was so very much more civilized.

On Sundays, he always took a tram from the suburbs, where he lived and worked, right into the heart of Rome, into the very centre of the world. Usually he went alone. He had no friends. Occasionally he felt obliged to take his sister but then he had to do what she liked. She always wanted to go to St. Peter's to try to see the Pope. But afterwards they did what he wanted. They crossed the Tiber river into that other Rome where they walked up the great majestic avenue that Mussolini had created alongside the Roman Forum, which linked the historic world with the present. Paolo always wished he could leave his sister behind, down amongst the ruins at the Colosseum end. She usually tried to take his arm and he was sure passers-by must think she was his wife or his fiancé. She was fifteen years older than he and had never been beautiful and now she was ugly. In one hand she always carried an outsize bag with nothing in it except a handkerchief. Whenever possible he bought her an ice cream to keep her other hand occupied. Then he could walk several paces ahead of her so that people would not really know if they were together or not. Only when they reached the glaring white Victor Emanuel monument, which foreigners insulted by calling it the wedding cake, when it was, in reality, the symbol of the new Rome, only then did they stand side by side in Piazza Venezia and stare up at the balcony where Mussolini appeared when he had something important to say to his people. Even though she was only a woman, his sister seemed to understand the significance of that balcony. But he had never had his sister with him when the Duce was due to speak. On those occasions he had to be completely anonymous and become just part of the crowd.

Going down town would be different when he took Clair. He would buy her a new dress and insist she take his arm so that people would have no doubt she belonged to him. He would never let her go out alone. He would not even let her do the vegetable and grocery shopping unless his sister went with her. Poor Marietta was going to be upset when he brought a wife to live with them. But maybe it would be alright if Clair treated her as though she were really a mother-in-law. Paolo went on up the hill, thinking about having Clair in Rome, not noticing the

Assisi he was walking through. He reached the Piazza Comune and there he sat down outside the bar facing the temple of Minerva and ordered himself a drink.

They had told him in the pensione where he was staying that the temple of Minerva had been built fifty years before Christ and that it was nearly two thousand years old. It was still dominating the very centre, the very life, of Assisi. They had had their history here, too. The great culture of the past had given this city other temples, a theatre, an amphitheatre, public baths and water piped and channelled through the streets to the Forum, which now lay beneath his feet. Assisi had been like so many other small towns, a prosperous little replica of Rome itself. Then in the Middle Ages the People's Tower had been built alongside the temple of Minerva. He did not know the legend of the black stone and he would not have believed it anyway. The date of the building of the tower did not coincide with any Saracen invasion in these parts.

The clock on the tower struck every fifteen minutes; first all the heavy strokes of the hour and then a light one for the quarter; all the heavy strokes and two light ones for the half hour, all the heavy followed by three light for the three-quarter. Paolo drummed out the strokes with his fingers on the table as though to be sure the clock did not make a mistake. He ordered himself another drink. He was on holiday, wasn't he?

He had been in Assisi only once before, with his parents in 1926, on the seven hundredth anniversary of St. Francis' death. Special trains had been put on for pilgrims that year. The whole city had been cleaned up and this piazza in particular. It was then that the clock had been given to the People's Tower and the battlements restored in true Ghibeline style. The palace next to it had had its battlements redefined in the Guelph style. These two different types had been for centuries the symbols of the domination of Emperors and Popes. Now, restored side by side, they were to become the symbols of the same old church together with Mussolini's new State.

Paolo spent the whole morning in the Piazza drumming out the echo of the clock's chimes with his fingers. There were no local boys idling at this time of day. He saw only an occasional tourist like himself and monks and nuns, black and brown robed, of different Orders and of different nationalities. The few housewives hurrying from one street to another, with their loaded shopping baskets of vegetables and loaves of bread, kept their heads bent as though guilty of being out so late. Their neighbours must already have been out at dawn to pick over the best of everything, leaving them to put on the table, for their husbands and children, only the over-ripe, slightly soiled left-overs of the market. A few workmen in overalls passed across the Piazza from one street to another. A postman left the post office with a mail bag on his shoulder. An old peasant, his trousers tied up with string, tugged a mule which still had a few faggots of unsold kindling fire-wood on its back. The mule tried to stop to drink at the fountain and was beaten and sworn at.

At last the clock on the People's Tower struck mid-day. The sound found its echo in the stomachs of all the men working in the side streets, on the building sites, even beyond the boundaries of the city walls. Suddenly the Piazza was filled with these men, some going up, some going down, to their houses. There was no time for talking; just a shouted, cut-short, greeting or a grab of the arm if they passed within reach of each other, because minestrone soup was already cooling in the plates and spaghetti, due to come out of the boiling water, must be eaten immediately before it went soggy.

Paolo went back to the little pensione where he was staying and had lunch and then went up to his room and lay on his bed waiting for the cool of the evening and the time when he would see Clair again. He could hear the clock of the People's Tower chiming in his bedroom too. All afternoon he lay there counting the hours and the half hours and the quarter hours.

Eventually he got up and had dinner in the pensione and then went out. It was still too early. He had a cup of coffee in a bar.

Clair down at the bottom of Via Fontebella could hear the chiming of the People's Clock. It must be half past nine. She began to count the strokes. Before the last one Paolo was standing in front of her.

"You see I always keep my word. I'm always punctual," he said.

He watched her as she put away the ceramic cups and plates and flower vases, umbrella stands, wrought iron work, the artisan-made souvenirs of Assisi. He saw that she was quick and neat by the way she folded the embroidery. She would be a good housewife if his sister ever allowed her to touch the linen. He helped her close and lock the great wooden shutters and noticed that she put the key in her pocket, showing that she was trusted to keep it for the night.

She wanted to walk too fast up Via Fontebella. He put only the tips of his fingers on her arm to slow her down. It was like an electric shock. She seemed to shrivel up away from him.

"You have a beautiful name," he said.

"Dozens of girls in Assisi are called Clair, Chiara or Clara or some version of it, or else Francesca."

"Of course. In little provincial towns like this most of the inhabitants must be baptized with local saints' names. The original inhabitants grow old and die but the names remain alive in the next generation and the next and the next. I come from Rome. People from all over Italy come to live there. I'm one of the few whose name really belongs. You haven't forgotten have you? My name is Paolo after St. Paul who died with St. Peter in Rome."

They'd reached the Piazza Comune and Clair's head bent lower and she seemed as though she wanted to scuttle across and run up the steps on the far side until she was out of sight of the boys who were watching her from the tables in front of the Minerva bar.

Again Paolo put his fingers on her arm and she felt the shock run all the way up to her shoulder. She blushed. They would be sniggering behind her back already, at her new boy friend.

Paolo did not look at her but he knew she was trembling. He was trembling too. He believed she must be feeling the same as he himself.

They were both out of breath at the top of the steps. Paolo's hand tightened on her arm, until he was hurting her. He made her stop and rest.

"My house is only a little way up here on the right," she said. "You'd better go now."

He refused to leave her. He wanted to know exactly where she lived.

At the fountain on the corner, Gina from Capobove, the adjoining street, was filling a pail of water. She had a child, her eldest boy, there to help her carry it. He was sitting on the ground watching her as she heaved the bucket out of the fountain. She was hugely pregnant. She looked up as Clair and Paolo passed. "Buona notte," she gasped. She nudged at the child with her foot, making him stand up and then brushed down the seat of his trousers with her hand before they picked up the pail between them.

"That's a cousin of mine," Clair said. They had reached the street door of her home. She would not let him follow her up the inner stairs to the very door of her mother's apartment. She blocked the entrance. His fingers squeezed her arm again. He hurt her.

"I'll see you tomorrow. When do you go to work? I'll walk down with you."

"I leave very early."

"Tell me how early."

She shook her head.

"Then I'll come down to the shop later in the morning. What time do you go to lunch?"

"We don't close, my mother has to bring something for me to eat in the shop."

"Your mother? I should like to meet your mother, but not now, not yet, it's too soon. You'll let me walk home with you again tomorrow evening, won't you?"

"I suppose so. If you like . . ."

"I'll be at the shop at half past nine. Goodnight. God bless you." His fingers relaxed and he was walking with his quick, precise little steps down the street the way they had come.

For the next five days he sat in the Piazza, did a little halfhearted sight-seeing and walked at least three or four times a day past the shop in Via Fontebella. She was always sitting with her head bent, refusing to look up from her embroidery. She allowed him to be with her for only half an hour in the evening and then she refused to loiter on the way home but tried always to race ahead of him.

He could not carry on like this. He could not sleep at night any more. This was not like courting the girl next door. His holiday would soon be over, almost half of it was gone already. He was sure of her innocence. The way she behaved with him meant that she was not used to having men, but he still had to be certain that her family was honest and respected. Then he had to be accepted into her house and be her official fiancè so that they could walk arm in arm down the Corso, the main street from the Piazza Comune to Piazza Santa Chiara, for all to see and know that their relationship was serious, just as the barber Peppe would be doing with his Maria on Sunday afternoon. Not that he had to put himself on the level of a barber; he would be raising Clair above that, but the conventions must be observed. Before he left she had to understand that she belonged to him and that her life had changed. Everybody in Assisi must know that she was promised, so that in his absence nobody else should approach her.

On Saturday morning he dressed in the dark, before five o'clock. As he walked up through the streets it was only just beginning to get light but already there were sounds of movement in many of the houses; shutters were being pinned back; bedclothes thrown across windowsills to air. A cart passed, pulled by a mule with its stinking load of human excrement, that the local farmers collected regularly from the shallow pits in the basements of the poorer houses. In the Piazza Comune there was Gina, Clair's cousin, not walking, but trotting as though already late, with a great basket of dirty clothes on her head. She disappeared off down the back streets past Chiesa Nuova.

Paolo climbed the steps to Via Santa Rosa and stood in an angle of the house opposite Clair's. The shutters were still closed on all the floors. A couple of women came up to the fountain on the corner to fill bottles and buckets of water. They did not notice him.

Paolo remained motionless in his corner. It was nearly seven o'clock when Clair left home. He heard her footsteps on the inner stairs and was already moving to meet her as she stepped out into the street. She was startled. He was a little stiff.

"Good morning."

"You haven't been here all night?"

"Not exactly. But I expected your 'very early' to have been before this."

"I'm usually much earlier. I overslept. I must hurry. I'm late."

He had to double his pace, running down the steps to the Piazza to keep up with her. At the bottom they nearly knocked over Gina who was staggering up, her load of clean washing, heavier now that it was wet, on her head.

The clock in the Piazza started to strike seven.

"Oh Mamma Mia. I should have the shop open by now. You're alright Gina, aren't you? I'm so late or I'd stop and help you."

Clair began to run again. Paolo had to run too if he wanted to keep up with her. He tried to slow her down, to hold her arm or her hand.

"I'll protect your from your proprietress," he panted.

She ran faster. It was ridiculous and undignified. There were people in the Piazza, in the streets, at the open windows. Paolo slowed down.

There were no excrement carts now. Most of the farm women who sold fruit and vegetables had already trundled into the market with their barrows and were surrounded by early housewives choosing grapes, plums, pears, the ripest tomatoes for the spaghetti sauce and baby marrows and cucumber and salad. A man leading a mule loaded with fire wood was sauntering up Via Fontebella.

Clair was struggling to open up the shutters of the shop when Paolo joined her. "They're so stiff and heavy."

Paolo pinned them back for her and began helping her to carry out the embroidered blouses and hang them on the wall on either side of the shop entrance.

"You'll have to go now," she said. "You can't stay here."

"But I must see more of you. Almost the only words I've heard you say are 'You'll have to go now'."

"I can't help it."

"I'll stay until you get your first customers. I'll go immediately someone comes."

"No, no, no. no."

Paolo left her. He'd already made up his mind. Today he was going to meet her parents. He had to declare his intentions. Her mother or father must ask permission for her to have at least tomorrow, Sunday, free, and a few hours in the afternoons of the days that were left to him. If her employer refused he would persuade Clair's parents to take her out of the shop for a few days anyway. If she lost her job as a consequence, then she and her parents would be even more grateful to him for the marriage he proposed. They would be as eager as he that it should not be delayed.

After Paolo had gone, Clair went into the dark interior of the shop and sat down behind the counter. She rubbed at her arm and the back of her hand where that horrid little man had touched her. If it had not been for trying to escape from him she would have stopped to help Gina up the steps.

She picked up her embroidery. Gina had taught her how to do this simple cross stitch of Assisi but the outline design of the tablecloths and centre pieces and cushion covers sometimes took days of concentration. Gina never had time to do embroidery now, nor to stand and chat, nor to dance in the street and sing and laugh the way she used to do. Poor Gina, all day she was slaving for her family, washing, cleaning, patching old clothes, cooking for them, waiting at table, even pouring her husband's wine into his glass for him and never sitting down herself. Every year she went through hours of screaming agony of labour. The idea was horrifying, terrifying, not to be thought about. "Dear Mary. Mother of God, protect us now and at the time of our death. Amen." It would be better to live in a convent, become a nun.

CHAPTER 11

Poor Gina. Clair had not really understood when she had left her standing there at the bottom of the steps leading up from the Piazza. The little man she was with had not offered to help. Why should he? He was a stranger and who had ever heard of a man offering to carry a woman's washing?

Gina leaned against the wall and brushed the hair out of her eyes with her free hand, a hand swollen and sodden from more than an hour's scrubbing and thumping and beating of clothes in cold water. The remains of a block of yellow soap showed damply through her apron pocket against her swollen stomach.

She gave a little sob. She didn't know if she could make it to the top of the steps. She felt damp all over and smelling of her own sweat. There were a hundred and fifty steps to get up and then, if the children were awake and had started fighting and were wrecking the house, she would have to begin immediately shouting at them and dressing them and feeding them. And she was due to go into labour. She did not bother counting months or days any more. She had not done so since the third child was born. Like an animal that has to prepare its lair, she knew she should have got extra water last night for the midwife. She would have to ask her sister, her mother and the relations to take the children and feed them and keep them away from the sound of her screams until it was all over.

Salvatore had not come home. He knew she was due. It was always the same. He would not come home until it was all over; not until there was a blue or pink ribbon on the door.

Peter came striding down towards the Piazza. He did not see Gina leaning against the wall until he had bumped into her and nearly knocked her off balance. He grabbed her and steadied her with one hand. Her grip relaxed on the basket of washing she was holding on her head and he caught it with his other hand as it was about to fall.

"I'm sorry," he said. "Are you alright?"

She did not answer and he looked at her face, at the lines and the tears and sweat. "I'm sorry," he repeated. He looked down into the Piazza. From where he was standing there was nobody in sight who might help her.

"Come along, I'll see you home," he said.

Gina shook her head. She tried to hang on to the basket but she had no strength to resist. He took it from her and put it under his arm, holding it against his hip. It was heavy even for him.

"Come on. Tell me where you live. You were going up the steps weren't you?"

Gina looked up the steps. With or without the basket, she would never reach the top. Peter half pushed, half carried her with his free arm around her waist. When they were on the flat of the street above, they paused.

"Thank you," Gina whispered. "I can manage now."

"Don't be silly. I said I'd see you home."

A woman opened a bedroom window and started shaking a piece of matting immediately over their heads. She looked down and saw them and recognized Gina.

"Are you alright then? What's happened?"

They heard her clattering down the inner stairs of the house to the street door. Other women heard her calling and came out. By the time they reached Gina's house there were seven or eight women out in the street.

"Call Agnes. Someone call Agnes."

"Yes," Gina whispered. "Please."

"Agnes. Agnes. Come quick."

A woman came out from behind a curtain that hung in front of an entrance next to the street door of Gina's home. Agnes's house was one of the few that had the kitchen-living room on the ground floor. She had been eating a hunk of bread with the remains of some cold cooked greens left over from the evening before. She wiped her mouth and the oil from her fingers on the curtain as she came out.

"Madonna Mia. Have you got pains already then? Must I call the midwife?"

Gina shook her head. "I felt faint, that's all."

"Because you haven't eaten or drunk anything yet this morning, stupid girl, in your condition. Why you can't ask some of us to help you, I don't know."

"I know," said one of the women. "By the time any of us get down to the fonte, somebody else has been there and the water's no longer crystal clear."

"And dirty water's not good enough for her children's clothes," another woman added.

"You all have your own work to do," Gina murmured.

"Of course we do. But if somebody just can't cope do you think we wouldn't give a hand?"

Peter watched the women. Most of them were older than the pregnant girl, comfortably plump; several had teeth missing. They were all wearing aprons or faded house dresses because they had been doing their chores and had not expected to be seen out in the street. Their voices rose, shrill and scolding.

"You'll be alright now? You don't need me any more?" he said.

"Of course, of course. Thank you." The woman called Agnes took the basket of washing from him. She was the oldest, the most authoritative, even though she was so scraggy with narrow bent shoulders like a clothes hanger, flat chested and all skin and bones.

Gina smiled at Peter and opened the street door of her home. At that moment the door at the top of the inner stairs opened and a child, too small to walk, came sliding and bumping down on his backside. When he reached the bottom he pulled himself to a standing position, using Gina's legs and knees for support and put up his arms to be lifted.

Gina stooped, picked him up and kissed the top of his head.

"I don't know how you have such beautiful children," one of the women said. She tried to take this one from Gina but the child clung with arms and legs and put his head down on his mother's shoulder.

"Do you want me to carry him up the stairs?" Peter said.

Gina shook her head. "He won't let you. He won't let anybody touch him but me."

"Little parasite," Aunt Agnes said. "They all are. Suck all the strength out of their mother and give nothing in return."

"What do you expect of them? They're all so small still." Gina hugged the child to her and kissed him again.

The little boy stared, unsmiling, at Peter over his mother's shoulder. He had dark red hair, long black eyelashes and bushy eyebrows too thick for a child.

Peter turned to leave. As he went down the street he could hear the women talking about him, their voices high and shrill, not waiting until he was out of earshot.

"Does Salvatore know you've got a new cavalier?"

"He's that foreigner."

"Speaks peculiar."

"You can understand him though."

"You mean he's that artist fellow everybody's been talking about?"

"He needs a haircut and a shave."

"These foreigners don't care what they look like the way our men do."

"Fausto said he spent a whole morning with him up on the mountain. Fausto said he's a genius, maybe another St. Francis, maybe a prophet."

"The prophets all had long hair, didn't they?"

"What ordinary man would help a woman carry her washing?"

"That's what I'm saying."

The clock in the Piazza started striking. "Mamma Mia, how late it is." The women did not stop to hear how many times the clock struck. They scuttled off down the street, disappearing into their houses. Only two remained to take the basket of washing up the hillside behind the houses and spread the clean clothes out on the low bramble bushes. Gina had no garden or back yard.

Gina gripped the handrail attached to the inner wall and began pulling herself up the stairs, the child clinging round her neck. Aunt Agnes gave her a push from behind as she followed her up.

"There was pandemonium just before you got back. There's silence now. They must be doing something they shouldn't."

The children were eating bread, sitting on the kitchen table, barefoot, in their pants and cotton vests just as they had got out of bed. There were crumbs in their hair and sticking to them all over, the table and floor smothered in crumbs. They looked guilty but they went on eating.

"We were hungry," the eldest boy said.

Gina pushed two of them apart to make room for the child she had been carrying and sat him down amongst the crumbs. "Haven't you left a piece for Roberto?"

"Or for your mother?" Aunt Agnes said. "Don't any of you think of your mother? Hasn't the milkman been yet? Don't you give them bowls of milk with their bread in the mornings?"

"Of course I do, if I'm here when they wake up," Gina said. "The milk's probably still at the foot of the stairs. I didn't think to look. One of the children can bring it up later. It still has to be boiled. Now they've finished the bread, they'll have to drink it as it is. I've got nothing else to dunk in it. Oh dear, oh dear, and Roberto still hasn't eaten."

"You'd better let me do your shopping for you," Aunt Agnes said. "I've got to do my own. I'll take one of the children to help me carry it."

Gina nodded. She had a pain. Either it had been too much effort getting up those last stairs with Roberto round her neck or she really was beginning labour. "Laura can go with you. My purse is up there on the shelf. I bought four kilos of bread yesterday and there are only crumbs left. You'd better get five loaves and the usual vegetables for minestrone. What are you waiting for Laura? Go and get your dress on." Gina began walking about the kitchen.

"Sit down," Aunt Agnes said.

Gina sat down for a moment and then got up and began walking about again. She was so tired but it was impossible to keep still. She had another pain just after Laura and Aunt Agnes had left. She climbed up the next flight of stairs to the girls' bedroom. When they were dressed, she climbed up another flight to the boys' bedroom. Giovanni could dress himself. She only had Roberto to do. She ought to go up to the very top of the house where she and her husband slept, to make the bed, dust the room and pass a wet cloth across the floor—in case—in case—She had another pain. Then there was no doubt.

"Giovanni, we'll go and get more water now."

"We got water last night, there's enough."

"No, the midwife always wants more."

She had to carry Roberto up to the drinking-water fountain on the corner between Capobove and Via Santa Rosa. The children were all thirsty and before she could fill the bucket she had to help them up onto the edge of the fountain so that they could get their mouths beneath the tap. It was all that bread they had eaten and she still had not boiled the milk.

She filled the bucket and then as she heaved it down onto the ground she felt the moisture pouring down the inside of her legs. It was neither from the bucket nor the fountain.

"Oh Mamma Mia." She squeezed the skirt between her legs. She could not have it here in the street. "Help," she began to call. "Oh Mamma Mia, help, help. Madonna help, help." Her voice rose.

Clair's mother came out of her house. She was on her way to the doctor's. She was sure her blood pressure was higher. She could see spots dancing before her eyes. She felt dizzy and her head ached. These were all the symptoms the doctor had asked her if she had the last time, and now she had them, all of them. If she were not a poor defenceless widow and Clair did not have to work she could have been accompanied by her daughter. It was probably dangerous to be going about alone. She heard Gina as she came out into the street. She could not help hearing her wailing, as she leaned against the basin of the fountain there, surrounded by her children.

Clair's mother turned to go in the opposite direction but Gina had seen her and was calling her by name. "Anna, Anna."

She would be late at the doctor's. There would be a whole crowd ahead of her. It might be the death of her. She sighed and waddled down towards Gina.

"What's the matter, what's the matter, then?"

"She's all wet," Giovanni said.

"You spilt the bucket? Couldn't you get the children to help you? Giovanni, aren't you any good at lifting?"

"My waters," Gina said. "My waters have broken."

Anna threw her hands up above her head. "Oh Madonna mia, Madonna mia," she wailed. "Here in the street, what a disgrace, what a disgrace. Pain and sorrow, trial and tribulation, that's all a woman's life is."

"Take the children up to Piazza Nuova," Gina begged. "Just take the children up to my sister. Aunt Agnes will be back from shopping soon; she'll call the midwife; she'll stay with me. Please take the children."

Anna looked up the street.

She could see none of the women who had been there earlier. They were all down in the centre of the town doing their shopping; buying their daily one and a half ounces of parmesan cheese and a dab of jam on the paper on the scales, and a dab of tomato conserve to thicken up the spaghetti sauce. There'd be old Antoinetta holding up everything by demanding three salted sardines with the salt scraped off so they wouldn't weigh so much and Berti, the shopkeeper, having to wipe his fingers on a towel before he could handle the bread to give to the next customer. The loaves were always either over baked or under baked and poor Berti would be squeezing them, breaking the crust on them with the heel of his palm, insisting they were all the same. Mafalda would be buying mortadella again and people would be saying when she left the shop—"She still doesn't believe it's only an old donkey. She will when her kids' ears start growing straight up."

Most of the women would have brought their own quarter litre bottles to be filled with olive oil. Little half daft Luisa could never remember what she'd come to buy. She'd be standing there with her fingers in her ears as though the buzzing of voices was disturbing. Nobody ever knew what they were going to give their husbands for supper. Every morning the women discussed what they'd cooked yesterday and the more important gossip of Assisi—whose wife or whose son had done what that was

79

disgraceful, their arthritis in the winter, varicose veins in the summer, who was pregnant and who was dying and the price of next year's wine. All those women just talking, just waiting their turn to be served. Not around when Anna and Gina really needed them.

"And now how'll I get to the doctor myself and I may be dying at this moment? Oh Madonna mia. How'll I carry the little one? Where is he?"

Roberto was half way home. It was down hill, he could manage down hill. He did not crawl but bumped himself rapidly along on his bottom, taking all the seat out of his trousers. Giovanni ran after him and picked him up and staggered back with him. He screamed and kicked. Gina kissed him on the top of his head.

"Be a good boy. Be a very special little boy for Mamma, please Robertino, pet, be a good boy."

Giovanni had to put him down. He was too heavy for him.

Gina had another pain. "Oh Madonna mia." She clutched her stomach.

Anna said. "Alright, alright. We'll manage somehow. Go and get onto your bed. I get dizzy if I stoop down. Giovanni you'll have to pick him up again and give him to me. I'll carry him somehow. We'll take it slowly. Get away with you Gina. Go."

But Anna was unable to manage. Roberto was fighting her, beating his fists against her face. He slipped out of her arms and was off down the street again on his bottom. He did not get very far because round the corner came the Saint Prophet man.

Gina saw him scoop Roberto up and hold him above his head and shake him and then swing him onto his shoulders, and Roberto didn't struggle. He laughed and put his arms round the man's neck. It was a miracle. It must be, his appearing like that when she was desperate, now for the second time. She had no need to worry about her children any more, only about herself. She went off, running, hobbling down Via Capobove, clutching her skirt between her legs.

She picked up the milk from the foot of the stairs. If it was not boiled immediately it would go sour; perhaps it was sour already. She could do nothing about it now. She put the jug on the kitchen table and dragged herself up the three flights of stairs to her room. She might have the baby there and then. She might bleed to death. She could scream and scream and nobody would hear her. She was alone. There was nobody to help her. She had all that pain to face again.

"Hail Mary, full of grace, the Lord is with thee, blessed art thou amongst women and blessed is the fruit of thy womb, Jesus. Holy Mary, mother of God, pray for us sinners now and at the hour of our death, amen. Hail Mary . . . Francesco . . . Mamma mia . . . Hail Mary full of grace . . . Man of the Mountains, Saint Prophet man, whatever your name is . . . Oh dear God . . ."

Aunt Agnes arrived and then the midwife. The midwife examined Gina. "You're not three fingers open yet, what's all the fuss about? You've probably got hours to go. What did you call me so soon for?"

"But my waters? They've never broken so early before."

"That doesn't mean anything, just you shouldn't have been heaving buckets around. And what good's it done? You didn't get the water into the house even."

"Oh Madonna, the bucket's still up at the fountain. If somebody steals it . . ."

"Don't make me laugh. Who's going to steal your old bucket? Who's going to carry it down for me's more to the point."

Aunt Agnes and Laura carried the bucket back to the house and Aunt Agnes lit the fire in the fireplace in the kitchen and stoked it up high so that the flames reached the blackened cooking pot that hung from a nail there. She poured the water into the cooking pot to boil. Laura went up to the bedroom to stare at her mother.

"See what trouble you get into if you make love?" the midwife said. "Just you keep clear of men."

"The child's six years old," Gina murmurred.

"Never too young to learn that lesson. Look at your mother now."

"No, don't stay," Gina said. "Ask Aunt Agnes to boil the milk and then, if it hasn't turned sour, maybe you could take it up to the other children at Piazza Nuova, so that it won't be wasted. You could manage to carry it, couldn't you? You won't lose your way?"

"How can she carry milk from here to Piazza Nuova without spilling it? Don't be a fool, Gina."

"No don't take it then, you might get it on your dress and then who'd wash it out right away? Don't get dirty. Tell the other children they've got to keep clean all day. They mustn't get dirty, you understand?"

Aunt Agnes came up with a glass of camomile tea for Gina and one for the midwife also. "Camomile's good at any time," she said. "I tried to boil the milk but it curdled. I threw it down the sink."

"So that's one great worry off your mind," the midwife said. "There's nothing more you can do to save the precious milk. If you tried to sleep you'd be better able to cope when the real pains start. You know you're not going to have this one so quickly."

Aunt Agnes took Laura downstairs with her. The midwife sat by the window doing her embroidery.

Gina said. "I took the herbs like you said. I boiled them and boiled them and drank the water. It was bitter, horrible but I went on drinking until I vomitted and nothing happened."

"You just shouldn't go with your husband."

"We don't, not for days, weeks. We lie here in this bed and we can't sleep and we don't—we daren't touch, not our feet, nor our flanks nor our finger tips. We lie in agony and listen to each other breathing and I pray and pray to the Madonna and St. Francis and all the Saints."

"And then you can't resist any longer and you come together and make up for lost time."

"He's no good at withdrawing. Anna only had one child and Aunt Agnes only had two. How did they manage?"

"What you mean is you cling so close, your poor husband can't get away in time even if he wants to. You won't let him."

"No, it's not like that. We just have to look at each other and there's another baby on the way."

"Fairy stories. You'll be telling me next how the stork flew in through the window. What you know very well is that once there's one on the way you're free to play about all you like for nine months without the responsibility of trying to prevent anything or anybody."

Gina groaned. She had a stronger pain. When it had passed, she said. "Next time, if I come to you after I've missed only the first month . . .would you . . .if the herbs, don't work? The other women say you can do it. It's not a sin in the first three months, is it? All the other women say it isn't a sin in the first three months. They say I wouldn't even have to confess . . . I wouldn't tell anybody, not even my husband . . . would you?"

"What are you talking about the next for? Let's get this one born first."

"Would you though?"

"You come to me. I won't make any promises."

Gina relaxed. If this were the last, she could bear the pain . . . this time, but not again and again and again."

CHAPTER 12

Whilst Peter was helping Anna take Gina's children through the upper streets of the city to Piazza Nuova, not knowing that Anna was Clair's mother, not knowing who Anna was at all, Paolo was down in the Basilica of San Francesco praying.

He prayed that his intention, his desire, should be understood by the Madonna herself. He begged St. Francis and St. Clair to be his intermediaries. Satisfied, he then went back to his room in the pensione. He polished his shoes and changed his shirt, putting on a brilliantly bleached white one. From the pensione he went to Peppe's to be shaved. Before he left the barber's he had a light cologne sprayed over his hair and neck.

The stale taste of a night without sleep lingered on in spite of the Holy Wafer that he had had on his tongue. He went to a bar and drank a tiny cup of dense black expresso coffee with three teaspoonfuls of sugar in it.

Now he was ready, the most respectable looking man in Assisi. He was clean, spruced, spiritually pure within, polished and perfumed without. It could have been his wedding day instead of only the one that he had chosen for the preliminary introduction to his future wife's family.

He walked with his quick, neat little steps up through the centre of the city, across the Piazza Comune and up the steps on the far side. Nobody took any particular notice of him. At the top of the steps he turned left into Via

Capobove. He wanted to have a few words with the neighbours of the street next to Via Santa Rosa before meeting Clair's parents.

It was late morning now. Most of the women had cleaned their houses, done their washing and their shopping, prepared their midday meal. Four of them were even able to sit out in the street with their embroidery for an hour before their husbands returned for lunch. The sun was hot. Since the storm on the day of Paolo's arrival in Assisi there had not been a cloud in the sky. Each of the four women had brought out a low stool and they sat together in a little group on the shady side of the street.

They were discussing again the morning's excitements. First Gina being escorted, her washing actually carried for her, by the huge, long-haired foreigner, the painter or prophet or whatever he was. Then her waters breaking in the street and the arrival of the midwife and now the waiting to be the first to know if it was a boy or a girl. They could only faintly hear Gina's groans from the open window at the top of her house. They would know when she was in her final stages of labour though.

"The last time, do you remember, you could hear her up at the castle almost?"

"She always has such enormous babies for a tiny little thing like her."

"She never has them easily."

Several children who had been playing quietly farther down the street now began quarrelling and screaming at each other. One of the women stood up and shrieked furiously at them, making more noise herself than all of them put together.

"Go on up the hillside. Gina's trying to sleep. I said before you couldn't stay around here this morning. Go on up the hillside."

Aunt Agnes came out of her house from behind her curtain to see what was happening. She too shouted at the children and shooed them, physically pushing them towards the steps that led between the houses up towards the castle. She stood and watched until the children were out of sight and then went over to where the women were sitting.

They didn't notice Paolo approaching until he was standing in front of them. "Excuse me," he said.

The women stared at him. "Please?" Strangers usually got lost if they ventured into these narrow upper streets of the city. All they ever wanted to know was how to get back to the centre or else to one of the Basilicas or to their hotels.

"Excuse me," and then, "Do any of you know a girl called Clair who lives in the next street, who works in a shop down near the Hotel Giotto?"

The women put their embroidery down in their laps and gaped at him. "That must be Anna's Clair."

Agnes, the one woman standing, was taller than Paolo. "What do you want to know about Clair?" she demanded.

"She's a very beautiful girl," Paolo said weakly.

"She is, you know. I think she's the most beautiful girl in the whole city just at the moment."

"Lots of people say so."

"What did you want to know about her?" Aunt Agnes insisted.

Paolo stretched his lips, cleared his throat. "I saw her the day I arrived, only a few days ago, yes. She seemed . . .She's different from other girls, isn't she? But she's so very shy."

The women began nudging each other.

"Yes, well, her family. I'm sure you could tell me something about them."

"Clair lives alone with her mother. Her father died two years ago," Aunt Agnes said.

"And the girl herself? She's never had any . . .any affairs with men?"

"Never, has she?"

"Never. I ought to know. My husband and her father were brothers."

"We've all known her since she was a baby."

"We'd have heard if there'd ever been any talk about her."

Paolo sighed, relaxed. There were no obstacles. "I'd like to meet her mother but . . . I don't know. It might not be correct. Unannounced."

Aunt Agnes stared at Paolo, a serious middle-aged suitor, thirty at least, his hair receding a little, not an age to play around. "Come with me," she ordered. She jerked her head towards Gina's house and said to the women. "I'll come straight back."

The women couldn't wait until they were out of earshot.

"Love at first sight."

"It does happen."

"Can you imagine, though? And Clair so timid."

"So beautiful, it's not surprising."

"Wait till her mother hears. She surely hasn't said anything to her mother yet."

"Anna would have told us."

"Isn't it what she's been wanting?"

"But now that it's actually . . ."

"It'll kill her or . . ."

"Can you imagine though, all in one day? Birth, marriage . . ."

"A new St. Francis."

"Only Fausto thinks he might be."

"Well, anyway . . ."

"Nothing's happened yet, not even the birth."

"Who knows . . ."

Aunt Agnes and Paolo turned the corner into Via Santa Rosa. They entered the doorway that Clair had barred to Paolo the evening he had first walked back with her and every evening since. They began to climb the stairs.

"Anna's a good woman," Aunt Agnes said. "She's always done the best she could for her daughter."

CHAPTER 13

Anna was about to change out of her good dress into her old house clothes. She was exhausted. She was standing in her bedroom remembering why she was so exhausted, thinking about dropping dead, when she heard the knock at the door.

She had not had to carry that child. The strange man who called himself Peter had done that. But after he had left she had felt obliged to stay and help. Maria had been alone in the house trying to finish making the dress she was going to wear when her Peppe came to lunch.

At last Maria's mother, who was also Gina's mother, came back from doing the shopping. As soon as she heard about Gina's waters breaking in the street, she had put her hands over her face and wailed, "Trial and tribulation, pain and sorrow, that's all a woman's life is!" Somebody had to go down to the centre of town again and buy more food. Would it be for lunch only or supper as well? The children could not possibly stay the night for there was nowhere for them to sleep. Roberto was left wailing beneath the kitchen table and the other children were shooed out into the street in front of the house. Maria sighed and put her sewing away and went to change into her street clothes to go out and do the extra shopping. She left the house door open and Roberto was away off in the direction of Via Capobove on his bottom, levering himself along with his heels. He had the instinct of a dog abandoned in unknown country; he could have found his way home from the other end of the world. Giovanni saw him and grabbed him and staggered back with him, screaming, and dumped him under the kitchen table again.

"Gina's too soft with him. Now in the hot weather she should leave him without any pants on then he wouldn't want to scrape the skin off his bottom. He'd soon learn to stand up and walk."

"I should be with Gina, a mother should be with her daughter at a time like this."

"It's not the first time; there's Aunt Agnes. Who else would look after the children? You're their grandmother, aren't you?"

"And their father? Does their father know? Oh Madonna mia, who's going to feed their father?"

"Poor little orphans."

"What do you mean, poor little orphans? Their father's a good man, don't you say anything against him. He works, doesn't he? What else has he got time for with all these mouths to feed?"

Roberto continued to wail. Maria came back at last and took all the children off up into the pine spinney leaving her mother in peace to prepare lunch.

When Anna left, it was too late for the doctor. He had finished his surgery and gone out. Thinking about Gina and looking after her children, she had forgotten about herself. But now, when she realized she could not see the doctor at all that day, she felt ill again—twice as ill as before and nobody was worrying about her. Other people had their troubles but they did not have blood pressure. They did not know what it was like thinking you might burst, blow up—just like that— drop dead. She had no time to rest. She had to change out of her street clothes and prepare Clair's lunch and then change again and take it to her. In this heat it would kill her going all the way down to the shop and back.

Whoever was at the door knocked again. It could be thieves, or gypsies or someone from the church asking for money. She always kept the door locked.

"Who is it?"

"Anna, it's me, Agnes. I've got somebody with me. Open up a minute."

Perhaps it was about the pension. Anna smoothed her hair with her hands. She opened the door and there was Agnes with a man standing just behind her. The man stepped in front of Agnes and held out his hand. He bent his head almost as though he were bowing. "Paolo Palmieri," he said.

There was a moment's silence.

And then Agnes said. "He's been seeing something of Clair. He thought it was time he met you, her mother." She gave a half smile, screwing up her face in a grotesque wink and nodded her head behind Paolo's shoulder.

Anna leaned against the wall supporting herself. "Oh." This time she really did feel faint. "Oh."

"Well, don't keep him here standing in the doorway, ask him in, offer him something."

"Of course, of course." Anna pulled herself upright. She had not changed out of her good dress and she did not smell of sweat because she had washed her body well that morning expecting to see the doctor. She had no need to worry about the house either; what there was of it was always clean and tidy.

"Come in, come in, please." Anna led the way directly into the kitchen. "We've no parlour as you can see. We're just honest, simple people. Please sit down. You too, Agnes."

"I can't stay. I've got to get back to Gina. You don't need me to talk about Clair."

"No, don't go and leave me, Agnes, you can't. Please stay, you must." Anna was all of a fluster. She went to the kitchen dresser and took out a bottle of vermouth and three glasses. She put the glasses on the table and started to pour vermouth into them, her hand trembling, and then stopped with one glass still empty. "But perhaps you'd prefer cognac. Men usually prefer cognac, don't they? And I've still got half a bottle. When my poor husband was ill, he'd have just a little drop of cognac. Only when he was ill. Now he's gone, God rest his soul." She crossed herself. "Since he died we don't have visitors. But if you'd rather have cognac . . .?"

"Thank you, I'll have vermouth." Agnes refused to sit down so they all three stood with their glasses in their hands.

Paolo raised his glass. "To your good health."

"And to yours, and to yours."

"Assisi is a very interesting city."

"Yes, I suppose it is."

"It's a very beautiful city."

"Do you think so? You haven't seen it in winter, of course."

Paolo twisted the glass in his hands. "Your daughter's a very beautiful girl."

"So you've met Clair?"

"I told you! That's what he's come about?" Agnes interrupted.

"But Clair hasn't told me anything. I asked her only the other day if . . ."

"Do you mind if I sit down?" Paolo said. His knees were shaking and there was no reason why they should be. He was vastly superior to these village women.

Anna sat down opposite Paolo. "Perhaps your daughter hasn't understood," he said. "I didn't tell her I was coming here today. She probably couldn't believe I was serious."

"You mean . . . Oh dear, do I understand you mean? Oh dear, if only my poor husband were here now. Agnes, what should I say ? I don't know . . . it's so unexpected. Agnes, help me."

"Clair's your daughter not mine."

"Oh dear, the trials and tribulations of being a poor widow. You'll have to excuse me. It's been such a terrible day and I'm not well."

"I've got to go," Agnes said. "Gina's the one who's having the baby, not you. Remember what you've always said you wanted for Clair."

Anna sniffed. "Yes, it's true. But so unexpected. You do understand?"

Paolo looked round the kitchen. What an offer he was making for such a humble girl. His apartment would seem like a castle to her. He had a parlour where he could receive people. It had straight-backed chairs and a polished table with a bowl of paper flowers in the centre.

Anna began fidgetting with her hands in her lap when Agnes had left. "Well, this is a surprise, I'm sure . . .Oh, if only my poor husband were here . . .Have a little more vermouth . . . Now please say exactly, exactly what you mean. I think, perhaps, I haven't understood."

"I'm making an offer for your daughter. I want your permission to court her. I want to marry her."

"But why? What do you know about her?"

"She's so pure, like a Madonna."

"Like a Madonna? Do you think so?"

"I think so. But she's so timid. And how can I court her if she's always in that shop? She says she works on Sundays too."

"It's true. Since my poor husband died, she's had to work. I'm no use any longer. The shop is better than going into service, but such long hours, such long hours and Sundays too."

"But she won't have to work when she marries me. You must understand. I have a good, safe, job. I work for the post office in Rome. I expect a pension. My family has always been respected."

"For the post office? Why didn't you say so before?" Anna sat up straight and beamed at Paolo. He was no longer a problem but a person. "Oh, how happy my poor husband would have been. That makes all the difference. My husband was a postman too. Only the most respectable people can work for the post office, isn't that so? Was your father a postman also?"

"My father was a school teacher and I'm not a postman. I don't deliver, I work in the post office itself."

"And that's even more important, isn't it? You must really be clever then, to have got that kind of a position and your father being something different too. My husband got his job when his own father retired. He had to have fifth grade elementary school of course. He had to be able to read all those names and addresses but he didn't have to take an exam because he just took his father's place. He was on delivering though, that was his trouble. In the summer it was alright, but in the winter he always got these terrible coughs. And here, you've no idea, when there's snow on the mountain and the wind comes down off it, freezing, channelling down these narrow streets, those post office uniforms are no good at all and he would go out. Even when he wasn't well, he wouldn't miss a day. That last day, I told him not to go, he had a fever and a high temperature. He knew he had and he would go just the same. That's how he got his pneumonia and that's how he died. If only he'd listened to me that day and not gone out. If only he were here now." Anna stopped and wiped the tears from her eyes and blew her nose. "He'd have been so pleased to have met you, you being in the post office too. Have another little drop of vermouth; it can't do you any harm. I will too. I shouldn't. The doctor said, "No drinks, not even wine. But today's a very special day, isn't it? She lifted her glass and Paolo lifted his, too. "Knowing Clair's got somebody like you, it's so, so . . . But you'll want to see Clair's trousseau. I'm sure she won't mind if I show it to you."

Anna led the way into the front bedroom and opened up the shutters to let in the sunlight. "We live very simply, as you can see, but we've always been respected." The great double bed in which she slept with her daughter had a hand-made, white lace bedcover that made it look like a showpiece, as if it were never touched. The only other furniture was one hard chair, a narrow wardrobe and a carved wooden chest. Anna went to the chest and opened it up. "Of course it's not complete yet. I've only twelve pairs of sheets, but they're all good linen, and the top ones are embroidered. Look at this one, that I did. Here's one Clair did herself. And this one, see how deep the embroidery is? This was given to her by Aunt Agnes on the day of her first comunion when she was seven years old." Anna took out the folded linen reverently and laid it on the bed.

Paolo peered into the chest as she emptied it. "Only twelve pairs?"

"Twenty four sheets in all, I know it's not very many. I'm just a poor widow, you know. I've not been bothering so much recently as I haven't been feeling well and there seemed no immediate need. But, of course, now I shall have to hurry up and add more. From where you come from girls have many more, don't they?"

"My sister has," Paolo said. His sister was forty five and was still adding to her trousseau. Recently she had bought herself a second chest and was filling it with linen that she would never use herself; yet nobody else would be allowed to touch as long as she lived.

"Look at these tableclothes," Anna said. "Isn't this a beautiful design? And here's a centre piece Clair did herself. Look how perfectly she embroiders! Look how she finishes off her work! This is the real Punto di Assisi."

Paolo took the embroidery in his hand. "Yes, yes, very well done. Yes, but she needs more linen."

"Of course, of course."

There were nightdresses too, intimate underclothing. Paolo looked away. He could imagine her standing in one of those white linen nightdresses. It would not be transparent but the neckline was cut low and trimmed with lace and the shape of her breasts would be clearly defined, for she would be wearing nothing else underneath, and it would be their marriage night. She would be standing there . . .He must not think such thoughts! Not yet!

"Oh, my Lord," Anna exclaimed hurriedly, putting everything back into the chest. "Here I am talking to you and there's poor Clair waiting for me to take down her lunch. I should have been preparing it and have taken it down already. She'll be thinking something's happened to me. Oh, my Lord. You'll have to excuse me. She'll be worrying."

Anna hurried into the kitchen. Paolo followed her. "You could ask the proprietress of the shop if Clair could have the day off tomorrow, couldn't you?"

"You know I think maybe I could," Anna said. "If I explain about you being in the post office and about this not being an ordinary occasion. Yes, I'm sure I could. Some people are frightened of the Signora but she's not a bad soul. I've known her for years, I could almost say we grew up together. Before I was married I used to be in service in her house; she was younger than I was but only a year or two. In the summer her family used to take a house by the seaside and they took me with them. I had to work of course, but they gave me free time. They never really treated me as a servant. The mistress used to say to her sometimes, . . .her name is Genevieve. Can you imagine, a name like that, Genevieve? . . .when she was being capricious, she used to say, 'Take an example from Anna, Anna knows better than you the proper way to behave.' I was quick in those days, I used to sing when I was working. That was many years ago. Then we both got married and now we're both widows. She opened that shop for something to do after her husband died. She didn't need the money, her husband was a solicitor. But then she didn't want to sit in it all day herself so she offered to take on Clair. She'd understand about tomorrow, I'm sure. Paolo, I'll ask. I can call you Paolo, can't I? Yes, I'll ask if my Clair can have the day off for you tomorrow. You've no idea how glad I am you're in the post office. It gives our families something in common right away, doesn't it?"

CHAPTER 14

Clair stood in the patio outside the kitchen, as she so often did when she came back from work, and stared up at the mountain. In a little while she might never see it again. She was numbed with the unexpectedness of her whole life being organized and changed. She was never to belong to herself again. Once she left Assisi she might never return. The thought of her mother getting rid of her like this and the idea of living in Rome was terrifying, and with that stranger. He'd always be a stranger. She never wanted to leave Assisi. She'd rather remain a spinster, here, than live in Rome with that man.

Only now, on her return home at ten o'clock at night, did she begin to know what had been going on up here during the day. She had been delivering a parcel to one of the hotels when her mother brought her lunch so that she knew nothing of the conversation with the Signora Genevieve nor her mother with that man, proudly showing off her trousseau.

She did not cry. Above the mountain, the sky was deep and full of stars. The Madonna and St. Francis and all the saints were so far away up there. If she prayed to them, how could they help her, trapped down here? Her mother was growing old and ill and dependent on her. How would she cope left completely on her own? Or did she expect to leave Assisi too and live with them in Rome?

Anna called to her from the kitchen. "Come in and shut that door. Just what you need now, standing there getting a chill. We should both get to bed early; we've got so much to do tomorrow."

Clair came in from the patio and sat down at the kitchen table and said, "Mother, we can't ask him to lunch. We know nothing about him."

"You mean you don't! Everybody else does. I've told you already, I had a long talk with him this morning and before that he'd been asking questions about you and about us. All Capobove and Santa Rosa, all Assisi by now, knows he's in love with you. Love at first sight. Everybody's talking about this romance. You're the envy of all the unmarried girls. You've no idea. And the Signora Genevieve thinks I should ask him to lunch and that it would be quite respectable. She ought to know, and she's been so kind. She said if you want more time off whilst he's here, you won't get paid of course, but you could have a few hours each afternoon."

"You're arranging all this as though I'd agreed. I don't like him. He's peculiar."

"Don't be so silly. You'll never get another opportunity like this again. How could I have such an imbecile daughter. I'm doing all this for you. Can't you get that into your head?"

"Is this what you really want for me?"

"Of course it is. Your father would have approved of him immediately."

"Papa would have wanted me to like him."

"If your father had been here to show his approval, you'd have seen reason. Why do you insist on this contrary behaviour when I'm struggling here alone, as if I hadn't enough troubles without your capriciousness. A girl has to use her head when she gets to your age. I shan't live for ever I keep telling you, and then what will become of you? What do you think is making me so ill if it's not worrying about you and your future? Anyway I've already asked him to come to lunch. We've arranged everything. He'll be here at the house at ten thirty, I think he said, and you'll go to Mass together at Santa Chiara. You'd better wear the pink dress with the roses on it, you look your best in that, and your hair! Oh dear, oh dear, you should have been washing your hair instead of wasting time! If you get up when I go to Mass myself at seven o'clock you could have it washed and dry. That's settled then. Now I can tell you what's been worrying me all afternoon and that is, what we should give him to eat at such short notice. At first I thought there was nothing for it, I should have to buy a chicken, but chicken's really too commonplace. And then I remembered, of course, we had the pigeons. They can be done in a hunter's sauce, the way I learnt when I was in service; you've never tasted them that way yourself; they're a speciality."

"Oh no, not the doves, Mamma, please not the doves."

"Don't be so silly child, they're just right, just what we need to make an impression. He won't ever have tasted pigeon better in his life."

"Mamma, please, they're so beautiful, we've had them since they were hatched."

"And we've been feeding them and fattening them up for a special occasion ever since."

"But you said yourself only the other day that they kept you company, out in the patio there, cooing, flying off and always returning. 'So white in the sunshine, so pure, St. Francis's birds,' you said."

"I said that once . . ."

"Don't you remember you asked Fausto to make you a statue of St. Francis for them to perch on just in front of the kitchen window so that you could see them better?"

"I'd forgotten that. He said he could carve a statue out of an old piece of tree trunk he'd already got in his cellar. Maybe it was too difficult for him. Anyway, it's too late now."

"Mamma, please, please, why? Just to make a good impression, why the doves?"

"Stop! Enough! Such sentimentality for a couple of old pigeons. I've had them killed already."

"The doves? I don't believe you." Clair rushed out onto the patio to look into the dovecote that Fausto had made specially for them, where they perched every night safe from cats or rats or any other form of danger. The dovecote was empty.

Anna followed her daughter out onto the patio and put her arm round her shoulders. "I had to have something special to offer your Paolo tomorrow, didn't I? I couldn't kill them myself and I knew you wouldn't be able to, so I got Agnes to do it for me. It's Saturday, so I'd never have found any of the men in the street to do it for me this evening, and tomorrow would have been too late. When they're plucked they're just a couple of pigeons. You know we've fed them so well, you should see the breasts on them."

Clair put her hands over her face, her shoulders hunched, making her body narrower, as if crushed, and the tears began to run between her fingers.

"Oh, come along now. You've got to look your best tomorrow. And for goodness sake, try to be light-hearted and smiling and proud when you walk across the Piazza with your Paolo."

Clair went to bed. She did not sob out loud. She did not move. She sniffed loudly several times and her mother, beside her, grunted.

Clair was so tired, so miserable. She lay quite still on her back in the darkness, not thinking any more, the only movement of her body her long black eyelashes blinking away the tears. Then she dreamt. She could see her body lying on the bed but she was not trapped in it and her doves were not dead; they were flying, and she was a dove with them, circling over the piazzas of Assisi, resting on the roof tops and then flying again. Round and round the People's Tower, their wings white in the sunshine they flew, and then settled again on the temple of Minerva itself. People did not laugh at the doves or try to capture them. Most people ignored them. Perhaps they did not even see them. Others said, "Look, aren't they beautiful," and left them unmolested.

CHAPTER 15

Whilst Clair dreamt, Peter lay awake with his arms behind his head.

After he had left Anna and the children at Piazza Nuova, he had continued on beyond the city walls, climbing up the track between the fir trees towards the top of Mount Subasio.

In his pocket he had two unopened letters. One was from his Aunt Sarah in Shropshire. He had an aunt similar to Gina's, all skin and bones and severity. His earliest memories of life in England were of her reading the Old Testament stories to him. She made him learn whole passages in the school holidays. 'And God created the world,' and the wickedness of Eve and Nebuchadnezzar and the string of impossible names of Hebrew kings.

The other letter was from his mother. She had never made him read or learn anything, as Aunt Sarah had done, but she left her own books all over the house. Sometimes when they were opened, face down, he picked them up to see what she had been reading. She liked poetry. In Florence he had remembered Shelley, 'If Winter comes can Spring be far behind.' Now part of a poem by Yeats came back to him. Something, something . . . and then . . .'how love fled and paced upon the mountains overhead and hid his face amid a crowd of stars.'

He did not know what love was. His father had taught him only the word 'Duty,' and his mother only 'affection,' when she had time for him. Once, just before he had gone to Oxford, she had talked to him about not getting decent girls into trouble and only allowing oneself to get attracted to the type of girl who would stand up to all the social tests. He had met plenty of all types and not been attracted to any of them. It was not love but he, Peter, who paced upon the mountains overhead.

Night after night, up here on the top of Subasio, he walked and walked, caged within his own body, with all that space of the mountains and the sky, around and above him, until his body was too tired to go on. Then he lay down and looked up at the stars. He was doing just that, now, looking up at the stars, the individuals and the millions, the thick white depth of them. It was very clear. For a fraction of a second only he saw a falling star, a reckless breaking away from the mass, brilliantly flashing into nothingness.

CHAPTER 16

Paolo satisfied, Clair dreaming away her misery and Peter still searching. And Franco? He was about to put into practice the only activity that was worth while according to him. He had always maintained that thinking and talking about love was a waste of time. You had to make love to know what it was all about.

That evening he and an American girl he had met earlier in the Piazza walked up to the castle together, their arms around each other's waists.

"Do you know why Latin Lovers are the best?" the girl asked. She spoke French. She had just spent a year in Paris and was now completing her education travelling with her parents on a cultural tour of Europe. It was this language that they had in common which had made it so easy for Franco to pick her up.

"Why are Latin Lovers the best?" Franco asked.

"Because they're superficial. They want to love the body, only the surface of the body; they're not interested in probing the secret places of the soul."

"Who told you that?"

"I read it in a book. When you're making love it's better just to concentrate on the physical emotion, not have thoughts at all."

"You shouldn't read books," Franco said. "Is that all you did in Paris, read books? Do you think that's how you learn about love?"

"About sex, you mean. That's all you boys think about, isn't it, when you're with a girl?"

Franco shook his head. "Not sex, love." He squeezed her waist with his arm. "We make love, we don't make sex, that's why we're the best."

The girl sighed. "I wish I could believe you."

"Why shouldn't you believe me? It's the truth."

"It's superficial love; love that doesn't last longer than the moment."

"It depends."

They were close to the castle now. They stopped and looked down over the rooftops of Assisi. "Isn't it beautiful up here in this balmy silence? Is it always like this?" the girl said.

"How else should it be in summer?"

"You live here all the time so you don't feel the magic?"

Franco shrugged. "Come over here under the wall of the castle."

"In a minute. Look, isn't that the Basilica of Santa Chiara with those great buttress arches?"

"Yes, and there above, with the round dome, is the Cathedral of San Rufino. There's the People's Tower just below us. You can't see the Piazza Comune very well though."

"It's so different from the daylight. During the day there's that warm pink glow of the stone that all the houses are built of, but at night the colour's been taken out and there's only the bulk of the buildings and their shadows and the street lights."

"Are you an art student?"

The girl laughed. "No, but I could become one if I stayed here long enough! Anybody could! There's nothing like this in the States."

"I'd like to go to America. Come up here under the castle wall and we'll sit down and you can tell me about America."

The girl said, "You want to go to America and I don't want to leave Europe. Isn't life contrary?" She was still gazing down at Assisi. "Where's the Basilica of St. Francis?"

"You can't see it from here. You have to walk on until you're standing beneath the look-out tower at the end of the long wall. But not now. Come and sit down now for a little while. Please, for a little while."

The girl let herself be led right up under the outer wall of the castle. He pulled her up the slope, her feet slipping, until they reached the slight hollow which he considered his place. There were a few low scrub bushes which gave it even further protection. Nobody could see them unless from the top of the wall above, and who would be fool enough to risk falling from up there at night?"

The girl sat with her arms about her knees. He tried to pull her back against the bank but her body became taut and resistant.

"You're not afraid of me?" he whispered.

"No, why should I be? I just like sitting here looking at the stars. Don't spoil it all, just the two of us looking at the stars."

"Romantic?" He sat up beside her and put his arm around her shoulders.

This was his first real season at the Latin Lover game. At the beginning of the summer he could count his conquests on the fingers of one hand only, even though he had boasted of many more. But then in June he had met Denise.

Denise had been like so many older, single women, coming to Assisi looking for religion and not admitting it was love they were needing and it was love of which they were starved. Not all of them were as lucky as she was. She had met him. He had cured her of her religion.

For over a month, he had used her, and gained all the experience he had lacked before. She had used him though; that was the point; they had used each other. That first time they had been up here together, it was not he who had begun to make love but she who had grabbed hold of him and pulled his head against her breasts as though he were a hungry infant. At the height of his climax she had whispered desperately. 'My son, my son, my son.'

Franco looked at the girl beside him. She was no more than his age, probably younger. He had learnt the gestures, the technique of love, and for her, he could be the true Latin Lover. He rubbed his cheek against hers and thought about the French woman.

That first time Denise had given him money he had refused, been insulted, but she had said, "This is my holiday, my convalescence, the best thing that's happened since my husband left me. We'll go out to dinner together and all the time you're not working we'll be together. But people must not see that I'm paying. If you accept the money now and pay for everything it will look as if it were you who were courting me." As though the people of Assisi could be so easily fooled and did not know that he never had a lira to his name! "Buy yourself a new shirt," she had said. "And new trousers, so that we'll be a good looking couple together."

In the end he had accepted but he was not a gigolo. If people did not understand it was too bad. He could not explain their relationship to anybody. His own mother had never understood him nor had had time to caress him and listen to him as this woman did. He had begun by being her son but she had taught him all the gestures of love. The telegram that made her leave Assisi came just when he knew she could not teach him any more, and just when he was beginning to tire of her maternal arms.

On that last night they had come up here and made love, but it would have been better if they had not, it was unsatisfying for both of them. She lay back against his arm afterwards and said, "My mother is dying and when she's gone I'll have lost everything except my typewriter. My arms will be empty. I can't put my arms around a typewriter. Think of me, Franco, sometimes! Remember me when you are with another girl. Don't worry, I shan't come back to disturb you. My mother may take months, even years, to die. She's had these attacks before, but I shan't be able to leave her again; my conscience wouldn't let me. Duty holds one to the past, to the older generation. Love has to be projected into the future, and I have no future."

"Perhaps your husband will return to you," Franco had said.

"Not now. The woman he's living with is expecting a child. It was a family that he wanted. He's proved that he's not sterile. I'm the one who is sterile."

They had sat here till dawn, until she had had to go and collect her suitcases and get a taxi down to the station. He had gone to the station to see her off. Then he had gone back home and slept in his own bed all day and his real mother had treated him like a prodigal son returned.

"What are you thinking about?" The girl beside him asked. His long silence had been tantalizing. It was a good preliminary to his gestures and a technique to be remembered. "You," he said. And then his lips were against her ear and down her neck.

"Don't," she whispered. "I don't want . . . I don't know you . . . We've only just met and I don't . . ."

He was whispering too, now. "I love you! You could be my fiancè." His lips moved across her face and found hers and he had pushed her back against the bank. She was wearing only a simple cotton dress with buttons down the front. Nothing could have been easier. His fingers didn't fumble, but were caressing, caressing all the time and she didn't resist. She was like a cat, almost purring, and he felt the urgency in himself and she began to respond and they reached the stage where nothing could have stopped them. He loosened his own clothing.

The moon was higher now, directly over them and they were in full moonlight.

There was a movement on the wall above them and a stone rolled down a little distance away, and then there was a scuffling sound as though someone were crawling along the wall. Franco jerked his head up but he could see nothing and he could not have stopped now even if all the world were watching. He was on her now and in her and she gave a great gasp. The French woman had never been like this. Then they heard a terrifying howl, like that of a chained dog that senses an earthquake seconds before the destruction. It was directly over their heads and a stone, or some object, nearly hit them and then there was a further sound as of a person retreating along the top of the wall, slipping, rattling stones, and then a thud that could only have been made by a body falling.

Franco grabbed for his trousers. His hand touched the object that had fallen near them. It was a pair of binoculars. The girl saw them too.

"My God, I'll kill him! I'll kill him, the devil! If he hasn't killed himself already! I'll kill him!"

The girl clung to Franco's arm. "Don't leave me! You can't leave me here alone!" She was trembling and sobbing.

He helped her button her dress. "I'll find out who it was," he said. But he knew already. Only Fausto had a pair of binoculars like these in Assisi. He had found them up here two years ago, left behind by some tourist. Fausto said he took them up the mountain to watch birds, animals, nature.

"I don't want to know," the girl said. "Take me back to the hotel. Please take me back, quickly."

Franco ran the girl down the slope, holding her up when she stumbled, down through the upper streets of Assisi. In Via Capobove they did not meet a soul. Their footsteps sounded loud and insistent, as though they were thieves. They were sure people must be rushing to the windows to see who they were. There was a large blue bow of ribbon on the street door of Gina's house; the sound of her husband's voice came from the open bedroom window high above. The news had reached him. He had returned home.

Franco avoided the Piazza Comune and ran on, down past the upper church of the Basilica of San Francesco, down into the piazza in front of the lower church. They paused under the portico.

The girl freed herself from his arm. She was out of breath, still trembling. She had not tried to speak as they ran through the city. Franco kissed her and she began to sob.

"Don't worry, whoever he was, he won't dare talk."

"I'm not afraid of being seen . . . it's what we did! Supposing I become . . ."

"Was that your first time?"

"Does it make any difference to you? Does it count as a greater conquest to a Latin Lover if the girl's a virgin?"

"I thought you, living in Paris, away from your parents . . . You talked of love as though you knew."

The girl shook her head. "It was my fault," he said.

"And mine! I wanted . . . I wanted . . . O Franco . . ."Her shoulders began to shake and she was sobbing out aloud.

"Sh . . . sh . . . Do you want everybody to hear you? I'll come and fetch you tomorrow. I'll take you to see more churches if you want."

"Churches? After what we've just done?"

"What do priests know about love like ours?"

The girl kissed his hand.

"I'll come and wait for you tomorrow."

"I'll be with my parents."

"You can give them some excuse; get away from them. Don't you want to see me again?"

The girl put her arms around his neck and began passionately kissing him on the lips. He pressed his body against hers. "Tomorrow, I'll come for you early in the morning and we'll go up the mountain together. Tell your parents something, anything you like, and we'll spend all day on the mountain together."

The girl still clung to him. He loosened her arms from around his neck. He could have her again, when and how he liked, tomorrow. "Go back into the hotel now, there's a good girl," he said.

He walked back up through the empty streets towards Piazza Nuova. He was thinking, calculating. She was a pretty little thing, passionate, but nothing special. American girls were probably all alike and there would be plenty more. If they did not come to Assisi he could go and pick them up from outside the University for Foreign students at Perugia. But that was not the point. This girl's father was rich. Supposing he could make her think she could not live without him and wanted to marry him? Why not?

He was sick of Assisi. He was sick of being closed in. He was sick of suffocating in this stagnant piety. Everybody was so righteous and hard-working. Tomorrow he had promised his mother he would be home for lunch when Maria's Peppe came and the following day he should be starting work up in the stone quarries. His father had got him the job, as he had got him his other jobs that had never lasted for long. His father had said that if he left the quarry, he would have to join the army, he could not go on feeding him any longer. His brothers worked; everybody in the family wanted to work except him. But it was always this physically hard, deadening, manual labour. The stone of Subasio might be polished up and used for beautiful marble flooring for the Pope to walk over in the Vatican, or for some aristocrat in a palatial home; or just for repaving the streets of Assisi. What did he care?

Whoever walked over the stone he had hacked out of the mountainside would be walking over him, treading down his youth and his tired muscles until they became compact old age. In America everything would be different. America was the twentieth century! America was life! And with a rich wife? ... If it did not work out with this girl, America was full of pretty, rich girls, wasn't it? Once over there, there was divorce.

Franco crept into the room where he slept with his brothers. He slipped off his trousers and then as he started unbuttoning his shirt he felt the strap of the binoculars and the weight of them against his side. "My God!" Up there behind the castle wall there must be Fausto still. After a fall from that height he must be dead or dying. Franco dare not go up to the castle alone, not in the dark. He lay in bed sweating, waiting for the dawn. Eventually he fell asleep and it was full daylight before he awoke.

He jumped out of bed. He was afraid of what he might find up at the castle. He made his younger brother go with him but he did not explain why they were going. Where he believed the body must have fallen there was a dark patch on a jutting out piece of stone that could have been blood. The ground beneath the wall was dry, hard and burnt by the long summer sunshine. There was no body, no mark or imprint. Nothing!

Franco sent his brother home, still without any explanation, and went down into the Piazza Comune. If there were any news of what had happened that night the men already there would tell him immediately.

There was the usual Sunday morning crowd greeting every new arrival, gossiping and talking politics and about the money that some people earned and others did not, and of costs and debts and who owed what and to whom. Nobody mentioned Fausto.

"Did you hear the radio this morning, about Czechoslovakia?"

"And what about the English and the Germans?"

"Here's Franco. Ask him what foreign girls think about Italy's position."

"What about the French, Franco? You could tell us something about them, couldn't you?"

"Have you seen Clair's new boyfriend?"

What the hell did he care about Clair's boy friend, or the English or the Germans or the Czechoslovaks? If he went to America he would escape all this useless idling in the Piazza; he would escape work, wars, and peeping Toms like Fausto. To hell with Fausto too! He could not be dead! That much seemed certain. It was not he who had pushed him off the wall, so why should he worry?

He went to the hotel where his girl was staying, to keep his promise to her and deliberately forget his promise to be home for lunch.

CHAPTER 17

Up in Via Santa Rosa, Anna had woken up before five and dressed and cleaned the kitchen and put water on the stove to heat for Clair to wash her hair before going herself up to early Mass in the Cathedral. When Paolo came, Clair was looking more beautiful than her mother had ever seen her before.

Clair and Paolo were equally self-conscious as they walked down into the Piazza Comune on their way to a late Mass in Santa Chiara. Paolo had taken Clair's arm possessively the moment they had left the house. She could not help knowing that they looked good together, that all those idlers in the Piazza Comune were watching them and talking about them as they passed. Perhaps he was not so peculiar; perhaps her mother was right. Walking arm in arm with him, the men must realize she was not such a fool, after all, to have rejected the local boys.

But at lunch time there were her precious doves on the table, no longer pure white; flying free over the city but smothered in a brown sauce in a brown casserole. She felt sick and ate only a little of her mother's home made tagliatelle and some salad. The fool Paolo tried to feed her from his fork, little scraps of her precious doves, as though she were a fledgling herself. He must think it was love for himself that had taken away her appetite. She pursed up her lips and restrained herself from screaming and became

118

as mute as a sulky child. Her mother muttered at her under her breath and then began laughing and talking with Paolo.

After lunch her mother washed up and would not let Clair help, shooing her out onto the patio with Paolo. Paolo took two chairs out and they sat there. The door into the kitchen was open so that Anna could look up from the sink and watch them. The sun was round the other side of the house now so that the patio was in the shade and there was a slight breeze from the mountain. Paolo pulled his chair closer to Clair and took her hand and began stroking it. His fingers worked up her bare arm. Clair felt sicker than before and tight and frightened inside. Out in the Piazza she had held her head up and felt proud, but now, even with her mother watching her, she was too much alone with him. This was what it would be like when they were married, this intimacy. Yet intimacy meant more than this, much more. Oh Mother of God! Nobody had ever talked to her about what it meant! She sat there with her eyes on her lap, her head bent, unable to look at him, only aware that he was gazing intently at her face, almost eating her, as he had eaten her doves. His fingers went on stroking, up and down, up and down her arm, communicating to her his own nervous electricity.

Suddenly they heard a great commotion out in the street. Although they were on the other side of the house, the noise penetrated to where they were. There were shrieks of 'Mamma Mia, Mamma Mia,' 'Who is it?' 'What's happened?'

Clair jumped up and rushed down the stairs, Paolo and her mother followed.

Fausto was being carried towards his home. He looked dead. There was a great gash down his cheek and caked blood all over him. One leg, the little shrivelled one, dangled at an unnatural angle.

Everybody came out of their houses into the street. It was Sunday lunch time, so the men were home and the children, the women, everybody collected outside Fausto's house. The doctor came and said Fausto must go down to the hospital immediately and Gina's husband, Salvatore, who had found him and carried him so far, picked him up off his bed and carried him out again, down the street and through the crowd.

"He moved his head."

"The doctor wouldn't have told them to take him to the hospital if he were dead."

"He'll never walk again now. Did you see how his leg hung there?"

"His poor mother. Those beautiful children that died, do you remember? And this cripple with his nine lives."

"Poor old Fausto. There's no end to his disfigurements."

"To his disablements."

"What happened?"

"He looked as though somebody had beaten him up."

"Like the beatings up there've been in Milan and Turin and Rome . . .?"

"The political . . ."

"Sh . . . that doesn't happen here."

"Not in Assisi."

"He's never been mixed up in politics."

When Peppe heard he was not so sure about the politics. Fausto was a close one. Who knew what he was really up to in that cellar of his. There would be plenty to talk about down in the barber's shop anyway.

That afternoon the Carabinieri went to visit Fausto in hospital. He was conscious. He had been all the time, but he was pale from loss of blood, unshaven with the gash on his face roughly stitched. His leg was broken in two places but as he had never been able to put any weight on that leg, it would not make much difference how or if it were set. He told the Carabinieri what he repeated again and again to all those who visited him whilst he was in hospital.

He had gone out to look for mushrooms and he had fallen against a rock and slipped into a deep crevice and had taken all morning struggling down towards Assisi.

Where were there such crevices on Mount Subasio? He was as sure-footed as a goat for all his deformities and knew the mountain better than anybody. How was it he had got down from the top of the mountain in that condition? His mother said he had not been at home all night. Why had he stayed out all night? Nobody believed his story.

Franco had the binoculars but he did not tell anybody how he had got them nor did he go to visit Fausto in hospital.

PART II

CHAPTER 18

For weeks Peter knew nothing about Fausto's accident nor Clair's engagement nor that Gina's baby was a boy.

He'd found an outcrop of rock like a throne where he could sit and look out across the valley. He was painting very little now. He was not consciously thinking. He was like a field lying fallow, accumulating strength, generating a new fertility. Christ spent forty days in the wilderness; St. Francis on the island in Lago Trasimeno; Peter did his time on Mount Subasio. But he could not see or plan a future as Christ and Francis had done. There was no prophecy yet, only his memories filling in the vacant areas of his mind and slowly, very slowly maturing his thinking so that he knew he would soon have to begin living actively again. But not yet. He was not ready to go down into the valley yet.

As a boy, he had sat for hours on the Longmynd, all alone amongst the heather and bracken, day dreaming of Crusader Knights, himself a hero defending right against wrong, the impossible ideals. He had sketched and painted the stream running down the valley; the spinney opposite. With swift elementary lines he had drawn the pigeons as they flew in from the corn fields on autumn evenings and the magpies in the hazel nut tree. If he sat very still rabbits came out and played in the clearings and he had sketched them too.

How many hours of his holidays had he been alone on the Longmynd?

He was not an only child but he had spent much of his childhood alone. His two elder brothers were twins, twelve years older than he. They spent nearly three quarters of the year at boarding school in England. When they came home they were treated as adults. Peter was not exactly a marital mistake but his mother told him she had hoped for a girl to keep her company, to dress up in pretty clothes. His father too would have preferred a girl, a dainty precious little replica of his wife to laugh and sing about the house, to offset his own masculine silences.

When Peter was a tiny baby, the family had lived in a not very fashionable part of Barcelona, in a small flat with no domestic staff sleeping in at night. His mother often said that that was the happiest period for the family, when they could enjoy being together and their time was not all taken up with business and social engagements. He had been too young then to remember the time before they had moved.

His father's business grew and grew. He imported and exported everything imaginable. British tennis rackets, golf balls, football shorts, luxury breakfast cereals and icing sugar, heavy machinery, French cosmetics and motorcars, American literature, all these and more were shipped into Spain. He exported oranges and olive oil, sherry, hand embroidered shawls and fans, even coals to Newcastle on one occasion during the General Strike. He said there was nothing that could not be bought or sold with the right kind of contacts, the right kind of persuasion, and giving eighteen hours or more a day working at it. Not everything could be done from the Barcelona office and he opened up new branches in other parts of Spain and in other countries. Until the elder boys were old enough to help him, he felt he had to go everywhere and make every important decision himself. He needed the support of his wife more, and took her with him when he travelled.

When his parents were at home, there had to be so much entertaining. In their new huge house there were always strangers at table; strangers enjoying the patio garden, port and cigar smoke and talking late into the night.

Peter's earliest memories were of nurses and governesses and meals in the kitchen. His first real friends were Josè and Maria's two sons, but he had lost even them when he had had to go away to school in England. Of course, like his brothers, he was given the very best education. Banishment was a privilege that only the rich could afford, and there was never any lack of money.

That first term, when he was so homesick for a waft of his mother's perfume, for Maria's scolding and the smell of a Spanish kitchen, he ticked off the days on a calendar, knowing each morning that he was a day closer to the holidays. Then his mother wrote saying what a pity: just when he should be arriving home, she and his father and his brothers would be going away on another business trip. So just this once, he would be spending his holidays with his aunt and uncle on the farm in Shropshire.

That was when Aunt Sarah started making him learn great chunks of the Bible whenever she could catch him, and his uncle taught him to ride Longmynd ponies and tried unsuccessfully to make him shoot rabbits. The only thing they never told him he would be good at was shooting. He always aimed too high to hit anything!

His mother's 'just this once,' was repeated and repeated. He got to know his aunt and uncle better than his own parents and Shropshire better than pre-civil war Spain.

Mount Subasio was like the Longmynd. It was an adult version of the same countryside. As he had grown up, the Longmynd had seemed to shrink into foothills but now he had found Subasio, a man-sized mountain.

Physically, he was man-size by the time he finished at his public school, though, to his father, he was still imature because he said he wanted to go to an Art Academy to study painting, sculpture and design. His mother would have let him, but his father came of different stock, his forefathers had been builders of the British Empire, pioneers, explorers. His father had said he would never finance any son of his who wanted to waste his adult life dabbling with paints. Peter's brothers had gone to Oxford and then into the family business and Peter should do the same.

Down in the valley the soil was being prepared with dung, falling leaves, rain and sunshine. Soon there would be frost to break up the plough and in the spring the ground would be sprouting a new crop. As Peter stared across the valley, he remembered that first year at Oxford. His father had not insisted that he study law or economics; he had been allowed to choose history. It was the next best thing to art and he began to enjoy his lectures and use the libraries and read and research beyond what was expected of him.

Then came that first long vacation when his whole understanding of life shifted to a new dimension. He was no more studying history for he was living it, in one of its sharper moments. At the time, the periods of waiting seemed longer than any events and all that was happening of importance was out of sight and only just within hearing.

In that first long vacation, he returned to Barcelona and his parents welcomed him as they had never done before, as if they had even been looking forward to his return. Of course, the other two boys were no longer living at home. Michael, who had always behaved like the elder twin, had been married for four years and was running the Madrid office; just at the moment he was in England with his wife who was about to have her second child. David, too, had married and was in charge of another of their offices in Teneriffe in the Canary Islands.

But it was not only that the family had dispersed. Spain itself had changed. The night after Peter arrived one of his father's acquaintances was shot in the same street where they lived. He was a man whose chief fault, as far as they knew, had been only that he bored everybody by too frequently and too loudly voicing his anti-Communist sentiments.

There was talk of assassinations almost every day. Occasionally Peter thought he heard single shots.

Then it happened. News came of some kind of military take-over in Morocco, followed by the news of army garrisons rising, in favour of a General Franco, in many of the major cities of Spain. The next morning, waking at dawn to the sound of gunfire in Barcelona; a succession of individual shots and then machine guns and a cannon; and the firing did not stop but became more intense.

The street onto which their house faced was deserted but, on both sides of it, people were at the windows or out on their balconies in their night-clothes.

Nothing happened in their street all morning.

Peter remembered now, all the details. He and his parents got dressed, drank their breakfast coffee at the end of the dining room table and then went up to the third floor where, from the balcony, they could see over the convent immediately opposite, over the roofs of all but the tallest houses, over the railway station, as well as down into the street below. They left the radio on in the room behind them.

The sound of shooting continued and by ten o'clock the radio was being used for calls for doctors, nurses, blood donors. It was being used also for the incredible, wild, hysterical speeches of the Anarchist extremists. Not only men, but also women, were shouting that the time had come for fire, death and destruction in the name of the people, and the radio voices were being obeyed.

From almost every quarter of town, the gunfire could be heard and the smoke could be seen. It was not in their street though; until mid-afternoon their street remained deserted.

It was Sunday. Concetta, the girl who usually came in to clean the bedrooms and wait at table when they had guests, did not appear. Peter's mother went down to the kitchen to tell Josè and Maria not to worry about lunch for there was enough food left over from the evening before that could be eaten cold. She stayed a long time chatting with them, trying to make it seem as though she believed what was happening was unimportant and would all be over soon. They had two sons, one in the army, in one of the cities whose garrison was probably already under General Franco's control; the other was in Barcelona, an active member of one of the left wing political movements. These were the boys who had been Peter's only real friends when he was small; one was just a year older than he; the other a year younger.

In the early afternoon his mother went to lie down in the cool of her bedroom. She told Peter afterwards that she could not rest, but got up and went to her writing desk to begin a new diary in an exercise book. "Events get blurred so quickly," she had said. "The day, the time, the sequence of events, the impressions, that have nothing to do with the history written by research students from official documents and from other people's memories." She had started diaries before and left off when the important moments stretched out into months of trivialities. "So often," she had said, "Big ideas get lost amongst the debris of little necessities."

Whilst she was in her room, Peter had gone out onto the balcony again with his father. "We should have known it was going to come to this," his father said. "We did know. We just didn't want to believe it was possible. All politicians should be shot."

"They are being shot."

"I don't mean shot by unknown assassins in the street. They should all have been dumped on an island long ago, told to come to an agreement or shoot each other, but leave the rest of us alone."

His father, a man of the world, was lecturing him again, talking at him, not to him. "There is no clarity of right or wrong, only chaos. Power hunger, egoism, incompetence destroy all human charity, all human dignity. You don't know what's been going on here. You're only a boy but you ought to know, there's no justification for what's been happening. In March the left wing parties, for the first time, combined. There is no doubt the Popular Front had a legal majority but then they were not satisfied. The Parliamentary Committees set up to examine the regularity of the election certificates found some excuse to unseat almost every one of the right wing opposition and when the Government was finally formed,, 'purged', the first thing they did was to demand the resignation of the President. When he refused and insisted that the question be brought before the High Court, he was unconstitutionally deposed. One of the few remaining right wing members of the Government, Calvo Sotelo protested too loudly and too courageously and he was assassinated. Matteotti in Italy was murdered ten years ago for speaking out against Mussolini's fascist take-over of complete power. This political murder of Sotelo was even more blatant. No attempt was made to disguise its meaning. One group of people determined to dominate all the rest and if in Italy it is called Right Wing and in Spain it is called Left Wing, what difference does it make? Oh, certainly, the Right Wing have not been blameless here. The extremists on both sides have been killing each other off and both sides have attacked the few honest judges and journalists, and others who've tried to tell the truth, remain neutral and objective and live and act according to their consciences. There was bound to be an attempt to restore order. David warned us when he was here last month. Franco was preparing in the Canary Islands and everybody over there knew. Thank God Michael's in England with his family and the Canary Islands are far enough away."

Peter remained silent. He had never had any conversation with his father. He had been expected to listen, not contribute any ideas.

At the end of what would normally have been siesta time, that same day; such a long day, the noise of cars and lorries approaching could be heard before they could be seen. His mother came out onto the balcony and sat between her two men, her husband and her son, holding them each by the hand. The cars and the lorries raced beneath them down to the end of the street, disappeared out of sight and then came racing back again. Up and down, up and down. Most of them were padded with mattresses but every part of the paintwork that was visible had the initials of some worker's syndicate scrawled across it. They were all there. The C.N.T., the U.G.T., the P.O.U.M., the F.A.I. Of the insurgents, some looked grim and carried their guns as though they were experienced and knew how to use them, but the majority were young and excited, holding their guns tensely or waving them carelessly, shouting and laughing. Some of the men were dirty and unshaven, wearing worker's clothes, but many were too young to need to shave, their clothes crumpled as though they had slept in them but never worked in them.

"Look at that third lorry, there. What villainous looking ruffians."

"They've probably been released from some prison."

"What about the women?"

Some of them could be distinguished from the men only on the second or third time past. They were just as grim and dressed the same. Then there were the girls who were out for the ride.

"Look at them, dressed for a Fiesta."

"They're wearing lipstick, rouge, their faces a mask of cosmetics."

"And nail varnish."

"Revolutionary fashion."

"Straight from the whore house."

"Not all of them. Look at that pretty girl there, the one with the red kerchief on her head, laughing."

"And the boy beside her, he can't be more than fifteen."

A cat crouching in a doorway was shot at, missed. It tried to rush down the street but was killed by the fire of a dozen rifles. The lorries in front stopped abruptly, guns were waved up to point towards the balconies and a hidden enemy. There were shouted explanations and laughter and the lorries and cars continued on, disappeared out of sight and returned. The lorry from which the cat had been shot swerved to run over the body with front and back wheels. The lorry behind did the same and the next and the next and the next, the drivers no longer knowing why they were swerving because they had been too far behind when the cat was shot and the body, now paper thin, was only a dirty mark on the street.

"We'd be wiser to go inside," his father said.

"And close the shutters?"

"No, leave them open."

There was nowhere they could go and nothing they could do except wait like everybody else. They did not go out onto the balcony until after they had heard the news that General Goded had surrendered and then his voice came over the radio appealing to his troops to lay down their arms and save further bloodshed.

"No-one can hope for protection now."

People who had nothing to do with what was going on were out on their balconies. The street below was once again deserted.

Their next door neighbour had never gone inside but seemed fixed to the railing he was leaning on, still wearing a pyjama jacket over his trousers. He was close enough to talk to and had often exchanged polite and formal remarks on normal days but now he did not hear the good-evening that was called to him, neither the first nor the second time.

After dark Peter and his father and mother climbed out onto the roof. They could see the whole panorama of Barcelona and in all directions there was smoke and the red glow of flames, but the heavy sound of machine gun and rifle fire had ceased and there were only occasional isolated shots.

"There's no resistance, no resistance whatsoever."

The night passed and the early part of the next morning.

"We'll have to think about getting out for food," his mother said. "There must be some shops open somewhere."

"Surely we've food for a few days."

"Nothing fresh; no bread, milk, meat."

"We can do without. I don't want even Josè to go out. Make a movement, say a word that draws attention, it doesn't matter who you are, and your life'll not be worth more than that of a cat in the street."

Then they heard the lorry driving up fast and come to a stop in front of their house. They had to see, they had to know, but not exposed out on the balcony. They stood back in the room with the shutters almost closed. The men who jumped off the lorry, all armed with guns, pulled great petrol cans out but they did not come to their house, seemed unaware of their existence. Their object was on the other side of the street, the little Franciscan church and convent. The people living on either side shouted and protested; their houses, the local shops, all would be endangered if a fire was started in the church. People came down into the street, for the first time angry. They surrounded the men with the petrol cans, outnumbering them, and the church was not burnt, not that day. The next morning the attempt was repeated and the people were kept at a distance by the guns that were pointed at them. The door of the church was broken down and the altar cloths, images, chairs, stalls, the bell from the belfry, all were thrown out into the street. When the fire was started it attracted, from God knows where, a mob who danced and sang. The organ was not thrown on the bonfire but was out on the pavement and all those who danced around it made music, strumming discordant or sacred music. They had all been brought up Catholic hadn't they! So they interrupted rag-time with sacred music again and again until the strumming was a sacrilege. The Madonna of the Palm from the altar was dragged up and down the street clutching a red flag instead of a palm before she too ended on the bonfire.

Voices called from the street. "And now the Convent, and now the Convent."

And from Peter's balcony, "The nuns?"

"They must have got out. Let's hope to God they took yesterday as a warning and got out in the night."

Then from the street, the sing song. "The bonfire's dying down, stoke it up, stoke it up."

From Peter's balcony. "Oh but look, they're going to throw on the books from the convent library, all those priceless manuscripts."

Josè and Maria had also come out onto the balcony when the singing and shouting started. Peter's mother put her arm round Maria's shoulder. "Our poor tragic Barcelona, our beautiful Spain," she said. His mother in her delicate, feminine soft, floral patterned dress and Maria, in her heavy dark kitchen skirt and apron, mistress and servant, just two little middle-aged women with tears in their eyes.

The glow remained, the glow of ashes remained for hours.

Another night passed and another day came.

The railway station was locked and there were no trains running. The only vehicles moving were those which were loaded with armed insurgents. The tram lines glinted in the sunshine and no shadows passed along them. As the day got hotter the perfume of summer flowers from hidden gardens grew stronger and stronger.

The shops remained closed but the children could not be kept indoors any longer. A number of little ones shuffled around in the dead ashes and debris of the bonfire and got cut on splinters of stained glass and so suffered the loss of precious blood for the glorious revolution too. Older children played football farther down the street.

"Goal!" "Foul!" "You don't know the rules of the game!" "Yes, I do!" "No, you don't!" There was laughter and blasphemy and so many feet running after the ball across the sun-dried paper body of the dead cat that crumbled, and by the evening was dust like the ashes of the convent books.

Parents watched from behind the closed glass doors of their houses or from their balconies but they did not come out into the street themselves and did not talk to their neighbours.

On the fourth day two large cars padded with new mattresses on the bonnets drove slowly into the street. In them were young militiamen standing upright and young militiawomen sitting alert, all in blue dungarees, with pistol holsters on leather belts around their waists, all with rifles held securely, easily. These young Crusaders were clean, their hair brushed, red scarves knotted around their throats.

They called, as they drove slowly past, that from now on all peaceful citizens must keep the shutters of their windows open day and night and nobody should go onto the roofs of their houses. The radio repeated their message.

The next day the same young militiamen and women drove slowly through the street again and called out that all peaceful citizens must show a white flag. The people of the street who had always before been too respectable to hang their washing out where it could be seen, now had towels and pillow cases and pieces of sheeting drooping from their balconies.

Peter's father said, "I'll have to go and open up the office, if I still have an office."

"Wear those old trousers you were going to give Josè for gardening."

"Don't wear a tie."

135

"Nor a jacket."

"I'll come with you," Peter said.

"No, you won't. You'll stay here with your mother."

His father did not come home until late evening and then he was not alone. He had a woman and three children with him.

"They took Fernandez yesterday afternoon," he said. Fernandez was his father's right hand man in the Barcelona office.

"Arrested him?"

"Took him away."

"Why?"

"Both his brothers are in the army, remember. Perhaps that's the only reason. Anyway for the moment his wife and children had better stay with us." They were talking in English. Peter's mother took Senora Fernandez by the hand and led her into the house and chatted in Spanish to the children who were following. She called Peter and Josè and Maria to move furniture and make up beds so that the youngest child could sleep in the same room as her mother and the other two in the room adjoining.

"We've not brought any night clothes, we've not brought anything."

"We must have plenty of pyjamas belonging to Michael and David we can find. They'll be too big, but that doesn't matter. You children don't mind wearing my boys' clothes just for a night or two, do you? Just until all this nonsense is over."

"You're so kind, you're so kind," Senora Fernandez kept repeating. "After they'd taken my husband they shut us all in the kitchen and then burnt or took everything— the shutters off the windows, the furniture, pictures, carpets, even the sheets off the children's beds and everything out of the wardrobes. The children slept on the floor last night but I didn't sleep. How could I? And my husband, they didn't say where they were taking him." She began to cry.

"Sh." Peter's mother said. "You've got to remember the children. Maria's going to bring something for you all to eat and drink up here and then you go straight to bed and have a good rest. There's nothing we can do tonight. Tomorrow we can talk and I'm sure we can find out where your husband has been taken and get a message to him, let him know you're safe with us."

The British in Barcelona had always kept themselves apart from the Spaniards. They did business with them, invited them to formal dinner parties; a few of the English speaking ones were beginning to join the tennis and golf clubs but they were never intimate friends. No Spanish guests had ever slept in Peter's home before. All the barriers were being crossed over, broken down, removed, becoming non-existent; all social, religious and national barriers, all, within a few days.

Peter, his mother and his father sat in the dining room that evening. They did not go out onto the balcony again.

"What's happening beyond our street?"

"Most of the burning has been of churches, convents and monasteries. Santa Maria del Mar, Santa Maria del Pino, San Pablo del Camp and I don't know how many others have all been damaged. Not all the nuns and priests have been as lucky as ours opposite."

"Do you remember those churches, Peter? So much destruction."

"And Fernandez?"

"He's been taken to the ex-convent of San Elias. I managed to find out that much. His wife doesn't know. Better that she shouldn't for the moment."

"And the office?"

"It hasn't been touched. I left my handkerchief hanging from the window on the end of a golf club. It looks very small from below but I hadn't anything else. Thank goodness there are no tourists around with cameras to publicize our shame. The few people I saw all looked like workers."

"Like yourself."

"You know who I mean by the best dressed dandy in Barcelona?"

"The Marquis?"

"He was wearing alpachas, rope soled alpachas, an open neck shirt that even his gardener would have refused to wear to work in, and carrying a shopping bag. He pretended not to recognize me."

"What about the foreigners like ourselves?"

"I went to the British Consulate. There's a British ship standing off shore already."

"You mean people are leaving?"

"Everybody's leaving."

"The remaining tourists or all the British Colony?"

"Everybody. The French and Italians have both got warships waiting to take off their nationals."

"Churches and monasteries have been burnt before. We won't leave."

"You will, you and Peter will if I tell you to."

They went to bed early.

Peter slept late. When he went downstairs next morning he found Maria giving the Fernandez children breakfast in the kitchen. Josè was telling them stories, trying to make them laugh.

"Is my mother not up?"

"She waited until your father had left the house and then she went out shopping."

"Without telling me?"

"You must stay at home, she said. Nobody would harm her, everybody knows her around here, but not you. You must stay in the house, she said."

"Where's she gone?"

"Don't go, please, master Peter. She said on no account were you to try to follow her."

When Maria took coffee up to Senora Fernandez in her bedroom, Peter went to look for his mother. The shops were open and there were women and children in the streets, unsmiling, aggressive, going into the shops and coming out again without anything in their hands. He found his mother in the market. She had just been driven away from an empty stall where the butcher had handed over the last skins, bits of bone and lights, to the woman in front of her.

"I came to help you carry the shopping."

"Carry what, my dear? The stalls are all empty. I wanted milk for those children but there isn't any and there's no meat. You're very naughty to have come out, I told Maria not to let you." She took his arm. He was much taller than she was. She stretched up and whispered. "Now you're here, come with me to buy some flowers."

"Flowers? At a time like this. We've got our own flowers."

"Sh."

They went beyond the market to a fenced-in garden area where there were fruit trees with no fruit on them, a bare vegetable patch and a variety of flowers dying on their stalks, as though nobody had any use for them any more. They came out and he was carrying a large bunch of these flowers, and tucked underneath them was a small dead rabbit and a duckling, carried hidden, as though stolen.

"We paid too much."

"What does it matter. This situation can't last. Just one more thing. Do you remember those little sweet almond biscuits you used to love? The shop on the corner of our street always had them. They were so expensive; maybe the luxury things haven't all been sold. We could get a few for the children."

The shop was open and there were a few biscuits and they bought all that were left. The heavy everyday shopping Josè had always done but when there were guests, his mother enjoyed coming here herself to choose the cakes and pastries. She tried now to chat to the shop keeper as she had done in the past. "Do you remember the station master used to come on Saturday evenings and buy these same biscuits for his children? Every Saturday I used to meet him here. The station's still closed. Have you heard when it will be opened again? We've not been out since the trouble started."

The shop keeper neither smiled nor answered but wrapped up the parcel and took his money. There was nobody else in the shop. Peter's mother looked him directly in the face and he raised his eyes for the first time and stared back at her. "The station master was shot. They gouged out his eyes and cut off his ears before they shot him."

"Who are they? It can't be true."

"Senora, please." He turned away, pretending to be putting something on a shelf behind the counter and Peter and his mother left the shop in silence.

His father came home looking tired and he neither spoke nor smiled.

Peter's mother did not want to tell him about the station master. She began describing how she had used all her wiles and feminine charm to get the rabbit and duckling. Nonsense chatter. He interrupted her.

"Fernandez is dead. You'll have to tell his wife."

"How do you know?"

"I wanted to visit him. They said he'd tried to escape. His body was brought in from along the Rabassada road. There are twenty bodies together with his in the hospital clinic waiting for identification. They were all shot in the back."

The government could not or did not try to control the Anarchist patrols and every day bodies were collected from the Rabassada road and brought to the hospital clinico for identification, a hundred, sometimes two hundred, a day. Peter's father helped Fernandez's widow and children to get away to France where they had relations.

There was no food coming into town. An Army, like the First Crusade, of unarmed women and excited young men with guns they couldn't fire, set off to take Saragossa. They left Barcelona amidst cheers, waving bottles of wine that their friends and relatives thrust into their hands at the last minute.

141

Josè and Maria left too. Going into the country,."and no tears now. It's only for a little while." They all knew that 'little while' was probably going to become like that 'Just this once' of Peter's school holidays.

The British authorities announced that all British women and children had to be evacuated and Peter protested that he was not a child. But his father said, "You're not twenty one and this isn't your war. You'll leave with your mother."

"And you?"

"I have to stay to take care of my interests, don't I? I survived the 29' slump. I can survive this too. It can't last long."

He transferred his necessary clothes and papers to the Marine Club where all the foreign business men were planning to stay. Peter and his mother went on board H.M.S. London and from there to a British destroyer back to England.

In the autumn, Peter returned to Oxford.

CHAPTER 19

It was autumn again now. Two years had passed since the beginning of the Spanish Civil War. 'It wasn't his war,' his father had said.

From his throne of rocks on Mount Subasio, Peter could see how the approaching winter was changing the valley below. Wood smoke from bonfires and farmhouse chimneys hung heavily and there was more mist. Sometimes there was fog down there whilst he was above it all in sunshine; sometimes clouds like fog enveloped the whole of Mount Subasio too. In the summer it had been only the sky in the West at sunset that had made it seem as though all the world beyond the horizon were aflame. But now, there were often red skies in the East at dawn. Then, like a follow-up of smoke, he would see the storm clouds rising over and above the Apennines, approaching and bringing, not snow yet, but a downpour of chilling, driving rain.

He could see Assisi from his throne, so small, enclosed in its surrounding walls. Fausto had not been back to see him for weeks; nobody from Assisi seemed to want to venture out from the safety of those walls or have any curiosity about what was happening in the world beyond. For almost forty days now, he had been up here without seeing anybody except a few peasant women in the village of Armenzano when he went to buy bread and wine. Just occasionally he saw the shepherd. He had not gone down into Assisi, even to the post office to ask for letters. Was his mother still in Spain? Could that war possibly still be going on?

His mother had gone back to Spain before him, without telling him she was going. She had no difficulty with passport control, as he might have done, because she was going to join her husband who was now organizing aid for refugees. Only after she had reached Barcelona did Peter know that she had left England. For a little while she began writing regularly to him.

She used her letters to him, instead of her exercise book, to fix on paper her own particular little view of developing history.

"You know your father never really intended to get involved. He started giving just a little money to the poor relations of the crippled children who had been moved into one wing of the Anglo-American hospital. Then he found he himself had to procure what they needed. As the food shortage in Barcelona became more acute and the numbers of refugees from Franco held territory increased, so the number of women and children coming to the hospital garden increased and soon most of them did not even pretend to be related to the patients in the hospital. When your father wrote and told me what was happening, he did not beg me in so many words but I knew of course, that he wanted me there to help him. That first day after I arrived, my dear, I was appalled. There were Catalans, Castiilians, Andalusians, from all over Spain, women and children whose menfolk were dead or fighting on one side or the other or in prison. It was raining. The paths and the brick bordered flower beds of that garden were already trampled into mud and these people refused to go away. They just stood there expectantly. Your father was so unhappy and depressed. But we talked and talked that evening and as we talked he seemed to recover all his old energy and he began planning. He knew he had got to do something better. You know Peter dear," and now she really was using her letter to him as though it were an intimate diary, "your father's only a man; he isn't a complete human being without me. Way way back in the pre-history of evolution it must have been necessary for two backbones, facing each other, to protect the soft vulnerable inner organs from the pressures of the outside world. I'm being absurd, I know. But I feel now together we make up one complete self again."

She was so tiny, he so physically enormous. Together they had taken over a vast covered garage opposite the hospital and turned it into a kind of milk bar where, not tens, but soon hundreds, and then thousands, came every day for a glass of hot milk and a handful of biscuits and just sometimes a little rice to take home.

Michael in England, who had inherited the most of his father's organizing ability, formed a theatrical troup of Flamenco dancers, singers and guitarists, all Spanish exiles, who travelled from town to town raising the money to buy the powdered milk and biscuits and rice. Before each performance Michael stood on the platform of the cinema or town hall he had taken over, and spoke just dramatically enough, just sincerely enough in his appeal, while his own tiny daughter, dressed in full Spanish costume, with one hand clutching the high backed comb that kept falling out of her hair, toddled down the aisles helping to carry the collecting boxes.

David was cut off in the Canary Islands, the only member of the family to keep the name of the business alive from the only office branch still open.

Peter remained in Oxford. His father who had said it was not his war, had sent him home like a child to finish his education and he remained in Oxford for another full year.

Very soon students he knew went off to join the International Brigade, as unprepared as the Spanish heroes who had set out to take Saragossa or sailed to recapture Majorca. He tried to tell these students it was not their war either; certainly it was not an all-right against an all-wrong type of war, for every idealist to get involved in but they would not listen to him.

Peter finished his second year at Oxford and spent his long vacation with Michael, following the troup around, helping back stage, and running errands like a good, obedient, younger brother.

He went back to Oxford for his third and last year, to continue to cram his mind with past history whilst present history was being fought out. But he could not concentrate as he had done before. Social life had the taste of stale tobacco smoke and student debates and arguments were as senseless as ball games, backwards and forwards on the same square patch of ground.

He joined a flying club and there he met Miguel.

Miguel was not very tall but so handsome, dark hair, black eyes, he seemed a romance image of a young Spanish aristocrat. He was learning to fly because he had to get back into Spain to look for his father and find out for certain what had happened to him.

146

"My father had a mistress," Miguel said, "My mother won't accept that he's still alive and that he's taken this opportunity to desert us. She prefers to think that he's dead. He was well enough known. Somebody would have been able to tell us if he were really dead, wouldn't they?"

All Miguel cared about, to start with, was taking off and landing. Flying was fun and the first time he was allowed up alone without the instructor he did a couple of acrobatic rolls and when he came down he was laughing. Just as soon as he found his father he would join Franco's forces. Then when all the troubles were over in Spain he would become a stunt pilot and draw bigger crowds than a bull fight.

Miguel came from Barcelona too. He was so certain that Franco was right. "Don't just take your father's word for everything that's happening. Don't read the newspapers. Grow up. Come with me and see and judge for yourself." He told Peter of his plan. He knew where he could pick up a little plane in France not far from the Spanish border and where he could land on the other side, just within Republican territory. He had worked it all out. All he needed was company for the journey.

Peter went with Miguel to France. He was not going to return to Spain to help his parents. If they were one self, they would not want him to divide their togetherness. If they had needed him they would have sent for him already. He was not going to fight but begin some kind of search for the Truth. Miguel was right. Every man should stop listening to the preaching of others and work out his own Truth. That was what life was all about.

His mother still wrote to him, though not so frequently. He knew about the street fighting in Barcelona and how in

June the Communists had won control, condemning their earlier allies of the Trade Union Movements. The criminals and the idealists alike were shot or in prison so that the order that Franco would have wanted could be restored. The last letter he had received, she had written. "Things seem to be settling down. If it were not for the refugees and the problems of feeding them we could say almost back to normal. Your father is once again wearing a tie and his alpacca jacket!" Was the other side saying the same? Was there really no difference?

Peter and Miguel took a haversack each, and a blanket. Peter took his camera and at the last moment he put a sketching block and a handful of charcoal and soft pointed pencils into his haversack amongst his rolled up sweater and spare trousers and shirt. They made out an official looking permit for Peter to move freely in any part of Spain, pretending he was a journalist and smothering the permit with indecipherable rubber stamp marks. Maybe he really could be a journalist.

They were being irresponsible, immature. What they were planning, and the way they were planning, had nothing to do with the serious adult situation and they began to enjoy themselves. They went to France in a fishing boat like smugglers, Miguel carrying no identifying documents, no change of clothes but a haversack bulging with English bank notes, enough to buy an aeroplane. They reached the little private airfield by train and local bus and Miguel emptied out his haversack; in return he received a fragile two-seater biplane painted bright yellow.

They took off at dawn with no trouble at all; it was a beautiful take off. But the instruments were not working.

They did not know their height or their speed and they had no way of telling what difference the wind was making to their direction. The only flying either of them had done was around Oxford, flat country, and here they were, with the Pyrenees seeming only a few feet below them and pushing them up higher and higher. The plane wobbled and shuddered enough to make a sailor queasy.

After an hour's flying Peter shouted. "Have you noticed the fuel tank is still registering full?"

Miguel did not hear.

"What do we do about landing if we don't find your airfield?"

"Look at the map." Miguel shouted.

"I have been. It was made for people driving along roads not flying over mountains."

Somehow they got beyond the main ridge of the Pyrenees and were flying down towards pastures and cultivated land.

"We're in Spain. Can't you smell the difference? See the difference?" Miguel shouted.

"We've no idea where we are. We've got to find a place to land."

Miguel began singing. He brought the plane lower. It was a beautiful morning, late autumn; not quite winter. They could see villages, clusters of farm houses, a church, fields divided off from each other by hedges or stakes, a narrow country road and then a small town where they could see the women in the streets. The aeroplane was noticed; faces were turned up; children pulled quickly into the shelter of doorways. And then the engine started spluttering and cut out completely and Miguel managed to glide out over the last roof tops between two trees into a field that was flat with hardly any bumps. He made a perfect landing.

They got out and stretched and weaved around as though drunk and clapped their hands and stamped their feet. They had not realized how cold they had been. They began to laugh.

"We made it, we made it."

"And the plane's not damaged at all."

"What was that town?"

There were people coming across the field towards them. Peter thrust his passport into Miguel's hand. "You'll be safer to be English until we know where we are."

"Do I look English, for goodness sake? Do I look like your photograph?"

"I'll do the talking. We're both mad English; we got lost; we won't even say we're journalists unless we have to; we're nothing to do with the war."

"Let's get away from the plane before any authorities arrive."

"Abandon it?"

"Fast."

The people's immediate interest was in the plane not them. They hid until dark and then found a farm house where there was an old man and his wife, and a young woman who stood by the fireplace watching them, holding a baby against her hip as though it were a bundle of old clothes. They asked for food to take away and they were given it in two separate packages, and two bottles of wine. "As though they knew we were going in different directions," Peter said when they left.

They had never planned to stay together. They split their map of Spain in half, Miguel taking the Eastern part,

Peter the Western. They came to a road that they both intended using as a guide line to start with, walking close to it but not always along it. There they clasped hands like Englishmen and then embraced like Spaniards, smiled foolishly and walked off in opposite directions. They both forgot, for several hours, until they were too far apart, that Miguel had Peter's passport still and now it was Peter who had no document, except the forged permit.

"But I'm searching for the Truth at last. My Truth, not anybody else's, starting from the beginning without any identity." Peter sat down right there beside the road and began drawing, before he should forget. That peasant girl, holding her baby against her side like a bundle of old clothes was his first impression on this return to Civil War Spain.

It was ridiculous; crazy; but then the whole venture had been from the start; a student escapade that was no longer funny. For the next few days, the only people he saw were women and children and old folk. There were no young men to help maintain the fruitfulness of the land or the further procreation of the family. It was the beginning of a winter of trees without leaves, of fields with no new crops growing in them, nature at a standstill. When he came to where the fighting had been, there, nature itself had been destroyed. The trees had branches ripped off; trunks were wounded with great gashes in their sides; cart tracks were so pitted and full of holes that nothing with wheels could possibly pass along them.

He walked up on to high ground to get a sense of direction and came across abandoned trenches. Nothing had been left except the litter, cigarette ends and rusted food tins and rags, amongst the churned up dried out excrement and mud. There were patches where the ground was burnt, where fires had been lit. In one patch were the charred remains of old boots. He went down the steep slope, across rusted barbed wire that had been cut and had coiled back on itself, into what must have been no-man's-land. There was a body; what was left of it, a soldier. But from which side? Abandoned by his comrades or searched for and never found? The skeleton and the clothes that were now only rags and the rusted gun which looked as old as the one his father kept in a glass case, left over from the Boer War. Peter spent all morning scraping a shallow hole with his penknife; the knife he used to cut his bread. There was just enough earth to cover the skeleton but then there was nothing he could find to mark the grave, no wood, not even two twigs he could lay in the form of a cross. He stuck the gun into the ground, a symbol of war; but perhaps the unknown soldier had fought for some ideal.

He went on down the steep slope and at the bottom there was a clean, clear stream. He knelt to drink and then climbed up the opposite side and at the top there were more trenches. Supposing Jose's sons, his friends, had been here? Too far apart to recognize each other, and too far apart to hit each other, unless either side were ordered to make an assault. Then probably creeping as close as possible in the dark before the rush forward and the noise of guns and screams and jabbing bayonets and the fury of killing so as not to be killed. On this side too there were the same rusted tins, the same dried excrement and mud.

For the next twenty-four hours he did not meet anyone, saw only the remains of farm buildings, tortured trees and the wasteland of uncultivated fields. There were no wild or domestic animals or birds. It was as though he were the survivor of plague in the Middle Ages. He was starving and talking out aloud to himself when he eventually saw a village. It was like a mirage and he stumbled towards it without wondering which side he had crossed into, or out of, and into again.

There were no villagers but Italian soldiers who surrounded him; a living creature; a diversion; their own pet prize spy. They took him in triumph to their commanding officer who was furious with them, and with him, because he did not know what to do with a British spy.

"England and Spain aren't at war but there's a war on. All kinds of foreigners are mixed up in it. How can you be so unintelligent as to go wandering around the countryside with notebooks and a camera and call yourself a journalist?" He picked up the false permit. "This isn't a document. Where's the photograph? Where's your passport? You must be a spy." He shouted suddenly and one of the young soldiers who had captured Peter rushed to his side. "What's going on here then? Aren't we going to eat?"

The young soldier was nervous. "The chicken hasn't laid its egg yet."

"What do you mean? It's always laid it by mid-day before. Go and look again."

A cottage kitchen was being used as headquarters. The soldiers referred to their commanding officer as 'Old Tagliatelle.' Now he put his head in his hands and his elbows on the kitchen table. The alarm clock in his stomach had gone off and the gastric juices had started dripping on his ulcer; the ticking of the clock past meal time.

The soldier came back. "Still no egg."

"Someone's stolen it. I'll have them shot. Get out and take this fool with you and bring me something to eat, do you hear, immediately."

Two other soldiers were waiting outside. They led Peter down the village to where the cookhouse had been set up. The streets were churned up but the houses were not damaged. The inhabitants had all left before the Italians arrived. There were still a few patches of feathers where some chicken that had been left behind had struggled frantically in a last effort to survive.

"There's been a guard on that hen all morning. Nobody could have stolen its egg."

"It's been embarrassed, that's the trouble, being watched all the time."

"It misses its companions."

"It's going broody, I know the signs. It hasn't seen a cock since the day we arrived."

"Since we had that dinner."

"Old Tagliatelle can fill up his stomach with mess spaghetti like the rest of us, can't he?"

"Make him his pasta without egg for once."

"At home he always had at least two eggs in his tagliatelle. It's a great sacrifice to have it with only one. He'd never touch it with none at all. He'd see how pale it was."

"Put flour in the tomato sauce so it sticks, then he won't see the colour of the pasta underneath. He'll never know the difference."

The soldiers did not know what to do with Peter. They had had no orders. He ate with them. They had put flour in all the tomato sauce and it stuck to the long over-cooked mess spaghetti like congealing blood. They walked him round the village in the mud and below the old walls and the deserted swallows' nests. The swallows had flown even before the inhabitants.

"You should just let me escape, walk away," Peter said. But they could not do that. In the evening he sat with them while they played cards. Old Tagliatelle had kept his haversack but he borrowed a piece of lined notepaper and began sketching with a stub of pencil. They all wanted to have their portraits done.

They had been in that village for two weeks, doing nothing. They wanted to go home. They had not seen any girls for how long? Not even in the distance. The war should have been over last year. It would have been if they had taken Madrid.

"They said we didn't take Madrid because there were traitors amongst us. Some officers had men shot, as an example of discipline, without knowing if they were traitors or not. They stopped ambulances and tipped the men on stretchers into the road and ripped off their bandages to see if their wounds were real or if they were deserters. I saw it happen with my own eyes."

"They said it was the Duce himself who ordered it."

"I reckon this isn't our war. We shouldn't be here at all."

"Old Tagliatelle hasn't had anybody shot."

"Not yet, but his ulcer's getting worse."

"He'll not have this spy shot, he likes the English. He spoke to you in English, didn't he?"

Peter nodded. Knowing Spanish he understood the Italians well enough.

"We'll keep you away from him before lunch. He's a different man after meals."

"It all depends on that chicken."

The next day the chicken laid its egg and Peter's life was saved. Old Tagliatelle sent for him after lunch. The contents of his haversack had been tipped out. A small pile of dirty clothes lay on the floor and strewn across the table was his false permit, the film out of his camera, an English newspaper cutting, an empty notebook and numerous sketches. Old Tagliatelle kept looking at the sketches but he picked up the permit and the newspaper cutting and handed them to Peter. "Did you write that article?"

Peter shook his head. It had been printed two weeks before he left Oxford. He looked again at the large heading, the words Barcelona, Refugees with the photograph underneath. His mother was unrecognizable. They had inked in false eyelashes and a false line to her mouth so that she looked like a smirking film star. The great soup ladle in her hand looked as though it had been added afterwards too, it was ridiculously large. The huge height and bulk of his father came across better. Black and white was alright for him but his mother needed the bright bourganvillia of her clothes and her natural smile. "The epitome of British Charity," Peter said.

"Read! Did you recognize those two? Their surname's the same as the one written on this permit thing of yours."

"Of course. Why would I be carrying around that piece of paper otherwise? They're my mother and father. They're nothing to do with the Republican Government or the Communist Party or anything else, if that's what you're thinking. They don't ask the politics of the people they are feeding. They're just trying to help the victims of this war from both sides, the women and the children, and they're not doling out soup but milk and biscuits."

"They're in Barcelona, aren't they?" Old Tagliatelle walked around Peter, round and round like a small, very aristocratic dog around a lamp post, muttering. "I should have you shot. I should have you shot."

"My father's great at organizing, anything and anybody. What's wrong with his organizing Christian charity? Whose fault is it if the peasants abandon villages like this and then find themselves safe, where there's no fighting and no food?"

Old Tagliatelle went back to the table and looked at the sketches. "You're not a journalist! You did these, didn't you, this Madonna and Child?" He picked up the first sketch that Peter had done after leaving Miguel, the young peasant girl holding her child like a bundle of old clothes. It had become his symbol of Civil War Spain. She would not get her husband back. She would never grow older or wiser, her child never learn to walk. "I hadn't thought of her as a Madonna," Peter said.

"Of course she's a Madonna! Every woman holding a child is a Madonna." Old Tagliatelle began muttering to himself, not to Peter at all. "Good, good, very good, but he's still got a lot to learn and when will he learn if I have him shot? What am I supposed to do with him anyway?" He looked up suddenly. "The greatest artists in the world are the Italians. You know that, don't you? I'll send you to Italy, if I don't have you shot now! That's what I'll do. You must go to Rome, and Florence, work backwards through the Renaissance to the very beginning. You must stay at least a year. My mother lives in Perugia; She'll help you."

Peter began to laugh.

"There's nothing to laugh about, you fool. Do you want to die or do you want to become a real artist? You'll take this Madonna and Child as a gift to my mother and I'll write her a letter explaining who you are and she'll help you." Peter was dismissed and sent out to join the ordinary soldiers, carrying his dirty clothes under his arm.

The next day there were rumours that there was fighting ten kilometers away; maybe fifteen; maybe fifty. Nobody knew who started the rumours or what the truth was.

"They don't tell us anything."

"What do you want to know?"

"If you're going to be sent into the trenches tomorrow?"

"If they've decided it's time you died?"

"Better to get it over quickly instead of sitting here rotting."

An ambulance came in that evening, bringing the wounded.

"How far had they come? Where was the fighting? Where were they being taken?"

Old Tagliatelle sent for Peter for the last time. "You've driven a car?"

"Yes."

"We've solved all our problems then. There's an Italian ship leaving Cadiz in the next few days, perhaps tomorrow night. You've got to get these wounded onto it, and you've got to get there in time. The regular driver is already tired. He can't drive non-stop for twenty four hours. He's got to bring the ambulance back and I'm not sending one of my own men. You'll go on board with the wounded, as a volunteer Red Cross worker, son of a British friend of mine. And don't let anybody ask how near the truth that is."

"And if I refuse to leave Spain?"

"You have no choice, And be grateful for what I'm doing for you." He came round from behind the table and put a hand on Peter's arm. "We should have had time to talk, but it's too late now. You think I'm a soldier just because I like giving orders? You'd prefer anarchy, the wiping out of Europe's culture, her history, her achievement? That's what's happening in Russia. The new generation are taught that everything began with their glorious Revolution, before that there was only slavery, an empty desert. But the real empty desert is the Revolution itself. We've preserved Italy from such lies and we're going to save Europe. I'm even saving a fool like you. Who knows, one day perhaps you'll be famous and I'll have you to paint my portrait and I'll be famous too; my portrait will be for posterity as the man who recognized your talent and didn't have you shot."

Old Tagliatelle would never have his portrait painted. He was dead. He and his boys died like heroes his mother was told.

CHAPTER 20

From way down on the road that ran through the valley below Assisi, not far from the village of Rivotorto, Peter's rock could be seen but from such a distance his figure was not visible against the dark background of the mountain.

Fausto had spent the night in the church of Rivotorto; in the church that had been built to cover the little stable where St. Francis had slept with his first companions before ever he had gone down to Rome to ask permission from the Pope to be allowed to form his religious Order. The priest had not known that he had shut Fausto in on the previous evening and he had slept on the floor of the stable in the place where St. Francis himself must have slept.

He came out into the early morning sunshine, stiff and cold and shivering, because it was November and there was no warmth in the sunshine. People said he was crazier than ever since his accident. He knew he must be, to have felt pulled down into the valley instead of wanting to climb the mountain. But now he must find the will and the energy to get back up there somehow. He had to find Peter again.

He got a lift up into Assisi on a cart that was being pulled by two great white oxen. They seemed to take all morning to cover those few kilometers. They stopped to rest near the spot where St. Francis had insisted on being put down on his last journey from Assisi into the valley to die. It was the spot where St. Francis had looked back and

160

blessed the city, and not only its native inhabitants but also those who came briefly to visit; people like Peter perhaps.

The city was laid out like a postcard. On the left the huge Basilica of San Francesco with its two churches one on top of the other being only a small part of the great fortress-like structure. The arches leading on from supporting the monastery right through to supporting the lower piazza in front of it. The castle stood detached on the top of its hill against the skyline and beneath, working across right was the People's Tower and then the blue-green dome of the Cathedral and farther across still, the tallest tower of all, that of the Basilica of Santa Chiara. St. Francis had not seen these landmarks, for none of them had been built until after his death; but the houses had been there; simple people's houses like his own, and the streets had been there and the piazzas. Peter would know how to paint this better than any postcard.

The oxcart was overtaken by three young men from the mountain village of Armenzano leading half a dozen bullocks. They had been south of Rome to fetch them, to sell them in the market that was held every month outside Porta Nuova. They had been eight days on the road coming back, sleeping in farms where they had friends. They would be returning again in a few days. Prices were lower still in the south. The profit they could make up here was worth the long journey barefoot. They walked for only a little while alongside the oxcart talking to Fausto. They knew Peter. Was it not from their village that he bought his bread and wine?

"He doesn't even ask for salami any more."

"And people say he's got money enough to eat steak in a restaurant every day."

The men hurried ahead. They would not be home for hours yet but they knew, over the open fires in their kitchens, there would already be great cauldrons of beans and porkfat, simmering very slowly. That evening they would be sitting in the warmth of their own kitchens eating huge platefuls of hot, stomach filling beans.

When he finally arrived up in Assisi, Fausto went home for lunch and his mother cried over him and scolded him because he had not been back the night before. She said he was crazier than ever since he had had that bump on his head and he was driving her mad too, worrying about where he was. He would not speak to her. He ate the cold white rice she had prepared for his supper that previous evening and then left her muttering about her pain and sorrow, trial and tribulation, like all the other miserable women in Assisi.

He had to take his mushrooming stick with him. He could not even walk from his home to the bar in the Piazza any longer without his stick. People kept consoling him, saying he was lucky to be walking at all.

He met Peppe who was on his way back from lunch to open his barber's shop again. "Where've you been? You look as though you'd slept in some Franciscan hovel. You'd better let me clean you up before any of my respectable customers arrive."

"As though I'd got some fiancè like your Maria who cares what I look like!"

"Don't be a fool!" Peppe took the stick from him, put his hand under his elbow and walked him down to the barber's shop and sat him in a chair and put a towel round his neck.

Fausto closed his eyes. He could not look at himself in all that expanse of mirror. Peppe lathered his face all over, even his forehead and around his ears and then shaved very carefully, avoiding the scar on his cheek and then he patted him dry and washed his hair. Fausto relaxed and before Peppe had finished he was asleep. He woke to hear men's voices talking about St. Martin's Day.

"We'll take Fausto along too! He's never missed! We'll borrow a donkey or a mule or something to get him up to the Hermitage."

Fausto opened his eyes and swung round away from the mirror. "I don't need a mule or a donkey."

"So you've had your beauty sleep then? Don't get offended. I wasn't saying you couldn't walk to the Hermitage but just that you might find some excuse for not wanting to try."

Fausto put a hand in his pocket. "How much do I owe?"

"Forget it," Peppe said. "Just make yourself responsible for finding two or three kilos of chestnuts. Maria's father shot a hare and we're going to have steaks; a real feast. We've got everything organized except the chestnuts. St. Martin's Day is only the day after tomorrow, or had you forgotten that too?"

"Who's going to be there?"

"The usual crowd. Who do you expect? We're going to make it a leaving party for Franco."

Fausto went back to Via Santa Rosa, to his basement workshop. He had the twisted root of a tree propped against the back wall, that he had picked out from the firewood three years ago or more. It was almost as tall as a man, a very small man. St. Francis had been a very small man but not twisted like this root, like himself. He could never get a statue like the one in the Basilica cloister out of it. Yet, that knotted bump, just where the waist should be! Perhaps he could groove out a hollow in it, so that it would become a nest in St. Francis's hands, like the statue at Santa Maria degli Angeli; or perhaps the hollow would hold water and Clair's doves would come and drink from it. He had promised Clair that he would give her two new doves, whiter and more beautiful than the ones that had been eaten. He looked at the wood for a long time and began humming to himself. Then he took his knife out of his pocket.

The wood was hard and his leg would not support his weight when he was standing. He tried sitting on a stool and gripping the wood between his knees, but one knee gripped and the other didn't. St. Francis was there in that piece of old wood; the outline and the detail; he could see the whole form but he could not get him out; he could not even begin. He slashed at the wood and his knife slipped and cut his hand. It was only a graze that hardly drew blood but he began to sob. His knife had fallen to the ground. He went on his hands and knees searching for it, dragging his shrivelled leg after him, amongst the junk and rubbish, the nails and bent wire and the firewood and broken crockery. He found the knife; he had it in his hand. He could cut his veins with it there and then. Other people did even here in Assisi; people whose lives were far easier than his. He looked quickly towards the door, and there was Roberto, Gina's little Roberto, sitting just inside the entrance with his thumb in his mouth, staring at him.

"What are you doing there?"

Roberto raised his shoulders the way his father did. He did not take his thumb out of his mouth.

Fausto dragged himself up off the floor. "I haven't got any little birds for you to see. They've all died or flown away. You knew that."

Roberto did not move.

"I suppose you've come scrounging for sweets then."

Roberto shuffled himself closer, still with his thumb in his mouth. Fausto felt in his pocket. He usually had sweets in his pocket for Gina's children. He had one left. He held it up. "You'll have to get on your feet and take that thumb out of your mouth if you want it."

Roberto pulled himself upright, using the twisted tree root for support, staring at Fausto's hand through his thick eyelashes. He grabbed at the sweet with his free hand and put it quickly in his mouth and then put his thumb back in again as though it were a stopper to prevent it falling out.

"You'll choke," Fausto said and made a movement to pull Roberto's hand away but Roberto wriggled out of reach, dropped to the ground and, using his heels, levered himself off down the street towards home on his bottom.

Fausto tugged the door of the basement closed and went up the outside steps into the house above. He walked through the kitchen, where his mother was, without looking at her and into the sitting room where he had his couch bed. He flung himself on to it, face to the wall. He pretended to be asleep when his mother came in. She began scolding because he was lying there with his boots on and fully dressed and his clothes were all dirty and she spent all her life washing and sweeping and cleaning and all she ever saw was dirt.

"I suppose you've been drinking again, if you can't even hear what I'm saying," she muttered. She tugged the boots roughly off his feet, twisting the weak leg as she did so. "Why I should be afflicted in this way I don't know, and me not getting any younger, Madonna mia, I know you're a good boy really, if only you'd just sit still quietly and not try to be like normal men but just accept that you were born different."

He slept in the early part of the evening but by midnight he was awake and could not sleep again. He put on the light and collected half a dozen parchment slips from the box by the window and began copying St. Francis' Canticle of the Creatures in a fine stylized hand. He knew this medieval Italian by heart:

Laudatosie, mi' Signore, cum tucte le tue creature.

Praise be to thee my Lord with all your creatures.

Specialmente Messer lo Frate Sole . . . Sora Luna e le Stelle.

Especially mister Brother Sun . . . Sister Moon and the Stars.

Frate Vento . . . Sora Aqua . . . Frate Fuoco . . . Sora nostra Madre

Brother Wind . . . Sister Water . . . Brother Fire . . . our Sister Mother

Terra . . . Quelli che perdonano per lo Tuo Amore, et sostengon

Earth . . . Those who pardon for love of you and support infirmitate et tribulations. infirmities and tribulation.

Laudato sie, mi' Signore, per Sora nostra Morte Corporale,

Praise be to thee my Lord for our Sister Bodily Death

Da la quale nullo homo vivente può skappare.

From whom no living man can escape.

Fausto went into the kitchen and cut himself the back end of a loaf of bread and put it in his pocket. He left the house whilst it was still dark. Using his mushrooming stick like a crutch he set off up the road towards the mountain. He could no longer hop-jump-run but only hobble, slowly, so slowly. It began to get light. He stopped to rest and looked up and was sure he could see a figure silhouetted against the sky-line, only a pin point figure, Peter?

He had no watch but he knew from the amount of daylight that he was too late for early mass at the Hermitage. Above the Hermitage he took the track that led right towards the ruined Benedictine Abbey and then left it for the short cut through the stoney gulley, straight up. When he came out onto smooth grass, he kept close to the treeline on the side of the valley of Spoleto.

There was a clear sky but very little heat in the sun. There was no sign of the shepherd and his flock nor of the cattle and horses that usually grazed up here in the summer months. But Peter was there. Peter was still there.

They embraced and laughed and patted each other on the back, just the two of them against the skyline.

They did not comment on each other's appearance. Fausto's face and his smile, which had compensated for all the other ugliness, was ruined too now; the scar had healed into a thick weal that was bright red at this moment after the exertion of his climbing. He collapsed on the ground, not only his crippled leg but every muscle in his body was shaking. Peter sat down beside him.

Peter had not shaved for weeks and his clothes were in rags. He had lost weight.

They were silent for a little while and then Fausto said. "Do you know how long I took to get up here? Hours and hours."

"But you arrived eventually."

"Yesterday I wanted to kill myself."

"But you didn't, and today you're on top of Mount Subasio."

"I came up here to find you. You've had your forty days. When are you coming down into the valley to start preaching?"

"Preaching?" Peter laughed. His voice had changed; it was nervous and rough as though he had a sore throat.

"I've been waiting all this time."

Peter put an arm round Fausto's shoulders. "You know I'm not a preacher."

"Like St. Francis, getting away from people, meditating, searching for your faith up here in the mountains. But Francis didn't allow his followers to meditate only. They had to do as he did. They had to go down into the valley and start preaching too."

"Fausto, I haven't got any faith. I've been talking to myself, to the wind, to the open spaces. Not even the birds would listen to me."

"You are painting? sketching?"

Peter shook his head.

Fausto pulled his bread out of his pocket and offered half of it to Peter. "You're thinner than you were. You haven't been eating properly. You'll get ill and then who'll look after you?"

Clouds had come up from behind the Apennines and were covering the feeble sun. Peter put his blanket around Fausto's shoulders.

"Perhaps you need more time. But you can't stay up here all winter."

"I know."

"I'll find you a place where you can sleep in Assisi. There's a widow who lives in the house next to mine. She'd take you in. She'd cook for you and wash your clothes."

"Not yet," Peter said. "I'm not ready to go down into the valley yet."

"You can always come back up here on fine days, and return to sleep in the Spring. Come down with me now."

Peter shook his head.

"Not tonight then. But tomorrow evening. Tomorrow's St. Martin's Day. I'm going to be up at the Hermitage. You know where it is, don't you? Meet me there tomorrow evening and I'll take you down to the widow. She'll have a bed ready for you."

"I'm not sure! Perhaps! I won't promise. I need more time."

Peter accompanied Fausto almost as far as the Hermitage and then returned to the top of Mount Subasio again. He needed more time. But time for what?

Only two or three weeks ago, it had seemed that if he allowed his mind to wander through all his past experience, this slow recollection would help him towards a new understanding of the world, events, himself. He had felt that if he waited a little longer the answers would come, perhaps suddenly, or perhaps slowly drifting into his mind like his memories. But the time of waiting had stretched into forty days and no great truths had been revealed. Something should have happened up here on

Mount Subasio, but there had been no miracles, no new inspiration. Nothing had happened,

That night was miserable and wet with the clouds that had accumulated during the day descending as damp, dripping fog the moment it got dark.

CHAPTER 21

The following evening Peter came down off the top of Mount Subasio just as it was getting dark. He waited a little while in the road outside the Hermitage and then entered the monastery precincts. He had only been inside once before, when he first came to Assisi. On that occasion he had been shown around by one of the monks. He had seen how the monastery was only partially man made, for the whole of the back wall was the rock face of the mountain and buttressed against it were the single cells of the monks, divided by partitions. It was still as primitive and lacking in comfort as it had been when first built in the early fifteenth century, two hundred years after the death of St. Francis. Yet each little cell had a chair, a bed and a table which was luxury compared to the bare rock of the cave where St. Francis himself had slept. Beneath the cells was the refectory with the original wooden benches and tables. The refectory led out onto a tiny courtyard with a well in the centre. To the left was the small chapel, built at the same time as the rest of the monastery and beyond that the earliest chapel, a mere hollowing out of the mountainside which had later had its rock surface covered by a fresco Madonna. There was a tiny choir. Steep narrow steps led down to the cave and tourists had to squeeze themselves as short and as thin as St. Francis himself to enter it.

Fausto had not been precise as to what time they should meet nor had he said anything about the St. Martin's Day-party. There was a sound of male voices and laughter and a smell of wood smoke coming from along a corridor on the right of the courtyard, opposite the chapels, an area Peter had not visited before. He went along the corridor and heard the last few words of a joke followed by the type of laughter that could not possibly have been that of any monk. He pushed open a door and entered a room; a pilgrim's refuge.

There was a shocked silence as the men inside looked up and saw Peter standing there in the doorway. Then they began exclaiming!

"Christo!"

"DioMio!"

"I haven't drunk that much yet. I can't be seeing visions."

Fausto hobbled over to Peter and took him by the hand and led him into the room. "You know who this is?" he said, "The painter, you remember? The one everybody was talking about in the summer. I said I was inviting someone extra tonight, but I didn't know for certain if he was coming. He hasn't eaten properly for weeks."

"I'm sorry," Peter said. "I thought I was just going to meet Fausto here, I didn't know . . ."

"Come in, come in, don't mind us."

The men made him take the haversack and sleeping blanket off his shoulders and pushed him to sit on a bench near the fire.

"He's coming to stay in Santa Rosa for the winter," Fausto said. "I've persuaded Anna to take him in. He's coming down with us tonight."

Again there was the stunned silence. And then a chorus of "No."

"Not like that."

"Anna's always threatening to die. She'll really have a heart attack if she sees him like that."

"That's if we manage to get him past the Carabinieri at Piazza Nuova."

"If they saw him they'd be certain he was an escaped criminal."

"An Anarchist."

"A Communist."

"Mind what you say about Communists."

"They can look as respectable as anybody."

"Present company excluded, of course."

"And we're not getting involved in that kind of discussion tonight!"

"You'd need sheep shears."

"Sh! There's no need to be offensive. How much does he understand Italian?"

"Everything," Fausto said.

Peter seemed dazed and was not listening to the conversation around him. There were two huge logs in the back of the fireplace that were giving off a lot of heat and he sat staring into the flames. It was so long since he had been with people, really felt warm. Before coming down off the mountain, he had washed in the sheep trough, wrung out his shirt in the icy cold water and then put it back on again. His comb had lost all its teeth long ago and he had used his fingers to pull through his hair and beard. He had no idea what he looked like. It had not mattered on Subasio.

"Fausto, the monks are friends of yours. Go and see if you can borrow a razor and a pair of scissors."

"For his own self respect."

"For Anna's."

Fausto put a hand on his arm. "Do you mind?"

Peter shook his head.

"Supposing he want's to look like Moses?"

"Not all off, just a tidying up."

Peter understood at last. "No take it all off," he said.

It became an initiation ceremony; his return into normal society. First they made him drink a full glass of red wine straight down and they drank to him too and then they crowded round him and commented and gave advice as Peppe set to work. Half a dozen hands patted wine on his face and neck as an aftershave lotion when Peppe had finished. Even so, in the glow of the firelight, Fausto noticed how pale and haggard his face now seemed.

Only one person had not greeted Peter or drunk to his health. Franco sat up on the window ledge in the far corner of the room, away from the fireplace. This was his farewell party. He had been the centre of attention, the hero of the evening, and now Peter had come and spoilt it all.

When he had first come up to the Hermitage that evening, he had looked around that smoky old pilgrim's room, at those crude, stupid working class men, his own father included. They were proud if they could boast that the family had a piece of boiling meat on Sundays, managing an occasional, a very occasional, guilty, clandestine feast like tonight. This was the height of their achievement. He had known how to do better since he was a child. He remembered the day when he had found his way to the German convent and looked up at one of the top windows and the Mother Superior had seen him and thrown a roll of bread out to him. He was only six years old then, but he had never been really hungry since. He had learnt that he had the kind of charm that women liked, specially older women. Until he was ten or more, every morning when he had finished what his own mother considered to be breakfast, he ran to the convent and if there was nobody at the window, he began chanting 'Hail Mary, Mother of God, Give us this day our daily bread,' and a roll came flying out of the window.

He was better dressed than any of these men here, wearing the clothes that he'd bought with Denise's money and in four days time he was off to America. His ticket had been bought for him by his future father-in-law and was in the kitchen drawer at home. All his travelling arrangements had been made for him. His girl had written that she was pregnant and could not live without her Latin Lover and must have him at all costs. And there would be costs because when he was married he would want to wear good clothes all day and every day, live in a big house. He would make the old man give him a car.

This was Franco's last real evening of celebration and the men who were supposed to be his friends had abandoned him the moment Peter had appeared—as though that tramp were Moses or Christ himself.

Franco had finished one litre of wine. He went to the table and collected another and took it back to the windowsill and nobody even noticed.

The day the ticket arrived he had gone to his old elementary school and asked the teacher to show him where America was on a map and his old teacher had

175

shown him not a flat page but a round globe. He had pointed out the distance between Italy and America and it was on the other side of the world. There was not just the Adriatic or the Mediterranian to cross but all that Atlantic. Why had nobody told him before about the Atlantic? The greatest expanse of water he had ever seen was Lago Trasimeno; he had never been farther away than that from Assisi. What happened if the boat sank? How would he ever get back from America if he did not like it? He would know nobody and he could not even remember what the girl looked like.

All that his so -called friends wanted to do was to make Peter feel warm and welcome. Franco might have gone out of their lives for ever and be already on the other side of the Atlantic! He drank three more glasses of wine on an empty stomach and felt sick and went outside to get some fresh air. Only then did his own father notice and begin worrying about him and go out to bring him back in again.

Peppe had finished with Peter. It was time to think about eating. The men poked at the logs and scraped the hot ash forward to the front of the fireplace. They put a grid over the ashes and slapped down a half dozen large tee-bone steaks and shook salt and pepper on them and poured on oil which they spread with their fingers.

There was a huge cauldron hanging over the logs in the back. A little of the water had been taken to shave Peter but the cauldron had been filled up again. It was boiling. The home made pasta was dropped in. Part of the hare had been used to make the sauce to go with it. The rest of the hare had been cooked by Maria's mother with rosemary and sage and pork fat and a little tomato and capers, with anchovies added at the last minute. It was in an earthenware pot in the hearth keeping warm. All the men except Franco pulled out strings of the pasta and put it between their teeth and gave their opinion as to when it was cooked and they all turned the steaks on the grill and poked at them with their forks. Then they dipped a little piece of bread into the sauce to taste it.

They filled a plate with pasta for Peter and then set-to themselves, shovelling it into their mouths and wiping up the last drops of sauce with hunks of bread. Then they ate the hare, once again mopping up their plates with quantities of bread. They divided the steaks so that everybody had a piece. They had not brought anything else to go with the meat, for they ate salad and vegetables every day of the week at home. There was a rusty old iron frying pan with holes punctured in it that they used to cook the chestnuts in.

Peter ate as much as any of them and drank every time his glass was refilled. He thawed out, became less remote, part of the group and began to notice the men as individuals, separating the voices, the physical shapes and sizes and clothing. The men forced Franco to sit with them at the table and put their arms round him and told him to cheer up. They loosened their belts and opened the top buttons of their trousers and patted their stomachs contentedly.

They had no inhibitions in Peter's presence. He was not a monk even if Fausto had told them all he was a pontential St. Francis. They drank too much, swore and told dirty stories and dug each other in the ribs and bellowed with laughter for no reason. They picked their teeth with their fingernails and burped, satiated; but they still had not eaten the chestnuts.

They began to tell Peter who and what they were. There was Peppe the barber, the tallest and best looking; then Franco, the youngest, just off to America; Franco's father, who'd shot the hare; Peppe's future father-in-law; and Salvatore, Gina's husband; two cousins of Fausto, labourers; and Marcello who was an artisan who did wrought iron work, and then Giorgio who owned one of the new hotel pensione that were beginning to become prosperous. There was another tiny little man, Sergio, whom it was difficult to classify until he started telling Peter his life story. He was a cobbler who had taken up watch repairing, following the changing fortunes of Assisi, he said. When he had first started some people had not even a pair of shoes for Sundays and now most people had them for every day. He had been able to afford to leave that kind of dirty work to others. Now he could maintain his family mending clocks and watches; there were plenty in Assisi to keep him busy. 'Clean and delicate as an artist, a watch repairer must be.' he said and he leaned towards Peter and whispered, "There's Salvatore, and some others I know, won't ever admit we're better off now than we've ever been before, but it's the truth."

Fausto was in charge of the chestnuts. When they were done he threw them out of the frying pan into the centre of the table. The men grabbed for them. As they peeled the skins off them, they juggled them backwards and forwards between their two hands because they were so hot.

Suddenly Franco retched loudly and vomitted all over the floor. It was the end of the party. The men threw grey ash on the vomit and swept it all up and put it on the fire and burnt the end of the besom to get rid of the stink. They put the bones and the chestnut peelings onto the fire too and damped it all down with the ash from the outer part of the hearth. Out in the courtyard, they rinsed over the plates with the pasta water.

They took it in turns to carry Franco. Fausto insisted on trying to walk at first but then allowed himself to be hoisted on to Peter's back. Fausto put his arms round Peter's neck, his head down on his shoulder, and slept like a child. Half way down the road towards Assisi, some of the men had to stop to relieve themselves. They had a competition; they chose a tree up on the bank and went to the other side of the road and aimed. As usual, Salvatore was the longest, strongest, most accurate shot.

At Piazza Nuova they separated. Salvatore and Peter, with Fausto still asleep on his back, continued on down towards Via Santa Rosa. When they reached Fausto's house, Salvatore tried the kitchen door. It was not locked and they crept through and Peter put Fausto down on his couch and took off his boots and threw a rug over him. "Is he going to be warm enough?"

Salvatore laughed. "He doesn't even need clothes. He's got hair like a dog, all over his chest and down his back. Haven't you seen? If you didn't know what a pious woman his mother is, you could believe God knows what about the way he was conceived! Let him be! You know your way to Anna's house?"

"Fausto was going to take me."

"You mean you're arriving in the middle of the night and . . .?"

"You don't have to worry about me."

"He promises to take care of you and then he goes and gets so damn drunk he can't do anything but snore."

"I can always find shelter. I've been sleeping rough for months."

"It isn't respectable! Like a beggar! Here there's only the floor. In my house there's even less room. We'll have to wake up the widow. You're going to be paying her, aren't you?"

They crept up the steep stairs from the street to Anna's apartment. There was a light showing under the door. "She must be waiting up for you." He tried the door. It was locked.

"Anna, Anna, it's me, Salvatore."

They heard the scrape of a chair and her shuffling to open the door. She stood, enormous in her old wrap and bedroom slippers, smiling and smoothing her hair and down her sides and rubbing her elbows that were sore and cold from the marble top of the kitchen table. She had been asleep with her head resting on her arms.

Peter recognized her. "You didn't stay up on purpose?"

"I didn't know, I thought you might not be coming so late but I didn't know. I couldn't go to bed and leave the door unlocked, could I? But I only just dozed off. Where's Fausto then? You'd like a little something to drink, wouldn't you, Signor Peter? And you too Salvatore? Madonna mia, Salvatore, you've no idea what's been going on in this street all evening. Gina's been in and out half a dozen times. I only just dozed off, that's all."

"What's the matter with Gina?"

"Did you tell her you weren't going to be home for supper? No you didn't. Well, somebody said something in the market this morning about all Communists being rounded up in Milan or perhaps it was Turin. I can't remember where, and the women keep telling her your politics are going to get you all into trouble one day and she thought this was the day and it had happened. Then there was something about some strange man who'd come to see you a little while ago and you wouldn't tell her what he wanted. He must have been a Communist too because he'd been seen walking between two Carabinieri this evening. Thank goodness,, thank goodness, then there's no more trouble! She went up to Piazza Nuova, running and crying and her hair all over her face and the Carabinieri laughed at her and said they knew all about you and you weren't important enough to take in. If you were missing so late at night you must be with some other woman. She came back here crying even more. Thank goodness then you're not in trouble and that's all over."

Salvatore swore and left to go back to his own home.

Peter was alone with Anna. "So you knew who I was when Fausto asked if I could stay here?"

"Of course! I couldn't be expected to accept a complete stranger, could I? I'll never forget the day you helped me carry those children. What can I give you to drink then? You'd like a little something?"

"Thank you but I've been drinking all evening."

"A little snack, a little something to eat?"

"Really, I'd just like to go to bed."

"Just a camomile tea to sooth your stomach, for your liver?"

Peter moved towards the door.

"Of course, of course. We can talk tomorrow, can't we?" Anna waddled ahead of him into the front room where she and Clair usually slept together. "It's not very grand I'm afraid, not what you're used to at all." She bent over the double bed and folded back the lace counterpane.

Anna left and Peter looked around the room. It was too clean. It smelt of cleanliness, when he got into bed he realized it was the sheets that were smelling of bleach. He got up and pulled back the fine lace curtain and opened the window wide and stood breathing the cold damp air, looking out across the roof tops towards the dark valley. It was a terrible mistake to have come down off Mount Subasio. It was claustrophobic. He had allowed himself to be trapped.

CHAPTER 22

Out on the mountain, Peter had always woken at dawn. He did so too after his first night in the house in Santa Rosa.

The widow had not told him where there was a bathroom; if there was one. He got up and went out into the corridor.

From the open door next to his own, there was the sound of heavy breathing and an occasional grunting snort. Beyond that was the kitchen and the door that opened on to the stairs leading down to street level. There was one other door. He crept along the corridor and opened it. It led into a kind of box room. He could just make out a dressmaker's model, a sewing machine, a trunk, a low sloping roof, no window. It certainly was not what he was looking for. He went into the kitchen then out into the little patio courtyard and jumped up on to the wall on the far side and, a little way up a track, he disappeared into the bushes. Then he continued on, up the track to the castle.

He went around the outside walls until he was beneath the look-out tower that had been built to watch for enemy movements from the direction of Perugia. He could see Perugia right across the plain on the far hillside, with the landmarks of the pointed church tower of San Pietro and the square tower of St. Domenico clearly visible, as they must have been to the soldiers standing guard here, in the days of the medieval wars. He looked down on the upper church of the Basilica of San Francesco to the deep gorge of the valley of the river Tescio and then at the pink and white marble of the tombs of the little square cemetery. There was a strong wind and armies of black clouds moved heavily across the sky. If the wind dropped, it would rain. He looked down on the Basilica of San Francesco again. It was time he went in there. It was time he started work.

For a last moment he lingered, looking down on the curved and crooked roofs of the houses where the people of Assisi lived, to the churches where they prayed and the cemetery, where they were all going to leave their bodies eventually.

He felt less depressed this morning than he had done the night before. That time on Mount Subasio had not been entirely wasted. It had helped to clear his mind and his emotions and eliminate old prejudices and doubts. A field that has lain fallow for long enough is ready for sowing. The Contessa had confused him by telling him to study the old Masters so that he could learn from them and absorb something into his own style. But Old Tagliatelle had said, "Work your way back through the Renaissance to the very beginning." And he had meant more than just line or colour or perspective. He had meant also the history and the religion and the life, even the geography of the country that had influenced the artists.

Peter had walked through that Basilica down there only twice, had only looked superficially and not really studied at all. He was an artist of the twentieth century and those artists down there were painting for a different age, he had thought. But how long ago was that age? Less than seven centuries; not more than about twenty five generations. Calculated in grandfathers, Francis was only about twenty seven grandfathers ago! Christ himself probably not more than sixty! Peter laughed aloud.

The wind kept the clouds moving and their shadows seemed lighter and swifter, racing across the valley. Suddenly the sun broke through over the dome of the Basilica of Santa Maria degli Angeli, just in that one patch, as though a sign from God, and all those fantastic religious paintings he had seen in art galleries made sense. Artists really had seen one church or village or patch of countryside illuminated whilst the rest remained dark.

It was possible to watch the sky for hours. But not now. All that period of doing nothing was over. He had left the mountain. If he was still to feel trapped within his body down here then it was because he was no different from any other mortal who must find release through work, or art. It was useless to wait any longer. His style, and his belief in what he was doing, must come whilst he was already working. He could feel the urgency to begin. Now. Immediately. Quite suddenly the racing clouds seemed like time itself. He ran down to the widow's house.

Anna gave a little shriek as he jumped down into the patio yard and entered the kitchen. She thought he was still in bed. What was the matter? Had he not slept? Was he not warm enough? She smiled and fussed around him and prepared him a soup bowl full of coffee and milk with thick slices of bread to dunk in it. She was still wearing her old wrap and bedroom slippers. What did he want for lunch? He did want lunch, didn't he? What time did he want lunch?

Peter escaped as soon as he could and went to his bedroom to collect his sketching block and then left the house and went down to the Basilica of San Francesco. He had not seen Clair yet and still did not know Anna had a daughter. Fausto had not mentioned her.

He went into the upper church first. It was dark so that even when his eyes were accustomed to the dimness, he could see very little. The sky outside was black and the narrow stained glass windows that had let through too little light in the summer months now seemed as solid as walls. He had a small guide book of the Basilica and he used it to get his bearings and begin to identify. The fresco paintings on the upper level of the walls of the nave were of the traditional Old Testament story on one side and the New Testament story on the other, so that the Priest from his pulpit could either point out the Temptation of Eve and the Expulsion from Eden or Christ changing the Water into Wine, according to whether he was preaching to chastise or encourage his flock. Beneath these were those much discussed frescoes that might or might not be the early works of Giotto, that had brought religious painting into a new perspective, into a realistic setting, right down to every day life. In the transepts behind the altar and on the walls of the apse, above the level of the carved wooden choir stalls, was the panorama of the work of Cimabue, perhaps his greatest, if he had not experimented with his technique. It was said he had watched the stained glass artisans and used lead oxide as a base for his colours, not knowing that to retain and fix their brilliance it was necessary to bake them. You could not bake the colours on a wall as you could glass. At first they seemed all that he had hoped for but, with time and damp, the blacks had turned white and the whites had turned black; all else had disappeared and now the effect was that of the negative of a photograph. Peter was impatient because he could see so little. He would have to ask the monks to give him light, as much light as possible.

He went down into the lower church and it was even darker. It was impossible to imagine how the painters had worked at all. He could see the arches and get the feel of the architecture, of the enclosed, cave-like protection of that lower church, all of it painted, every inch and every angle. Here the first school of painters were known simply as those of the Master of St. Francis. Then there were the great names again, Cimabue, Giotto, Simone Martini, Pietro Lorenzetti. It was here that as much as, perhaps more than anywhere else, Europe had become artistically fully awake after the long Dark Ages. It had happened, like the sun's rays breaking through over the Basilica of Santa Maria degli Angeli that morning. Only now there were no sun's rays. This lower church was too dark but still Peter could imagine and sense the brilliance and the magnificence. How could this contradiction of the preaching of poverty of Francis be justified. Because painters can never be as poor as preachers?

Words take up no space on solid walls and need no expensive colours from far away places. They need no scaffolding, no artificial light, no hours of manual application.

There were no other tourists. An occasional black-robed monk walked about but nobody bothered Peter. He looked at the relics of St. Francis, the sacking tunic, the piece of Subasio stone on which his skull had been resting when the tomb had been opened. He did not enter the side chapels on this first morning but went quickly down to the crypt to see the tomb. The crypt had only been excavated after the re-discovery of the tomb. There was no decoration. The walls were simple rough cut pink Assisi stone and the tomb itself a grey block lying horizontally inside what appeared to be a hollowed-out nitch in a column. During his life time, it was said that St. Francis had held up the church and here he was buried in such a way that, symbolically, he could do just that, to the architectural structure above him. The column seemed more than a basic piece of architectural support and was like the trunk of a tree that disappeared underground and Francis's body fed that trunk and above was the artistic flowering.

It was raining when Peter left the Basilica and Assisi had returned to the greyness of the Middle Ages, almost to the Dark Ages. He stopped at the post office on his way back to Santa Rosa. Money had arrived again from England so there would be no difficulty in paying the widow. There was a brief letter from his mother. The situation of the refugees in Spain was getting worse every day. Barcelona could not hold out against Franco much longer.

The site of the post office was where the little church of St. Nicholas had once stood. Francis had entered it with his first companion to open the Bible at random and read the words of Christ. 'He who wants to follow me must leave his family and give his wealth to the poor and take up his staff . . .' or words to that effect. Peter had gone into the post office to collect money not spiritual direction. He was going to give most of that money to the widow who was poor enough, but in return she was going to feed him and fuss him and . . . and he had left his parents; no, that was not true; his father had sent him away because he did not need him. That was in the past. But he had taken up no staff yet . . . unless his art? . . . There were no more doubts, no more ifs or maybes or unless. His art was to be his staff.

He met Fausto in Via Santa Rosa and asked when and how much he should pay Anna. Fausto took him to the basement below his house to show his own artistic works and the gnarled tree root that had the figure of St. Francis hidden in its wood.

"You could get him out of that," Fausto said. "I haven't the strength, but he's there. You could do it."

"I know flat surface only, I'm not a sculptor," Peter said.

"You've never tried."

Peter walked round the wood to look at it from all sides.

"You acquire experience. If you don't start you'll never have it."

Peter took the knife Fausto held out to him. "Try, try." He walked around the tree root again, touching it, feeling the knots in it with his finger tips. "I'll have to make sketches first to get my ideas clear. I'll come down again after lunch."

Clair was sitting by the kitchen window when he came in. She was sewing the last buttons on to a pair of men's trousers that were spread across her knees. Her head was bent, she had just snipped off a thread with her teeth.

Peter hesitated in the doorway. She looked up from her work, then looked beyond him as though he were blocking her way of escape. He could not see her face properly. The only light was from the window behind her. She collected the trousers hurriedly into her arms and stood up, muttering something. Peter moved out of the doorway and she fled past him into the dark box room.

189

Anna was standing over the stove. "Don't mind Clair, she'll get used to you. The water's just boiling. Spaghetti cooks quickly. In ten minutes your lunch will be ready." She put a clean, bleached, white linen cloth on the table and set one place at it.

"What about you, aren't you eating?"

"We never have very much at lunch. I'm on a diet, you know. We'll have ours afterwards."

"But I don't want anything special. Can't we eat together?" "I've put the pasta in now, enough for you only. We'll eat afterwards," Anna insisted.

Peter put his money on the table. "Will this be alright for a month?" he asked.

It seemed a lot. Anna hesitated and then picked it up and counted it quickly. It was more than twice as much as she was expecting. Clair had to have more trousseau. Her Paolo had written that he wanted the marriage to take place in the summer. He wanted the wedding in the Basilica of San Francesco. He wanted lunch in a restaurant afterwards. She had not known how she was going to do it. Then Fausto had said that this Peter man was looking for somewhere to live. She had said she would take him in only because she needed the money. She would make any sacrifice to get Clair properly married. This foreigner could not have any idea of how much or how little was necessary to live decently. She put the money quickly into her apron pocket.

Clair in the dark of the box room was shivering. Her mother had said that that great bear-like creature sitting at the table in the kitchen had been sent by Providence, if not by the Madonna herself. Even Fausto said he had been sent by God, but it was not respectable to have him in the house. It could not be. But how else could they pay for the wedding?

She crept out of the box room into her bedroom. It was just as dark. There was no window there either; it was just an enclosed space in the middle of the house between the real bedroom where she usually slept with her mother at the front and the kitchen at the back. She could not go into the front room to look out across the roof tops of the houses opposite, right across the valley to the mountains beyond. She could not go into the kitchen and out into the patio yard to stare up at Subasio. There was no light in any direction. She pulled the gold chain up from the neck of her blouse and kissed the crucifix on it. On the same chain was the little medal of the Virgin Mary that Paolo had sent her from Rome. She could not kiss that. It would be like kissing Paolo himself. "Holy Mary, mother of God, forgive me, forgive me," she whispered. She was tied to Paolo now, not only by the rosary but also by this image of the Virgin on a chain. He had wanted one from her, too. She and her mother had had to buy one exactly the same that he could wear round his neck to remind him of her. They had been eating cabbage and lettuce like rabbits for three weeks afterwards whilst they were paying for it. Now he had written to say it was time they went to Rome to meet his sister and see where he lived and where she would live. "Holy Mary, Mother of God forgive me. Forgive me for not wanting to accept God's Will."

She heard the chair scrape back in the kitchen and the Peter bear man's voice thanking her mother for the lunch. She saw the huge bulk of him pass in the corridor as he went to get something from his own front room and then he passed back again and out and down the stairs.

Her mother called. "Come and get your lunch now."

Anna was smiling. "So well educated and he eats anything. He wanted us to sit at the table with him. But it wouldn't be proper. Look!" She pulled the money out of her pocket. "Immediately after lunch you must write to Paolo and say we're coming to Rome. You mustn't mention this foreigner of course. He wouldn't approve at all. I asked the Signora Genevieve and she said two women alone in the house and you engaged to another man! Of course, it isn't correct, so we just don't tell Paolo, that's all! And if I never leave you by yourself in the room with this Peter man what can be wrong? On Saturday we'll go to the market and buy a piece of that good material we saw last week so you can make a dress for yourself and maybe we can find a remnant for a skirt for me. Look at the money he's given me for a month and Fausto thinks he'll want to stay all winter."

Clair looked at the money in her mother's hand. It was as much as she could earn in a year with her work in the shop and dressmaking.

"We'll ask Paolo to find us some respectable little pensione and we'll spend two whole days in Rome. We'll go on a Saturday before Christmas and we'll ask Paolo to take us to St. Peter's on Sunday so maybe we can see the Pope."

Clair said, "Did you put in the spaghetti to boil? Didn't you say we were going to eat now? It's nearly two o'clock."

Anna flung her apron over her face. "I'm killing myself for you, thinking only of your future, arranging everything and do you thank me? What do you want, I'd like to know? What more could a girl want than a marriage with a

192

respectable, good-looking man like Paolo? You'll never have another offer like this again, never."

"Alright," Clair said. "Please Mamma, that's enough."

After lunch Clair wrote to Paolo. Her mother dictated most of the letter. "Say we'll go down to Rome as soon as it is convenient for him. Say you're looking forward to meeting his sister. Say something affectionate that fiancès say to each other. Oh, I don't know, but say something to encourage him."

Clair could not finish her letter the way he did. She could not say she missed him or that she was living for the day when she could see him again. She could not say she dreamed about him every night. She had once, a terrible nightmare that she wanted to forget.

Her mother said, "Don't just sit there! Write something! And then go out and post it right away. I'll iron those trousers whilst you're finishing and you can deliver them also and then buy the thread and buttons you said you needed. Don't just sit there, for goodness sake!"

Clair wrote, 'Mother wants to see the Pope when we are in Rome and I should like to, too. I hope it doesn't snow before we can come down to Rome. I also wear the medal of the Madonna on the chain round my neck all the time.' Then she added, 'I remember you in my prayers.' It was true. She prayed she could learn to like him.

CHAPTER 23

Clair had to pass Fausto's basement on her way to the post office and there was the Peter-bear-man sitting in the doorway with his sketching block on his knee. Fausto beckoned to her.

"Which of these do you think is the real St. Francis?"

Peter looked up and straight at her. She blushed and lowered her head and wanted to hurry on but she could not. "So this is Clair," Peter said. Fausto had been telling him about her. He stood up and held out his hand. "If we can't meet in the house at least we can say 'How do you do' in the street."

She was like one of the cloistered nuns of Santa Chiara who wore black veils to hide their faces and spoke to people in the outside world only through a double iron grating, allowing no visual or physical contact. Peter stood there with his hand out and the silence and the barriers were ridiculous. He made her feel they were ridiculous and made her look up and straight at him. It was the first time she had ever looked into a man's eyes. He was not mentally stripping her naked or thinking of running his fingers, exploring, up her arms. She put out her hand to take his and they smiled at each other. He was so friendly and easy. Then he sat down again to continue his sketching and she moved closer to watch him.

Gina's children came up the street and crowded in behind him and they all stood there watching.

Peter sketched St. Francis with the birds and Francis did not appear to be preaching at them like a priest, he was singing with them. And then Francis was sitting on the outcrop of rock on Mount Subasio, where he, Peter liked to sit. He was staring across the valley, beyond the past, the present and the future, beyond time and space, just an ordinary little man who had found himself outside and above the world in this moment of meditation and vision.

Then there was a quick sequence: of the actor, drawing attention to himself, throwing the money out of the window of San Damiano that the priest had refused, believing it to be stolen; stripping himself naked in front of his own father and the dignitaries and clergy of the city; preaching, naked, in the Cathedral.

Other, older children came up the street and stopped to watch, and Gina, looking for her little ones, stopped; then several women who saw the crowd from the windows of their houses came hurrying to enlarge that crowd. They stared hardest at the nakedness but the children did not snigger and Clair did not blush. The nakedness was natural, symbolizing the man-made hypocrisy that had been stripped off. Any child or fool could understand that.

Just a few lines and each story was out on paper and Peter dropped the sheets on the ground beside him and Fausto and the women picked them up and passed them from one to another.

There was Francis, who was only middle-aged but looking old, with a thin scraggy beard and emaciated body, up in the mountains again, searching for his vision and seeing only disillusion. Even his own followers had misinterpreted his words to suit themselves and dressed themselves in a new hypocrisy, making use of him. All he had wanted to do was die as Christ had died, a martyr to a cause, but his cause was already perverted. They brought him back to Assisi, a hero, to be lodged in the Bishop's Palace. Peter drew prancing horses and noblemen and crowds, crowds indistinguishable as individuals, like the sheep on Mount Subasio. Yet, wasn't that Fausto there? and Salvatore? and Gina? and one of the monks from the Basilica, pushing around his litter to get a better view of the stigmata? Francis was a hero, an actor who had overplayed his part, and they wanted to possess him and would not accept what he had been telling them. They refused to accept that he was only an ordinary little man.

But, he died the way he wanted, in spite of them.

Peter drew Francis's body stretched out naked with the beard and the hair more straggly than before and his eyes sunken, semi-blind. His body showed the skeleton of ribs and bony arms and legs with joints gnarled and distorted by arthritis and stomach bloated and blotchy. Malnutrition, sleeping in caves on the damp rock. How else could his body have looked? It was a body to be left behind, discarded to manure the earth. He died, naked, on the naked earth, in his last theatrical gesture.

Peter stopped sketching. He had completely forgotten he was supposed to be preparing for a piece of sculpture; it was the story that had counted. When he had finished he was exhausted and limp. He looked at the people standing around him. He had been in a state of concentration so complete that he had ceased to realize that he was being watched and he had not noticed the time. He had brought his own inner knowledge to the surface, made it visible to himself, visible to others. He had got started at last.

He had been on that stool in the doorway of Fausto's basement all afternoon. It would soon be dark. He stood up and stretched. Anna had come down and found Clair lingering, watching him and had chased her away to the post office. Clair had sent off her letter to Paolo and returned immediately, forgetting to buy buttons and thread and had found her mother still standing watching Peter, as she had been doing herself. Only the smallest children had become bored and begun playing amongst the firewood, returning every time a new sheet of paper dropped to the floor to have a look at it too.

Fausto said, "Which one is in that piece of wood? Which St. Francis?"

Peter yawned. "I don't know. All of them, none of them. I don't know which one must dominate. I'm not ready for that piece of wood yet. I'm going for a walk. Clair, do me a favour. Take these into the house for me." He left them and strode off up the street.

Anna called after him, "When are you coming back? What do you want for supper? Would you like a good hot plate of minestrone soup?"

He did not hear her. He had to walk, walk, walk and unwind.

He reached the top of the montain and it was cold and damp. He went towards his outcrop of rock and for a moment it seemed as though his image of Francis were sitting there, but when he reached it all he could see was bare stone with clouds chasing in across the valley and the tree line immediately beneath him. He shivered and clapped his arms around his chest. He could not get his body warm, though inside he was glowing, for he had got started at last. He strode across the top of the mountain and down through the trees on the other side, around the circular wall of the fortress village of Armenzano and down past the church towards the small cemetery. The grass of the flat land just outside the cemetery had been cut in the summer and the hay piled onto a long central pole so that it looked like a tall mushroom without any stalk. He had found shelter here once earlier in the autumn. Now some of the hay had been cut away at the bottom so that the stalk of the mushroom was beginning to appear. The overhang above kept off the wind and the drizzling rain but his clothes were already soaking wet. He put his arms around his knees and dozed and shivered. At dawn he went up into the village of Armenzano and found one of the little old women who had given him bread before. She had baked enough for a whole week and she gave him a loaf. He refused the cheese and salami she offered him. She insisted he drink a glass of wine, pale red, vinegary, sour and cold. He had become used to it for the mountain grapes never produced such sweet wine as those of the valley. He ate the bread on his way down to Assisi. It had its own flavour of wood smoke and was a little heavy and doughy in the centre.

People stared at him as he walked down through the upper streets of the city, down past the Cathedral, along Santa Rosa.

Anna exclaimed, "Oh Madonna mia," when he entered the kitchen of her house. "Oh Madonna mia. You've been up on that mountain again. Can't you wean yourself of it?" She boiled up milk and made him sit at the table while she cut hunks of bread for him to dunk in the soup bowl in front of him.

"No more bread, please, I've just eaten a whole loaf."

"It'll be sitting on your stomach then. Drink the milk, it'll wash it down; it'll warm you. Take off all those clothes and I'll wash and mend them for you. How your mother could let you leave home I don't know. You've got a mother, haven't you? Or are you a poor orphan boy? I don't know, but somebody should be looking after you. I gave all my poor husband's clothes away when he died but they wouldn't have fitted you anyway, and I haven't even a pair of his pants left. Your supper was sitting in the middle of the table here all night, and you go giving me all that money as though you're rich and you haven't even a pair of underpants to change into."

"Oh yes, I've got a pair of underpants."

"And you think you can go walking round Assisi in a pair of underpants? It's a disgrace. What can your mother be thinking of? Go and get into bed then. Everybody in Assisi's been talking about you again. And what they must be saying of me I don't know, having you in the house, and in rags? You need a good thick sweater and a pair of decent trousers and look at your shoes, tied up with string."

He got into bed and the sheets still smelt of bleach. Whatever was the widow thinking of, putting him to bed in the middle of the morning? What was he thinking of, obeying her?

He had a spare set of clothes but they too had been worn day and night on the mountain, rinsed out in the sheep trough. He put them on but they were faded, crumpled, torn and even worse than the ones he had taken off.

He had to escape from the house without being seen. Clair and her mother were whispering in the dark boxroom. He went quickly along the corridor and was on the stairs leading down to the street before they realized he had left his room.

He did not go immediately to the Basilica of San Francesco but to that of Santa Chiara. He had to go back to the beginning, to the Crucifix that Francis believed spoke to him. That Byzantine Crucifix with a Christ who never died. That Christ with his eyes wide open, his feet straight down and his arms pinned flat and straight along the width of the cross, stiff as a piece of architecture. But with the spirit looking out through the eyes, Christ inhabiting a body as though it were a temple. Whether that belief had been condemned as heresy or not, it was there.

Francis had been so intense that he had seen the spirit in those eyes, showing through the architecture. He had heard a voice which spoke of the church as though only the architecture counted and he had misinterpreted everything at first. But Francis was not a fool, he used his intelligence as well as his visionary powers. He understood the total sacrifice of that symbol, the cross. Give away all, money, power, pride, even life. Any man could be the son of God who understood this. Christ's eyes remained open. What did it matter if that artist knew nothing of anatomy? He had not even tried. He did not want a bone and muscle, flesh and blood, Christ. He had painted an idea, a sacrifice, not a man.

Peter left the Basilica of Santa Chiara. The sun was coming out through a break in the clouds, pale, luke-warm. He strode down to the Basilica of San Francesco.

For the first time he went into the chapel of San Matino and here there was an art he had not expected. Why had he not studied Simone Martini before? This painter had taken the blurred story of the fourth century St. Martin and cleaned it up and reshaped it to fit the sophisticated, aristocratic experience of his own period. St. Martin leaned down from his high stepping horse and slashed his cloak down the centre so that he could give half to a beggar. It was an exaggerated, gallant gesture that a rich man could afford to make. In the next scene the self-righteous St. Martin dreamed that the beggar had been Christ Himself. St. Martin lay there, stiffly asleep in his beautiful Sienese bed with the white linen sheets and elaborately patterned counterpane, with his toes sticking primly up beneath its folds and a halo like a golden plate behind his head. On the far side of his bed a number of angels stood like servants, and, in their midst, a grateful Christ was wearing that half cloak around his shoulders and had come to thank him personally for such generosity to the beggar. In yet another scene St. Martin was being initiated into the consciously artificial world of chivalry. The symbols were being buckled on to him; the sword and the spurs. On one side of him stood huntsmen with their hawks on their wrists and on the other the musicians who had attended such ceremonies before, and knew that chivalry was just a parade of virtue, a show. They stood there with their mouths turned down cynically, there to play sweet music on flutes, on double flutes, on mandorlins; there to earn their keep. What other artist of that period had painted such knowing faces and such worldliness?

Then came the climax of the sequence which was a contrast to all that had come before. Martin stood now, simple and at ease in front of the fourth century Emperor, back in his true historical context, stripped of all the emblems of knighthood, wearing only a plain unadorned smock. The Emperor, on the field of battle had come to survey his troops, and pay them and encourage them to go forward and die for him, whilst he sat and watched. The enemy was there in the background: menacing spears and spikes and tents, faceless helmets; an unknown, undated, permanent enemy. Martin, quite at ease, was suggesting to the Emperor that he should go to meet them alone, without armour, holding only a tiny cross in his hand, the thinnest, narrowest brush stroke lines of a wooden cross. Why hadn't he taken his spurs off though?

Peter stayed in the chapel until a monk came and rattled keys beside him, shooed him out because he wanted to close the Basilica and go to lunch.

Peter walked down around the outer walls of the lower part of the city, through the olive groves to San Damiano but that was closed too. When he got back to Santa Rosa the water was boiling on the stove, Anna had the pasta ready to drop in the moment she heard him on the stairs. The table was set only for himself. Clair was hidden in the box room.

"You're not going to eat?" he said.

"We've eaten already. We thought you wouldn't come. Well it got later and later and the water was boiling away so we just ate ours very quickly and got it out of the way."

"I'm sorry. I didn't know it was so late."

"That's alright. It makes no difference. I've made a special sauce today. The spaghetti's the same but the sauce is different." Anna drained the spaghetti and piled it onto his plate and ladled on the sauce and sprinkled parmesan cheese over it. "Try it! Try it! It's really good!' She hovered around behind his chair.

"Please sit down. Just sit down."

Anna sat at the table and folded her hands in her lap and watched him eating.

"You wouldn't be offended, would you?" she said.

"By what?"

"Well, it was Clair's idea. She wants to make you a pair of trousers. She's got a piece of material; it's nothing special, but it's good strong cloth. She was going to make it up for Gina's husband but there's no hurry for him; he said next week anyway. She can get some more for him in the market on Saturday. After you've finished your lunch you'd let Clair measure you, wouldn't you? You wouldn't be offended?"

"Offended . . .?"

"What's the matter? You are offended then . . .?"

"Of course not."

"To tell the truth . . . well I must tell the truth. If I were your mother, I'd be ashamed of the way you go around."

"I'm sorry. I'd love Clair to make me a pair of trousers, but . . ."

"If it's the money you're worrying about, you don't need to. I've counted what you gave me again. There's more than enough for this month, we could get a pair of trousers out of it as well. So that's settled. Now eat up that spaghetti before it gets cold. It's horrid when it's cold."

Peter obeyed. The table was cleared and he stood patiently in the middle of the kitchen whilst Clair put her arms around his waist with a tape measure in her hands. She was very gentle and shy and did not look up at his face. Anna supervised and to get the measurement of the outside of his leg, it was she who held the tape measure at his waist whilst Clair went down on her knees to hold the other end at shoe level. The moment they had finished, Peter escaped again and returned to the Basilica of San Francesco.

CHAPTER 24

Long before the Catholic, Protestant split, long before the Renaissance, there were many, many different ways of translating the Christian story.

Peter was in the transept of the lower church with a powerful torch which the monks did not seem to mind him using. He picked out from the surrounding darkness the Madonna on her Throne, the only one of Cimabue's frescoes that still remained in good condition. Here there was no doubt. She was the Queen of Heaven, gentle but distant, untouchable, surrounded by angels as gentle and as remote from this world as herself. The figure of St. Francis stood a little apart, with his long sad face and sticking out ears and slightly crooked nose. Maybe it was the halo that made his ears stick out like that! Modestly he showed his stigmata, the signs, like those of the nails of the cross, that made him different from other men. Yet he was still only human; a little earthly creature raised to the dignity of Paradise.

Peter turned his torch to the ceiling above. There in the briefest of periods from the time of Cimabue's Madonna, was the Revolution. The Queen had lost her throne and her golden robes and had become a woman of the people; one of the humblest and least fortunate; having to give birth to her child against a background of barren rocks, an unhospitable earth, with animals in the foreground more friendly than mankind. Blessed be the poor for their simplicity of composition, for their realism is perspective and plasticity of form and their humility, the richness of colour. Following the sequence, Peter turned his back on the Nativity and saw, on the opposite curve of the ceiling, the flight into Egypt, with all its practical details of a family setting out on a long journey. There was the solid working donkey with the Madonna riding on it. She held the child in her arms, supporting his weight by a sling that went round his buttocks and was tied behind her neck as though he were a broken arm, as though the pain of having borne him, and the weight of him, would increase on the journey. The little angel guides, flying ahead, were looking over their shoulders to make sure they were being followed, leaving trails of speed behind them. And the tree bending over as Mary passed was nature itself bowing down before them. If this was not Giotto's brush it was Giotto's thinking and conception, Giotto interpreting St. Francis who had formed his ideas on Mount Subasio.

There was something else about this Flight into Egypt. Joseph was in front, but behind the donkey there were two men. Were they other members of the family or servants? Was it possible?

Peter moved his torch again and there were Simone Martini's portraits on a side wall. Here there was neither Paradise nor peasant simplicity but the sophisticated world of court life again. The saints were not so much inspired by God as deliberately calculating their own moves. Their slit eyes held no belief; their long narrow fingers had known no physical work; their heavy embroidered gold haloes were worth more than ordinary crowns, and here was the little figure of St. Francis, the merchant's son, who had climbed socially to the level of King Louis of France and Queen Elisabeth of Hungary.

Once again there was the rattling of keys. It was sundown, and time to close.

Peter arrived back in Santa Rosa when it was dark. Clair and her mother were busy in the kitchen. Clair was cutting out the material for his trousers on the table and Anna was sitting near the fire unravelling a shapeless mass of blue knitting in her lap.

"It's all for you, really," Anna said. "This cardigan's not old. I only wore it two or three times, just before my husband died. I couldn't put it on after; the colour's not suitable for a widow but it's good wool and when I've put it all into skeins, I'll wash it with a little vinegar in the water and you'll see, it'll be like new! The winter's here already and you with only that old jacket."

"Couldn't you have made something for Clair out of it?"

"It's too heavy. She likes fine delicate things, my lady does. And the colour wouldn't suit her as it'll suit you, with your blue eyes."

Clair glanced up quickly in Peter's direction. He grinned and winked at her. She lowered her head immediately and continued cutting along the chalk lines she had made on the material on the table.

He went into his bedroom and got his sketching block and pulled a chair to the other side of the fireplace opposite Anna. With his usual quick strokes he defined the kitchen, the heavy table with its clumsy, square legs, the sideboard, dark and heavy too, but stretched across the open shelf, a delicately embroidered runner. A ridiculously frilly piece of flowered material was pinned across the high wooden mantlepiece above the hearth. The fire was almost out and there was only a faint, pink glow to the grey ash which lay piled in its deep sooty interior. There was the shape of a black, cooking pot. On the wall hung a replica of Raphael's Madonna of the Segiola in a thick wooden frame; the colours, contrasting splodges of red and black; a street market version of the original.

"Clair, look at me," he said suddenly.

She jerked her head up, startled.

"Alright, I'm not going to eat you. No, not like that. Just carry on working then."

"And finish, Clair, Madonna mia, I want to set the table."

Peter helped poke and blow the fire until it burned brightly again. Anna warmed up some vegetable soup she had made earlier and dropped in little quick cooking rings of pasta, enough only for Peter.

Clair finished cutting out the trousers and laid the long strips of material over her arm and collected scissors and chalk and odd scraps of cloth and took all off to the box room and Anna set the table for Peter.

"This is nonsense," Peter said. "I've been here in the kitchen with you both for almost an hour and now you don't want to eat at the same table with me. If you want to know, I am offended now."

"We eat so little," Anna said.

"What difference does that make?"

"Well I don't know, but you'd better have your soup now because it's ready and we're not having that."

"And then you sit down."

Anna said nothing but put the plate of soup on the table and stood watching, following the spoon from the plate to his mouth. Suddenly she laughed. "It's good isn't it? You like my cooking and you like being here. You're happy, aren't you, in my house?" She called loudly. "Clair, come out of that dark place there! Signor Peter wants us to eat together this evening; he's going to be offended if we don't." She smiled broadly at Peter. "That'll bring her out of her hiding place. She wouldn't want to offend you."

Anna ordered Clair to get out two more plates and put cheese and sardines on the table and cut bread whilst she herself washed salad and, when it was clean, sprinkled oil and vinegar and salt over it and tossed it. Then she remained standing, hovering around Peter to take away his soup plate and pour wine into his glass and hand him food.

"Sit down, woman, for goodness sake," he said, and she laughed and obeyed. "You sound just like my old man."

"Mother hasn't laughed like that since father died," Clair said, almost inaudibly, not raising her head.

"Santa Maria! Give peace to his soul!" Anna crossed herself and they ate in silence, but only for a little while.

"You know Clair's getting married in the summer," Anna said. "Perhaps Fausto or somebody told you."

Peter shook his head. "I didn't know. Congratulations."

Clair didn't say anything.

"Her Paolo wants the ceremony to take place in the Basilica of San Francesco. Her Paolo works for the post office just like my poor husband did. He and his sister own a flat in Rome, just imagine. We've been invited down to meet his sister and see where Clair's going to live. We'll be going, not next week, but before Christmas anyway. You won't mind, will you? We'll only be away two days, or perhaps two nights and three days, with all the travelling, I don't know! You can sleep here, of course, and maybe Fausto's mother will feed you; or you might prefer to go out to some little restaurant. Fausto's mother puts rice into everything, lunch and supper, always rice, rice, rice. She's getting old, you know."

"I can go to a restaurant."

"You're sure? You don't mind? Maybe we need only be away two days. That's settled then. I didn't really need to tell you so soon but it just occurred to me . . . You wouldn't . . ."

"Be offended?"

"No, I wasn't going to say that. I was going to say . . . well . . . I have to take some present with us and I had thought maybe I could get a photograph of Clair but it might not come out well. Photographs sometimes don't look a bit like the person, do they? We'd have to pay for it, even if it wasn't good, and then we couldn't give it just like that. It'd need a silver frame and even a little one . . . I don't know! It just occurred to me you might paint her portrait? Only a miniature? I was thinking, if we make those trousers and sweater, . . . I know I said you'd paid for the trousers, with the money you have given me already, and the sweater isn't going to cost anything except the time to make it up . . . but a portrait wouldn't cost you anything but time either. Could we just say we make an exchange of presents?"

Peter put his hand out suddenly and touched Clair on the shoulder. "Do you want me to paint your portrait? Would you sit for me? Would you trust me to be able to do it well enough for your Paolo?"

Clair remained silent and her head bent lower. There were tears on her cheeks and her shoulders began to shake. She pushed back her chair and ran out of the kitchen into the dark bedroom and pulled her dress off and lay shivering and sobbing.

Anna sighed heavily. "You'll have to excuse her. Sometimes I think she's one of those poor creatures that's not quite right in the head." Anna stood up and brushed down her apron with her hands and began clearing the table.

Peter left the kitchen and went out into the little patio yard and jumped up into the bushes on the far side. He knew where the toilet was now, that shallow pit in the basement, but he still preferred the bushes. He climbed on up to the castle and looked out over the roof tops of Assisi. The dim street lights just showed the piazza of Santa Chiara and the dome of the Cathedral, making the countryside beyond seem darker.

Poor little Clair! So terrified of all that was outside her narrow radius of light. And Anna, motherly and calculating. The sketch he had done before supper was only a rough idea. He wanted those two women in the kitchen in colour, and the contrast of that heavy, ugly furniture and the frilly, tasteless ornament and even the crude Raphael, just as it was against the glow of the fire. And Clair alone. He knew already how he wanted to paint her portrait.

For the next three days, he was up early and down in the Basilica the moment it was open in the morning. He went first to the crypt where Mass was being said, to listen but not to take part. He had been christened and confirmed a Protestant, hadn't he? Wasn't that what he still considered himself to be? He could just hear puritan Aunt Sarah warning him against spending too much time looking at Saints and Madonnas and Crucifixes, all the visible signs of what she would call pagan Catholicism. He remembered his father lecturing him on the tragedy of the Latin countries that had been subjected to the domination of the Church. Even his mother, who had cried when the Madonna of the Palm was burnt, had once said, "Of course dear, the Spaniards have never understood the Trinity. They always insist on the Father, Mother, Son relationship. These Catholics have no place for the Spirit."

After Mass, Peter climbed the stairs to the upper church. Here the work of cleaning and consolidating the frescoes of the life story of St. Francis was about to begin. The flooring was going to be relaid, the old brick replaced by the marble stone of Mount Subasio, which would be polished and lustred until pilgrims could see their own reflections in it. After all, plain poverty can be so ugly, unadorned, humility so degrading. Better to bury such ideas even deeper than the body beneath the lower church. Certainly, if St. Francis was going to become Patron Saint of all Italy, he deserved the best. This Basilica must once again be a monument to be proud of.

Peter used his torch to study details and he began sketching, copying, now a face, now the outline of a scene. There was Francis, publicly renouncing his father's inheritance. The physical bulk of Francis's father, even the outline of his thigh and leg showed beneath his clothing and opposite him was Francis, not defying his father, but moving away from him. He was physically so much smaller, giving up the necessities of the body so that in the next scene he would be spiritually strong enough to hold up the whole Christian world. The structure of Christianity which was tumbling into corruption and disbelief, he was supporting with one hand, whilst the Pope lay dreaming in his alcove curtained off from the world. The Pope of that time, the most powerful man in Europe, who could excommunicate all his rival Heads of State, lay rigid as a stone effigy on his own tomb. The curtain of the alcove had been pulled back, and wound round a column, giving depth and third dimension to the scene. A pulled back curtain, a symbol of Revelation.

By the third day Peter had dozens of sketches. He was sitting cross-legged on the floor of the Basilica looking from the frescoed walls to his sketches and back again. Realism! Symbolism! Revelation! How much of this in the twentieth century could be used in art, be understood and accepted?

He had thought he had cleared his mind of doubts and prejudices when he came down off Mount Subasio but he was asking himself questions again. Was this search for Truth in his art really just for his art or was it part of his search for a religious Truth? And was searching for Religious Truth the same as Who am I? Why am I? Why is the world the way it is? Was going back to Spain to try to understand the Truth of what was happening in that war only the beginning of all these questions? Was the beginning of asking questions the beginning of growing up? How many people never tormented themselves in this way? How many others continued to ask the questions all their lives and never found the answers? He was talking aloud to himself. "Idiot. If in forty days you found no answers on Mount Subasio, how can you find the answers down here? Stop asking questions. Stop suffocating in the story of St. Francis too, wallowing in Saints and Madonnas and Crucifixes. Are you trying to become a Catholic convert? Are you aiming at taking the place of St. Francis?

Idiot! Stop looking at paint and stones that are seven hundred years old! Only twenty-seven grandfathers ago, my eye! Recognize what you can learn from the past and carry it forward and then, go on moving forward. You are a potential artist; none of the other potentials count. Your art has to concentrate all the symbolism, realism, truth, that is dispersed throughout time and space, like the sun breaking through the clouds, whose rays concentrate on one little patch of the valley like a Revelation. Sun through the clouds! Sun through a magnifying glass! Was that what the priest believed he was doing when he claimed he had captured Christ in that morsel of wafer? Fool! Talking to yourself! Going crazy! Get out into the fresh air! Go and try capture the spirit of Assisi!"

He went back to via Santa Rosa for lunch. Clair and her mother had got used to eating with him now. After lunch he had to be fitted for his trousers and measured for his sweater. He was impatient and he stayed no longer than he could help with the two women.

He was satiated with the Basilica. He had to get back to working out-of-doors, with life that was going on at present, not merely reproductions of the past.

He started a collection of sketches of faces of old people and children, of corners and angles and unexpected views. The streets were mostly cobbled and often running with muddy streams after rain. He got up before daylight and watched the cart come down Santa Rosa, stopping at the houses to collect the human manure from the pits in the basements. Some mornings he was in the Piazza when the market women came trundling in with their hand carts of vegetables and basketwork cages of live rabbits and chickens and pigeons. He did a whole series of donkeys

214

coming down from the hill villages and entering the city, and unloading their firewood and the women coming out of their houses in their aprons and collecting enough wood in their arms for a day or two's cooking only. And again . . .all to be repeated again and again. He was out in the Piazza on Sunday mornings when the women scuttled across on their way to Mass as though guilty of being seen out of doors, and the men stood around in their best suits, in groups, doing nothing except wait for lunch. Standing there in their good dark suits, like a lot of expectant crows, with black umbrellas up if it were raining, just waiting for the morning to pass, standing there in front of the old Pagan temple of Minerva, dominated by their past, not looking forward to any future beyond lunch. Only down in the streets near the Basilica of San Francesco there seemed to be a breath of life from the outside world, from the twentieth century, where the hotels were, and the little tourist shops and the tourists themselves, though there were not many at this time of year. Peppe's barber's shop was always bright and clean and cheerfully full of gossip. The men looking at themselves in the mirrors and smoothing their hair with their hands, rubbing the stubble on their faces, as they waited for the luxury of a shave or a cut, a shampoo and perfumed brilliantine.

Clair was no Savile Row tailor but the trousers she made for Peter fitted well enough. He felt restricted by their respectability. He would never dare sit on damp stone walls or go up Mount Subasio or use paints in them! The sweater took longer to do and in the end Clair took it over from her mother, to finish the front and the arms and sew all the pieces together.

When finally he put on both the sweater and the new trousers, the women walked round him, hitching at the waist line and the shoulders, turning back the cuffs. It was late afternoon already almost dark, great black clouds filling the sky though it was not actually raining.

"You should go down to the Piazza and see if anybody notices."

"No, no. I'd better change now before I get dirty. I'll have to buy a pair of decent shoes to go with this outfit. I should keep these clothes for Sundays."

"Now you're mocking."

"No, seriously."

"Just for once you could go down to the Piazza and sit without getting dirty like other men do."

To please them Peter left the house. He could go and collect Fausto and take him for a drink.

Fausto was not in his basement, nor in his house above. Peter continued on down to the end of Via Santa Rosa and turned into Via Capobove. As he came level with Gina's house he heard a whimpering animal sound and saw a small shadow in the doorway.

On the few occasions when Gina's husband was at home, other than at meal times, he could not stand the noise or even the movements of his own children. If he came home early it was because he was too physically exhausted to work any longer. He considered his wife too soft with the children and he had to bring discipline and authority into the house. He raised not only his heavy hand but also his foot and sometimes used his belt on Giovanni, the eldest boy. Peter knew all this from living with Anna. He went closer to the crouching figure at the door and it was not one of the little ones who had been turned out for being too boisterous, but Gina herself, whimpering.

"Gina?"

"Turn the light on on the stairs," she whispered. "If you help me into the house I'll be alright." She put her hand up to his hand and it was damp and sticky. "I knew you'd come. I prayed to the Madonna that you'd come."

He groped along the wall inside the street doorway and found the switch. There was blood where she had touched him.

"You've hurt yourself. What's happened?" He pulled her to her feet and there was a pool of blood, all her clothes had blood on them. She saw it herself.

"Oh Madonna mia, Madonna mia." She was limp and pale, her eyes closed.

"Where? Where's the wound? Where are you hurt?"

She opened her eyes. "No, no. The midwife didn't say it would be like this. She said it would be alright."

It was less than four months since her last baby was born. She couldn't have got pregnant again so soon. But she had. If he took her into the house she might bleed to death before he could get help. If he stood there she would die; perhaps she was dying now. He picked her up and ran down the steps of Capabove, across Via San Paolo, down past the church of Santo Stefano. He ran with her in his arms and only when he was near the hospital did he begin to meet people who tried to stop him and ask him what had happened and followed down the street behind him. There was a doctor about to leave the hospital and a male nurse appeared and a stretcher was brought. He lay Gina down on it and she opened her eyes.

"I'm sorry," she whispered. "I'm so sorry."

They took her away and Peter was left in the entrance to the hospital. His legs began to shake and he felt sick and faint. He sat down abruptly on a bench. A female relation of some other patient was sitting there already, looking at him. She went off down one of the corridors and came back with a glass of water for him.

"You ought to get those good clothes off straight away. If you wash blood out immediately in cold water it doesn't leave any mark at all."

Blood! Water! Pontius Pilot washed his hands symbolically to be free of the guilt of sending an innocent man to his death. Why did poor little Gina have to suffer like this? How could she be so sure he would come? He was asking himself questions again. How many more questions?

CHAPTER 25

Gina did not die and Anna managed to wash the blood out of Peter's clothes and on Sunday morning he went with Fausto to Peppe, the barber, to have his hair cut again and to be shaved. Then he wasted all the remainder of the morning in the Piazza, strolling from the fountain to the temple of Minerva and then to the post office, down to the piazza Santa Chiara and back to the fountain again. He spent all morning like a good self-conscious Italian cockerel, doing nothing. Anna thought he was becoming domesticated at last.

He knew there was something he should be doing instead of idling in the Piazza. There was something he had not seen; something he had postponed seeing in the summer and had forgotten about until now; it was in the back of his mind and he knew it must connect up with what he had been looking at in the Basilica of San Francesco. He had to go to Sansepolcro to study Piero della Francesco's Resurrection of Christ. The respectable trousers and sweater meant that he could once again travel by public transport without drawing attention to himself and the next day he was off.

Sansepolcro, named after the Holy Sepulchre of Jerusalem was only a little valley town, nothing like as old as Assisi or Perugia or Florence or many others. The civic building was not very impressive. But when Peter was in that room with Piero's fresco of the Resurrection he knew why he had had to come to see it. The painting was smaller than he had expected, confined to a flat wall surface, yet it had the magnetism of Mount Subasio, was as powerful in composition as Michelangelo's statue of Moses.

There were no 'Ifs' or 'Perhaps' or 'Buts' here. Piero's Christ had conquered death. Piero had not only believed that himself but everybody who saw his Resurrection had got to believe it too. It was not enough here to interpret belief in simplicity of colour and line and a guess at perspective. This was almost two hundred years after the painting in the Basilica of Assisi. So much had been learnt about art since then and Piero had employed all the intellectual, mathematical calculation of the Renaissance to convert his day-dream image into a visible Reality. Future artists might learn to do as well as this but nobody could ever be more convincing.

Peter copied and copied but he could not get it right. Christ with his left foot on the edge of the tomb was like a gladiator dominating a dead opponent; his left hand rested on his left knee, his right hand held a staff with a Crusader's flag on it, erect, as though it were a spear; the background was a desolate countryside like Civil War Spain; like Winter. In the foreground, at the base of the tomb, the soldiers who should have been guarding him were asleep. Where was the calculation, the lines that drew into the focal point of magnetism?—In the foot on the tomb? In the hand resting on the knee? The hand firm but not tense, drawing in the folds of his cloak that was a warm pink, the colour of life against the dark brownblack of the dead landscape? Or was the focus in the eyes, looking straight ahead, beyond the past and the present and beyond the future also?

Peter could not get it right. Just copying, that day and the next, he dropped sheet after sheet of paper on the floor. Only imprinted on his eyes, when he closed them, was the image perfect.

The Contessa had books on art criticism. Old Tagliatelle had said she knew all the people who might be able to help him. Surely she could find someone, persuade somebody to teach him how Piero had succeeded? Peter went from Sansepolcro to Perugia. He climbed all those crumbling stone stairs to her apartment and rang and knocked but nobody answered the door.

In the apartment below a woman heard him and called up to him. "The Contessa died. Didn't you know? The Signorina Battista's gone away. She didn't say when she'd be back. She's left everything locked up, just as it was."

Locked up! The Contessa's ancestral portraits in the corridor, her books on the floor, on the wall behind her bed his Spanish peasant girl and infant that she'd called a Madonna and child. And now Piero's Resurrection was locked away too, to be seen only when his eyes were closed. There was no sense in going back to Sansepolcro again. He needed to return up Mount Subasio to the silence and the open spaces. But when he arrived in Assisi and went to the house in Via Santa Rosa to change into his old clothes he allowed himself to be trapped by the women.

Anna began immediately with her Mamma mia-ing and "Why didn't you say you were going to be away more than one day? I prepared food and waited up late into the night and nearly called the Carabinieri because I thought something terrible must have happened to you." Peter looked at Clair while Anna was scolding and Clair half lifted her head and almost smiled as though she were glad

221

that he had returned home again. For a fraction of a second their eyes met and then she blushed and left the kitchen.

That evening he did not change out of his good clothes. After supper he remained in the kitchen with Anna and Clair. Fausto came up and they sat by the fire looking at all the sketches he had done of Assisi and the Basilica and Fausto kept saying how different, how much better he was than any other artist he had ever seen and he had really captured the spirit of the city. But Peter knew how much he still had to learn and he would have thrown them all on the fire if Clair had not collected them together and hidden them away in the boxroom.

Gina was still in hospital and her female relations had to take it in turns to sit by her bedside day and night and clean her house and feed her husband and children and wash their clothes. Clair and Fausto sometimes took all the children, except the baby, up to the castle to play and Peter went with them carrying Roberto on his shoulders. They sat under the wall of the castle, sheltered from the wind, and the children wanted Peter to draw their portraits and then tell them stories and illustrate what he was telling them and they climbed all over him whilst he did so.

He sketched Clair several times before he started on the miniature he had promised. To begin with her eyes were lowered; the lashes like medieval curtains still not ready to reveal her character. In the end he painted her, not the way Paolo had seen her, as the perfect Madonna, nor as the nun of his own first impression of her, but as a novice who had not yet taken her final vows, who probably never would, because she had just begun to understand that the world was not so frightening after all. It was true. In real life she was no longer so timid. She held her head up more often, laughed when they were with the children. One day when she thought she was alone he heard her singing.

In Clair's presence he was calmer himself. He too laughed when they were with the children together. Even.Anna's fussing did not bother him so much. He slept in a warm bed every night and came in to meals on time. He had never been so domesticated in his life before. For a little while it did not seem to matter that he did not already know everything there was to know about art. There were so many other questions that he had been asking himself that had, as yet, no answers.

He went with Fausto into his basement and looked again at that old tree root and now he could see Francis in the wood. But not in the way Fausto had. He turned the whole piece upside down, and then he began carving his first sculpture. The statue was to be for Clair. There had never been any doubt about that. Fausto had promised it ages ago.

The Francis that emerged was gentle, smiling, stooping slightly with his hands held out in front of him. The hands were a little too far advanced, too tense to harmonize with the rest of the figure. Only Peter saw these defects. Old Tagliatelle and the Contessa would have known how much he still had to learn. But everyone in Assisi who came to admire it thought it was beautiful and that Peter was a true artist.

Instead of just sitting up by the castle with the children he and Clair and Fausto began taking them for slow, rambling walks, all of them looking for likely pieces of wood that he could carve. On a special request from Anna he went down into the valley to paint the whole panorama of Assisi from the spot where St. Francis had blessed the city for the last time. That evening he propped a small mirror on a chair on the opposite side of the kitchen table and Anna and Clair watched, laughing, as he superimposed his own profile portrait on that panorama, twisting his head, rolling his eyes, contorting his body to see himself sideview in the mirror.

For a little while Assisi's present, which was really the past, seemed a stretching of time that need take no account of the future. Then, one night, when it was raining in the valley, it snowed on Subasio and on the mountains on the far side of the valley. Then for three days, there was frost and not a cloud in the sky and the clarity of the air made distances of over fifty kilometers seem a twenty minute walk. The sunsets burned redder than ever before, for half an hour and then they were extinguished. Darkness. Followed by moonlight as bright as day. It was much colder, autumn had passed into real winter now. Peter remembered that the changing seasons were only part of the movement of time and beyond the horizon lay the twentieth century. Having a drink in the bar in the Piazza with Fausto he half heard a radio news broadcast; only half heard. He had received no letters since coming down off Mount Subasio. There had seemed no point in going to the post office every day but now his next monthly money allowance was due and when he asked for it he found there were two letters from his mother that had arrived before he went to Sansepolcro.

The first must have been written long before the second. It began "My dearest boy, I expect my letters are taking a long time to reach you. I am having to send them by ship to England to be posted from there. All we have had is that address from Aunt Sarah. We so much want to know briefly what you are doing. The last time I wrote I was so happy to know where you were and that you were safe that I forgot to tell you about Miguel. If only we had known that he and his poor mother were not certain of his father's death. Your father recognized the body the day he went to identify Fernandez. He had been shot in the back in the same way, perhaps betrayed by his mistress because Miguel himself was nearly taken when he went to visit her. He was brought to us in a terrible state and we pretended he was really our son. Your father smuggled him onto a British destroyer wearing some of Michael's left-behind clothes with the school name tapes still sewn in them. He had your passport and promised he would post it to you. I sent him your address the moment I knew it. Has it arrived yet? We were horrified when we heard how you had flown to Spain together when we thought you were still in Oxford. We cannot imagine how you got to Italy without a passport. How much you will have to tell us when we are together again! As soon as you get your passport and can travel freely, please, dear boy, I beg of you, return to England. What about your degree?"

The second letter must have been written immediately after they had received the only one he had sent to them. "Dearest boy, you must forgive your father and me if we think your staying in Italy to paint seems rather selfish and frivolous. We accept that you have abandoned your studies for the moment. We do understand that you are different from your brothers and we can't expect you to settle down just yet, but you know, Michael is not leading such a conventional life either, nor are we, for that matter. Couldn't you help us? Come back and join Michael in his fund raising? He is still doing a marvellous job but this war has been going on too long and there seems no end to it and the misery it's causing. People in England are not as generous as they used to be and our needs are greater than ever. Sometimes we only have supplies for two or three days. So far we have not had to turn anybody away but there is always the fear that we shall be unable to carry on. If only you could see these poor, patient, uncomplaining people."

The next day there was a letter addressed to Anna and Clair from Paolo. He had arranged for them to go down to Rome the following weekend. The atmosphere in the house in Via Santa Rosa changed. Anna, who had forgotten about her blood pressure and about feeling ill now became flustered with all the preparations that had to be made for the journey and she was furious with Clair because she looked pale and miserable and would not make a good impression.

Peter paid for a taxi and went with them to the station in the valley. He was wearing his best clothes. He helped Anna up the high step and into the train, giving her great bulk a little push from behind. Helping Clair, for a moment he held her hand and she was trembling. Her eyes looked frightened and he wanted to lift her out of the train again but the guard came along slamming the doors. He waved to them as the train moved off and then he returned to the house in Santa Rosa and found it cold and empty without the women.

CHAPTER 26

He dreamed that night of Spain for the first time since he had left. There were bomber aeroplanes flying over Barcelona and the sound of gunfire and his mother was standing in the middle of a deserted street waving an enormous soup ladle at the sky.A soup ladle that grew bigger and bigger. A child with the face of Clair crouched at her feet and his mother went on defying all the forces of evil with her soup ladle.

"It is milk and biscuits and rice and sometimes a piece of soap to wash with but never soup. Can't you even get that right?" he shouted.

His mother shouted back. "Forget the soap and remember the Resurrection. You've not got your perspective yet. You think you're an artist when all you've done is one deformed little image of St. Francis. You've got to see sculpture from all sides; it is all the feeding breasts and the farting buttocks of humanity."

He woke and did not know where he was. Then he remembered. He was alone in the house, and Anna and Clair had gone to Rome. It was dark and there was silence. He turned on the light. His watch had stopped.

His mother's image remained: her soup ladle still raised; her voice, she would never have mentioned the farting buttocks of humanity; it was far too vulgar; the men of Assisi perhaps, but never his mother.

He jumped out of bed. Four tight walls like a box! Himself packed into it beneath the counterpane! His new trousers and sweater placed carefully on the chair where he had folded them himself! This was what the women had done to him!

He found his old rags and the sandals tied with string that Anna had wanted to throw away and he had said he would keep as souvenirs. He went down the stairs to the street and remembered that he would surely get hungry. He returned up to the kitchen and took out the loaf of bread Anna had left for him in the kitchen drawer. Then he went down to the street again and pulled the door shut. There was no sound, nobody, not even a cat. There was only one direction to take, up the mountain.

In less than two hours he was above the tree line, sitting on his rock in his rags, tearing off hunks of bread, eating ravenously, waiting for the dawn.

He was facing the valley looking down towards Spoleto and up towards Assisi and Perugia. The sun had to rise behind the Apennines, behind his left shoulder. There was that pre-dawn clarity in the air, a thinness, and then the mountains, way out across the valley became visible, touched, just touched, by the rays, whilst he himself was still in semi-darkness.

He could get his distance now, his perspective. The sun was getting stronger. He stood up. In a moment he would turn and face it. The sun rose and he looked and looked at it until he was forced to close his eyes. And then, with his eyes shut, he saw—The Sun! And then a Crucifix superimposed on the Sun! And then, 'Oh my God' there was his mother's soup ladle! He opened his eyes and flung out his arms and laughed and laughed at his image!

He closed his eyes again and it was still there. The glory of the Sun, blinding, and the flat Cross and superimposed on the very centre where Christ's stomach should have been, his mother's three dimensional Soup Ladle. What a Symbol!

He had nothing to draw with. He searched furiously, urgently and found what he was looking for, a sharp stone. And then he strode out, until he reached a flat smooth stretch of grass and there he began cutting deeply, incising his image on the top of the mountain as prehistoric man incised his images, and then he filled in the lines with stones. When he had finished he stood back and looked at it. It was huge. It was so big you could see it from an aeroplane.

He was starving again and he went back to his throne of rocks and ate the last of his loaf of bread.

He sat quite still for half an hour, an hour. He had no idea for how long. He had lost all sense of time.

The air was cold beyond his finger tips, beyond his feet. The Sun seemed to be concentrating all its rays on him alone. His body relaxed.

He knew something was going to happen to him now. All those weeks of meditation had not been in vain. All the life that he had known physically, all that he had been taught, that he had seen and heard and tasted and felt and not always understood, all this was coming together now. He was going to have his moment of vision. This was the miracle he had been waiting for.

It happened. He was not asleep. He was not dreaming now.

He could see his body sitting there covered with his old rags. He was outside it. The body was limp as though it were itself a piece of discarded clothing. He moved away from it and began to feel himself dispersing far beyond his own little physical experience.

Down in the valley, the seasons were changing, Springs, Summers, Autumns, Winters, with seeds germinating beneath the soil and sprouting and fruit maturing and falling and out in the fields and on the hillsides and in the houses children were growing, strong young men and women aging, the old dying. There were army movements in the valley, burning and destruction, rebuilding. Then sowing and burning and destruction again. Beyond the valley, beyond the horizon, all this was going on too. The rhythms of history were as constant as the changing seasons, like the tides of the sea. All history had a geographical pattern and cycles in time. As the sun and the moon controlled periods of blooming and periods of hibernation, high tides and low tides, so the patterns and cycles of history, the destiny of the world, were part of the rhythm of the universe. Droughts and famines and earthquakes, human ambitions and creeds, which seemed to be causes, were really only external, superficial signs of the great population movements that were bound to take place. When the forces beyond the earth's surface pulled, when the unrest began the tide had to flow, sometimes in shallow gentle movement, sometimes in overwhelming waves.

Wise men had always known this, that the destiny of the world was part of something far greater, that included sun and moon and stars, and the destiny of each individual was a part of the world's.

Peter was not seeing the past. He was part of it; and of the present as it happened; and of the future, too, dispersed beyond all limitations of period or place. Then came the narrowing again and he was coming in closer, closer, aware of his parents in their last days in Spain and himself back in England and he was approaching Mount Subasio again, looking down on that symbol he had carved on the mountain top, down on his own limp discarded body. He could feel himself returning to that body, pressing down into the feet, stretching out into the fingers, sensation in the corners of his eyes and around his mouth and in the hair at the back of his neck. He could feel the rhythm of his heart beat repeated in all the pulses of his body, in his ankles, behind his knees, at his wrists and elbows, at his throat and temples. He could feel the rhythm of his own breathing.

The sky was heavy with clouds. He had no idea what time of day it was or whereabouts behind those clouds the sun might be.

He stood up, all of himself complete, and shook himself, once again confined by his body to time and space. He faced towards the horizon across the valley and put his hands together, fingers and palms touching, and his elbows touching his sides. He could feel the force of his own magnetism rising up through his body, concentrating in his hands that were turning like those of a water diviner, moving from East to West. His arms began to lift away from his sides, to stretch out ahead of him, the palms began to open and the finger tips to come apart. As his arms spread wide, the clouds that had been in a direct line where his hands had been pointing, low down to the West, divided. The last rays of the evening sun were concentrated on that one little patch of the mountainside where he stood.

He alone had divided the clouds; he too could perform miracles; little ones. Fausto had not been so wrong about him. He too had the potential to become a prophet or be acclaimed a saint. But he knew, because he had seen the future, that this was just another of his potentials that would never be realized. He knew now that he was not even going to have the time to develop into a great artist. He knew that throughout human history there had been, were, and would be millions like himself whose potentials could never be fulfilled because their destinies were limited by the destiny of the world. So very, very few individuals were born at the right time, lived in the right space.

Peter collapsed on to his throne of rocks, exhausted, and did not know that there were tears pouring down his face.

It was completely dark. His body was shivering. He stood up and clapped his arms around himself and began to jump up and down but he seemed to have no internal energy left to keep his body warm and he continued to shiver.

He began to run and stumbling, falling, he continued to run across the top of the mountain until he came down round Armenzano and reached the cut away haystack near the cemetery. He pulled hay around himself and curled up beneath the overhang where it had been cut away and he slept and woke and slept, then slept and woke again until morning.

The rising sun gave off no heat. He was shivering, alternately hot and cold and muttering to himself, not knowing that he was doing so. He stood up and saw there was a white frost on the ground and so much swirling fog in the valleys that no landmarks were showing. He curled back into the hay and lay dozing, shivering, muttering. When he stood up again it was after midday and there was still no heat in the sun. The fog had settled into heavy artificial lakes in the valleys now, stirring only very slightly, occasionally rising to spill over one of the lower ridges as though a dam had temporarily opened. The air above the fog was clear and the range of the Apennines that could be seen from this side of Subasio was closer than ever before, sharp and white with snow. Mountain peaks were standing out clear above fog-filled valleys.

He had eaten nothing since the last of that loaf of bread that Anna had left him but he was not hungry any more. He staggered back to the top of Subasio. His image as he had incised it was still there. He knew now why he had made the Sun, the Cross and the Soup Ladle, large enough to be seen from an aeroplane, the white stones filling in the lines like the markings for a landing strip, to be seen from the sky.

The valley on the side of Assisi was fog filled too. Just the very tip of the dome of the Basilica of Santa Maria degli Angeli protruded. But as he watched, the dome was covered and the fog rose and took Assisi like an enemy and continued to rise until only the tip of the bell tower of Santa Chiara and the green dome of the Cathedral and the top of the People's Tower stood out; then they too disappeared and all that was left was the castle. The fog continued to rise and took the outer wall of the castle and seemed repulsed, flowing back outside and down the hill and then returned and this time got in and stayed and rose and covered everything.

There were no haystacks on this side of Subasio. Peter went down to the tree line, in amongst the firs. He scooped himself a hole in the ground and covered himself with twigs and pine needles and fallen leaves like primitive man, like an animal. He lay there shivering with his teeth chattering, hot and cold, muttering to himself, delirious, sometimes shouting aloud. Up there, there was no-one to hear him. Before sunrise on the third day he could see himself stumbling, zig-zagging, falling down towards the valley. Even while he was still there amongst the pine trees, he could see himself reaching the street door of the house in Via Santa Rosa.

CHAPTER 27

Anna and Clair returned from Rome. Anna talked to everybody in the compartment of the train and was happy to have an audience because Clair was silent and no company at all. She did not seem to have been impressed by anything she had seen.

It was already late when the train arrived at the station of Santa Maria degli Angeli and there was nobody she knew particularly well and there was not much time on the bus that took them up to Assisi. It did not matter, Peter would be in the house and she would tell him everything. The next day it would take her hours to do the shopping because everybody would want to know about the visit to Rome. What an experience!

The door at the top of the stairs was locked. The house was cold.

"It would have been nice if he had lit the fire for us," Anna said. "But there, why should he have thought of doing so? We'll have some soup. We shouldn't be hungry at all after all that food! Just fancy your Paolo taking us to that good restaurant. But I'm hungry, really hungry! Maybe it would be quicker to do some eggs! Oh Madonna mia, we've no bread! Don't just stand there! Run down to Fausto's mother and ask her to give us a little piece whilst I get my good clothes off and light the fire. I just hope our Signor Peter has had something to eat already this evening.

One shouldn't go away and leave the house like this, no fire and no food."

The door to Peter's room was open, the bedclothes thrown back, his clothes still folded on the chair.

"Madonna mia, the moment we've left him he goes off in his old rags again. We shouldn't have left him."

When Anna had changed into her house clothes and put on her slippers she lit the fire and then went and made Peter's bed. "He can't have gone to a restaurant in his rags. He'll be back and wanting supper." She was talking aloud to herself. Clair was still out at Fausto's.

Fausto had not seen Peter since they had left. Nobody in Assisi had seen him; he had disappeared.

Fausto's mother was a different shape from Clair's, she was very broad in the hips and thin in the shoulders. She tapered up to a tiny head with a scraggy bun on top. She had her ailments too that she was always talking about. Her collapsed uterus was the worst. She made Clair wait whilst she put extra rice into the broth she was making for Fausto and herself, so that Clair could take a plateful back to Anna.

"It's getting worse and the doctor says . . ."

"What was Rome like, then?" Fausto sat crouched half inside the fireplace.

"Imagine having to end your days like me and all your inards falling down between your legs . . ."

"What was Rome like, then?" Fausto repeated.

"Walking around doing the shopping and the cleaning and the doctor says . . ."

"Don't listen to her. Come closer to the fire. Tell me about the new home."

"Having too many children, that's what the doctor said."

"Shut up. You and your old inards all the time."

"She's going to get married, isn't she? She ought to know what happens to a woman's body after she gets married ... And all of them dying except this lame creature here."

"Don't listen to her. Come and get warm. Did you like Rome? You've been and I haven't. You're going to live there."

Clair was shivering. She went and crouched in the fireplace beside Fausto. "It was so big."

"Of course. And the people?"

"There were so many."

"And what about where you're going to live?"

"There's his sister there. She didn't approve of me, or Mamma. She was old and thin and never smiled. She hated us."

"You mean she wasn't friendly like Assisi people? She doesn't know you yet! Assisi people have all grown up together; they've always known each other."

Clair shook her head.

"And Paolo, was he as ardent as ever?"

Clair blushed and shivered.

Fausto took her hand and pulled her closer to the fire. "What's the matter?' he said.

Clair did not answer.

"A girl has to get married. I can't look after you. You haven't got a father. Do you want me to give you some more doves as a Christmas present? To sit on the shoulders, on the hands, of that statue of St. Francis that Peter carved for you?"

237

"I couldn't take the doves to Rome with me. There's no place for the statue there."

"You'll come back often, won't you? When you leave, your mother will look after the doves. You can see them when you come back to visit us."

Fausto's mother said, "Are you going to take this broth to Anna then before it gets cold? There's enough for both of you. Hot broth's what you need after a train journey."

"How do you know what's needed after a train journey?" Fausto said. "You've never been in a train! You've never even seen a train!"

"Yes, I've seen a train. From Piazza Santa Chiara you can see the train. My eyes are still good, it's only my inards . . ."

Clair took the soup and carried it carefully up the stairs to her own kitchen. Anna divided it between three plates. There was only a little each as they left some for Peter. He did not return and they finished it off themselves before they went to bed.

Clair lay awake. If she moved closer to her mother, the heat of her body would warm her, but any physical contact was horrible. She trembled and could not sleep, remembering the awful spinster in Rome and Paolo who had touched her, surreptitiously, possessively, all the time, her fingers, shoulders, his leg beneath the table in the restaurant. The electric current of his touch made her sweat and blush. It was worse than his sister's icy stare. And the way he had kissed that miniature that she'd had to give him, that she had wanted to keep herself because Peter had painted it. Paolo's thin-lipped mouth had suddenly seemed bigger and fleshier than those of any of the boys who had tried to kiss her in Assisi. It covered the whole face! he had almost licked it; as though it tasted good; as though he were hungry. He had done it when they were alone for a moment in what was to be their bedroom, when his sister and her mother had gone ahead to see the front parlour. He had said he would keep it by his bed and kiss it every night. Then he had turned and tried to put his arms round her and she had struggled free.

Anna had not told the truth about the portrait. She had said it was done by some old man who had known Clair since she was a child.

Paolo and her mother had talked about the white dress she would have made for her wedding in the Basilica of San Francesco. He wanted to give it to her as a present. Her wedding present to him, he had whispered later, she would give him afterwards, when they were alone together.

He had been at the station to meet them in Rome. He took her arm the moment they got off the train. They had to go by tram and then by bus, way, way out, into the suburbs to the place where he lived. When they had gone back to the centre of Rome, he still held her arm all the time. He was so dominant, repulsive. He breathed into her ear. "After we're married I'll keep you in the house so you're always fresh and ready for me. You'll be like a carnation in a vase. When we go out together on Sunday afternoons I'll wear you in my buttonhole and then when we return to the house I'll put you back in the vase again." He did not laugh for it was not a joke. He would keep her prisoner. He would never let her return to Asissi, not even for a day. "I'll buy you a new dress for when we go out together," he had said. "I'll never take my old sister anywhere ever again once we're married. Look at her there with your mother. We should take them both down into the ruins of the Forum, to the Colosseum and abandon them there amongst the cats! That's where they both belong." He laughed. That was his idea of a joke.

Peter did not return in the night.

Anna spent all next morning shopping. Everybody had to be told about Rome, about the apartment where Clair was going to live. There were three bedrooms and a parlour and a kitchen and a bathroom with a toilet that flushed the water, like a house of a grand signore. Paolo's sister would be living with them so Clair would never feel alone and Paolo had said she, Anna, would be invited to stay in the spare room, "The children's room," he called it already, and when there were children it would be big enough for her to sleep there too. Clair's Paolo was already thinking like a real family man. He took them to St. Peter's and the piazza with the balcony where Mussolini usually appeared when he wanted to speak to the people. "Fancy, he'd seen Mussolini himself, heard him speak standing close up to that balcony." He was very impressed by Mussolini. People do not all realize what great things he is doing for the country. Coming from a little place like Assisi, being women, we could not understand, he said. "A real intellectual, our Paolo is, just to listen to him. No, we didn't see the Pope but somehow, well, we learnt so much about Mussolini. We took a tram and went to that street where the grand people go and we walked there amongst them, and then we went to the fountain, I can't remember its name but it is famous, and he gave Clair a coin to throw in like foreigners who want to be sure they'll return, he took us to lunch in a restaurant. You've no idea, all in such a short visit. We never stopped and he was so in love with Clair, you wouldn't believe it, very respectful always but you could see the way he looked at her."

Anna set three places for lunch and they waited until nearly two o'clock but Peter didn't come.

"Maybe he won't return at all," Clair said.

"Madonna mia, why should he go off without telling us? Not even Fausto?"

"He doesn't belong in Assisi."

"He's paid for another week still. Fausto thought he wanted to be here all winter."

"He didn't say so himself. Why should he stay?"

"He wouldn't go off, just when we need his money. Don't say that."

"He left his new trousers and sweater."

"So he'll have to come back. How far could he go without any decent clothes?"

After lunch Anna wanted Clair to write a joint letter to Paolo and his sister. Clair sat at the kitchen table waiting for her mother to dictate.

"You've been to school You ought to know. If only your poor father were alive."

"Peter would have helped us."

"He's Signor Peter to you, and he's not here, is he? That boy alone, with nobody to look after him. Well, he's not here, so write. 'Thank you from the heart,' how does that sound? 'Thank you from the heart for your great hospitality.' I don't know. You write it. I'm not educated. Then you must send a separate letter just to Paolo, very affectionate. Make him know you care. Now you've met his family . . ."

"His sister . . ."

"She's his family, you stupid girl! You've been to his home. It's all official now so you could use the word 'love'. If he lived in Assisi you'd be walking arm in arm every day like I did with your father. Your Paolo would be courting you as is natural."

Clair sat all afternoon with a pen in her hand like a child who refuses to do her homework and in the end Anna slapped her face and put her coat on and went off down to Signora Genevieve to get her help.

Peter had not returned when she got back to the house and now with the wedding to plan for, she needed his money more than ever before. All the way up through the town and climbing the stairs she could hardly breathe. Her blood pressure was going to kill her before ever she got her imbecile daughter married off and she could not . . . She stumbled into the kitchen and sat at the table sobbing, her head on her arms.

Clair made her camomile tea and she fell into bed and went to sleep almost immediately, snoring, with her mouth open.

Clair went into Peter's room. She took his trousers from the chair into the kitchen and ironed knife creases down the legs and then took them back to the front room and put them on the chair again. It was too cold to go out into the patio yard. The kitchen fire was nearly out. She went into the room where her mother was snoring and found her lying across the bed so that there was no room for Clair. She could not get in without pushing her mother's great bulk, waking her.

She went back into the front room. After all, she had always slept there since her father died, until Peter arrived. Now he had gone, there was no reason why she should not sleep there again. She took off her shoes. The sheets smelt of Peter. It was not a dirty smell, not a perfumed brilliantine slickness like Paolo, but . . . it was not even a smell. She did not undress or get right into bed. She lay beneath the top cover and pulled the pillow down into her arms.

It was almost daylight. She had left the bedroom door open and a noise woke her. The manure cart passing beneath the window? No. The key downstairs in the lock. Only one person had the key apart from her mother. Of course he would not have left without telling even Fausto. She put the pillow back and pulled the bedclothes straight and put on her shoes and smoothed her hair with her hands and went down the stairs and he still had not got the street door open.

She pulled it wide and there he stood swaying in front of her.

"Poverino! You poor thing! Oh, you poor thing!" She put his arm round her shoulders the way she had once seen little Gina with her great big husband when he came home drunk.

She helped him up the stairs and sat him at the kitchen table. She put fresh kindling wood on top of the warm ash in the fireplace and poured some of the best oil over it to make the flame jump alight.

"Dio mio! You poor dear! Oh my poor dear! Just because we went to Rome. If we hadn't gone and left you like that. What can I give you? Something hot. Camomile tea with lemon and sugar. You'd like that and then you go to bed."

She went into the front room and pulled the blanket off the bed and returned and wrapped it round his shoulders.

He whispered, "Thank you," in English and she did not understand.

She touched his forehead. "I'll have to call my mother. We'll have to call the doctor. You're burning and you're still trembling."

Peter shook his head. He mumbled; she could hardly hear him. "Anna, no, not Anna."

He sat there slouched in the chair at the table and Clair brought the cup of steaming camomile tea and blew on it as Gina did when she was giving something hot to her children. She put the cup into Peter's hands. "Drink, please drink." Her face was close to his and she looked at him with her eyes wide and anxious, and he was too befuddled with fever and tiredness to see her. She put one hand on his shoulder and with the other guided the cup to his mouth. He felt the camomile tea warm in his throat; he felt her touch, her voice, her presence, all without substance.

He was dirty and smelt of dead leaves and there were bits of fir twigs sticking in his hair. His broken sandals had not protected his feet at all. He had worn no socks and his feet were scratched and black between the toes. His trouser bottoms were sticking with damp mud to his ankles. She could not let him get in between her mother's best sheets like that.

There was always a cauldron of water hanging in the fireplace. It was warm enough. Clair got a tin bowl and knelt and washed Peter's feet and then realized she should have washed his face and hands first. She went out into the patio yard and threw the filthy contents of the bowl up into the bushes and then got more water. She combed through his hair with her wet fingers. He seemed unconscious or asleep and his eyes were closed.

"You must go to bed now." She shook his shoulder. "Do you hear? I'll have to call my mother to help me if you can't walk alone." She put his arm across her shoulder again and tried to pull him to his feet. She repeated louder, more urgently. "Come along, you must go to bed. Please, please."

Anna woke, heard Clair's voice, pulled her old housedress over her nightdress and put on her slippers and stumbled into the kitchen and began wailing her Madonna mias. "He's got the fever like your poor father and your poor father died. Why didn't he go to the hospital when he knew he had a fever? Who's going to pay the doctor and the funeral and all the rest of it? And if he's here ill in the house for months? Where's the Prete then?" And for a moment Clair thought she meant the flesh and blood Priest for the last rites but she meant the warming pan that everybody always called the priest. "It's on the floor by my bed. Go and get it." Anna scooped hot charred wood out of the fireplace into the long-handled bronze warming pan and took it into the front room and began rubbing it up and down between the sheets.

Peter sat still in the kitchen, slumped across the table. He heard Anna's voice but he did not know what she was saying.

The two women put their arms around him and put his arms across their shoulders and they stumbled down the corridor together.

"Not on my lace counterpane in those trousers!" Anna shrieked. They put him onto the upright chair but Clair had to hold him steady whilst Anna turned back the bedclothes. They took off his jacket between them and Anna wanted to send Clair out of the room whilst she took off his trousers but she could not manage alone. They left him his pants even though they were damp. Then they put one of Anna's voluminous white embroidered nightdresses on him. They had nothing else. Anna was puffing and blowing with exertion and trying to talk at the same time. "And his mother? Hasn't he got any family? All this responsibility! As if I hadn't got enough trial and tribulation already. He must be mad! Nobody sane would keep returning up that mountain, and in winter, and in rags. He must be mad! Oh Madonna mia, and to think we took him in and didn't know how mad he was!"

When they finally got Peter into bed, Anna sent Clair off to call Fausto.

CHAPTER 28

Fausto stayed in the room with Peter as long as he was delirious, wiping the sweat from his face, trying to understand what he was saying. Peter spoke sometimes in English, sometimes in Spanish, but when he was aware of Fausto sitting next to him, then he spoke Italian.

To begin with he wanted Fausto to help him to get dressed before it was too late. He kept repeating how little time there was left. He threw the bedclothes back and tried to get up and Fausto had to hold him down and call Anna and Clair to help him. Peter tried to rip the nightgown off and Fausto could not keep him decently covered. Anna sent Clair out of the room and chasing up the street to call the doctor while she herself threw her whole weight on top of Peter.

The doctor came and gave Peter an injection and after a while he quietened and lay still with his eyes wide open, whispering in English as though he were in a trance. Anna went back to the kitchen muttering. Fausto closed the door and pulled the chair close to the bed.

"Say it in Italian, please. Let me understand. I knew you were different the first day we met. I'll follow you anywhere, do anything for you."

Peter must have heard him because he began whispering in Italian. "No disciples. No words. No time for painting. So much shouting from pulpits and balconies and only on the mountain the silence of knowing."

"Tell me what happened up on Subasio. Please. Just to me."

"The Truth. I went up Subasio to search for the Truth and it happened."

"What happened? Tell me what happened?"

"You leave your body, like clothes on a rock. All the rest is you—All accumulated experience and Will, Conscience, Reason, Emotion, Destiny—all that is intangible is you."

"Explain, please explain! I don't understand."

"Only my Truth."

"Please."

"The Wise Men of the East knew and the Etruscans and Christ and St. Francis, and many many others who never spoke out. They knew their own destinies and they knew that destiny was a part of themselves. A limitation in time and space the body, and the body and destiny one with the soul until death. Only Christ's body was visibly prolonged beyond death— The Resurrection—His destiny—to prove to the living—the individual remains beyond time and space even as it becomes part of the whole. Piero's Resurrection—Piero knew—Piero della Francesca's Resurrection—the lines of magnetism, the pink cloak, the symbol—" Peter suddenly caught hold of Fausto's hand. "The lines of magnetism, that other dimension!"

"Sh! Sh! Don't start getting agitated, now. Sh!"

Peter's eyes closed, he quietened again. "Not one doctrine or dogma nor another. From the beginning to the end, all variations on a single theme. But the Resurrection, the lines of magnetism, that other dimension. I was there, I didn't just see."

Fausto leaned right over Peter. "Tell me. You must tell me."

"The historical context, the artistic frame, that Flight into Egypt. The great light house off the coast of Alexandria and every night that warning beam coming and going, coming and going, coming and going. He's only a child but his room is filled with light and darkness, light and darkness, light and darkness and the rhythm is part of himself. Alexandria full of skilled artisans like his father and merchants, soldiers, philosophers from all parts of the Roman Empire and beyond. And there's all the understanding and all the ignorance of the world there. And there's the library to study in with the collected knowledge of all mankind since man first learnt the art of writing. And beyond Egypt there are the high mountains of India and farther, farther East where man first learnt to know himself. And from the beginning he understood his limitation, in time to collect up and distil like an essence of perfume. His limitation in space was the framework of Hebrew prophecy. An Artist, the wisest of them all." Peter stopped whispering. He appeared to be sleeping at last. Fausto too dozed off, for how long he did not know. When he woke up, Peter was whispering in a more normal voice about the sun.

Fausto went to the window and looked out. "It's raining," he said.

"The Cross, you can see the Cross, can't you?" Peter muttered.

Fausto climbed onto the chair and took the crucifix down from the wall above the bed and put it in Peter's hands. He called Anna.

"Maybe we should get the priest. Maybe he wants to confess."

"You think he's dying?"

Peter suddenly started shouting. "Where's the soup ladle? Where's the soup ladle then?"

Anna and Fausto laughed with relief. "He must be hungry. He's not dying if he's hungry."

"And I've got some broth all ready. It only needs warming just a little." Together they tried to force it down Peter's throat.

Peter flung his arms out and the bowl of soup went flying across the room. "Not soup, milk and biscuits, can't you even get that right?" he shouted. He was sitting bolt upright, his eyes staring.

Anna went into the kitchen to get a cloth to wipe up the broth that was all over the floor, all down the wall.

"Sh! Calm, calm!" Fausto said. "She didn't know it was milk you wanted."

"And sometimes a little rice," Peter muttered.

"And rice too if you want. But you have to keep quiet. You must keep calm. Lie down now." Fausto pushed Peter and he fell back against the pillows. "Quiet! Calm now! Calm!" Fausto kept repeating.

"Anyone can calm the storm; that's only a little miracle," Peter whispered. "But feeding the five thousand, that was a lesson; and walking on the water; not changing the tides, no altering destiny but calming the violence."

Anna was back in the room. "What's he saying then? You'd think he'd apologise for all this mess he's made."

"He's talking in parables," Fausto said. "He's been talking in parables all the time."

Anna snorted. "It's more likely he's got the devil in him, behaving like that, and he was such a good, respectful boy. Maybe we should call the priest to exorcise the devil in him like that girl from Santa Maria last year, do you remember? The one they said swore and blasphemed every time she passed a church and every time she saw a monk or a nun. They took her up to the Cathedral, behind locked doors, it was. I don't know what they did to her but they said she was better after that. Maybe tomorrow we should call the priest and see what he says."

"Sh." Fausto said. "He's asleep."

Peter woke and muttered and slept again. They did not try to feed him when he was awake and by the evening the periods of sleeping were longer and on the following day the doctor came again and said the crisis was past and there was no reason why he should be violent or delirious any longer.

Fausto returned to his own house for the night and Anna and Clair went to bed leaving the doors of both bedrooms open. Anna was exhausted and slept immediately but Clair lay awake listening to Peter's movements. She dozed and then woke with a start.

He was crying, sobbing. It was not possible. She went into his room. On the window ledge there was a candle in a red glass container like the ones down in the cemetery. The glow was just enough to see by. There were tears on his cheeks. She wiped them away with her finger tips. He took her hand and kissed the palm. His eyes were open, and he smiled and then went back to sleep, still holding her hand. The chair was out of reach and she could not remove her hand without waking him. She knelt down beside the bed for a few seconds. An hour? She did not know. She was aching and shivering and her head was resting against his body and her hand was still held by him on his chest, where she could feel his heart beats.

"Let me go to bed, it's so cold," she whispered.

He did not hear and she tried to tug her hand free and at last he opened his eyes and released her. She remained on her knees for a moment longer and his arm came across her shoulders and then he started stroking her hair. She stopped his hand and then suddenly kissed it the way he had kissed hers and then realized what she had done and their eyes met. She jumped up and ran out of the room and slipped into the bed beside her mother who was snoring with her mouth open again.

Clair could feel her whole body flushed, her face burning. She whispered his name, 'Peter.' He could not have heard in the next room yet she was sure, aloud, or only in her mind, there was an answering, 'Clair.'

Fausto returned the next morning and Peter was quite rational and was able to drink the tea that Anna brought him. Clair remained in the kitchen all day. She had to catch up on her dressmaking, Anna said. She had a skirt to cut out and a pair of trousers to make and Agnes's old coat to cut down for Gina's eldest girl. Going to Rome and then Peter being ill had made her all behind. The moment she had any spare time, she had got to start hemming another pair of sheets and make the lace edging for the top one. Her trousseau was not finished and there were only a few months to her wedding. Time passed so quickly and her Paolo was so particular.

Anna kept Clair out of Peter's room all day but at night,when her mother was asleep, Clair crept in, only to stay a little while, only to whisper goodnight. She sat on the hard, upright chair and he told her to bring it a little closer and he took her hand and held it. There was no candle and it was completely dark. They were absolutely still and silent until Clair began shivering and then Peter whispered, "Go back to bed," and she obeyed him.

Everybody in Assisi knew about Peter's illness. When the news got round that he was getting better, Peppe came to offer to shave him. Salvatore looked in on his way back from work. Gina visited carrying the baby with Roberto clinging round her knees. Aunt Agnes made him a bitter concoction of boiled artichoke leaves and chicory that he was supposed to drink on an empty stomach the moment he woke up every morning. The little watchmaker brought his own radio to keep him company. Fuasto continued to be his day nurse, going back to his own house only for meals and to sleep, and each night Clair crept into his room to hold his hand in silence.

He was still very weak. The doctor said it was a miracle he had survived the double pneumonia. He would have to stay in bed for days and keep warm in the house for weeks.

Fausto was certain he had not only had a physical illness. He was like St. Francis must have been before he began preaching. "You know when the doctor said you were delirious I knew you were speaking in parables. Couldn't you explain, just to me?"

"What am I supposed to explain?"

"About no words and no time for painting and all that. No man has the right to sit on a mountain and meditate and see beyond the horizon and then not go down into the valley and tell what he knows."

"Fausto, believe me, nobody would listen to me."

"The people of Assisi would, if not in words then through your art; even children understand your drawings."

"I haven't got time even to become a great artist."

"You weren't so pessimistic before your illness. When you're completely better, you'll think differently."

Quite suddenly Peter laughed. "Oh forget all this seriousness! I am better! Can't you understand? I want to get up!"

Fausto shook his head. "The only thing I understand is what the doctor said. You're lucky to be alive after you've been so ill, and I'm to keep your clothes hidden until he comes back and says there's no longer any danger of you having a relapse. We can play cards if you like."

Peter's passport arrived at last as he knew it would. His allowance came too, enough to pay the doctor and for Anna to keep him for another month. Anna was happy and immediately went out to leave a message for the salesman who went from house to house, travelling from Assisi to Perugia and Spoleto and all the neighbouring towns and villages, with trousseau. He came that same evening.

Peter was out of bed for the first time, sitting by the fire in the kitchen,when the salesman arrived and opened up his suitcases and began taking out tableclothes, sheets, towels and embroidered underclothes.

"I don't need anything more," Clair said.

"Your Paolo thinks you haven't got enough."

"Well, he's exaggerating."

"We want to please him, don't we?" She held up a nightdress. "It's cut so low. I suppose it's the fashion. Clair, you could add a little more lace yourself. Isn't it beautiful?"

Clair had been smiling, even laughing out loud and singing during the past few days. Now she left the kitchen in silence.

"She knows we can't really afford any more. I could pay half straight away and half next month, couldn't I? And you must give me two more lengths of plain sheeting that we can put the edging on ourselves."

That night, sitting beside Peter in the dark, Clair whispered, "I can't marry him. I can't."

"I know. You'll have to tell your mother."

"She'll never understand. You haven't met him. I'd rather be a nun."

Peter lay very still and then he bent down and put his arm round her. He was still too physically weak to lift her onto the bed but she knew that was what he wanted and in a moment she was lying beside him, beneath the covers, with only the top sheet separating their two bodies. She lay within the circle of his arm and put her head down where her hand had been that first evening when she had crept into his room. Now she could both feel and hear his heart beats, steadier and stronger. Peter remembered his mother's warning before he went to Oxford. "Out in the adult world, on your own, you may be tempted. I know when you were still at public school your father explained about growing up, becoming a man, all about that. But I hope you'll always bear in mind that a real gentleman respects all kinds of women. You must never get too fond of a girl you couldn't marry. Don't smile, it happens too often. I'm not talking about money. Look for a girl who could sit beside you at a formal dinner party, bring up your children, make a home to which you can invite your friends, be a companion in any situation. Beauty and attraction aren't everything. The wrong wife can ruin a man's career, his whole life." His mother had been living in the past, in another world that had nothing to do with his present in Assisi, with any future he had left. Her advice had applied to a world that had been destroyed the day the little Franciscan Madonna of the Palm had been burnt in Barcelona. That day even she had forgotten her British superiority, her puritan attitude to other people's religions, the difference between mistress and servant. That day had been the beginning of one enormous great wave of history that was moving upwards and forwards now. The deep mass from below was surging to overwhelm and throw down the fine spray that had previously ridden on the crest.

Clair crept up onto his bed and they lay together night after night during his convalescence. If Anna had come in and found them, she would never have believed that they were still both virginal, that they kept the top sheet between their bodies, that they only stroked each other's hair and faces and they dared not kiss each other on the lips.

Peter sat in the kitchen in the afternoons watching Clair as she did her sewing. He was still very pale and had a cough and it was too cold to go out. On Christmas Eve, the two women went to Midnight Mass and Peter waited for them to return and for Clair to creep into his room and snuggle up against him.

On New year's Eve, they would have gone to bed at their usual time but Peppe came to visit them with Maria and Maria's mother. They had bought a bottle of spumante, a sparkling wine like French champagne, and a cake. Fausto arrived with his two cousins from San Pietro who brought another bottle. Peter could not go out and celebrate so they had come to him.

Anna had never had so many people in her kitchen. There were not enough chairs. Peppe went down Via Capobove to borrow from Salvatore and Salvatore returned with him bringing Gina for her first evening outing since she had started having children. The men drank wine and played cards and Maria's mother and Anna talked about their daughters' trousseau. At midnight the bottles of spumante were opened and they drank to the two brides. 1939 was going to be a great year. Clair had tears in her eyes. Because her Paolo was absent? Because next New Year's Eve she would not be in Assisi? Only Fausto saw the way she kept looking at Peter and suddenly understood.

"Happy New Year." They kissed each other on both cheeks. Everybody except Peter and Clair; they just looked at each other and smiled and Anna was pleased. The other men in the room were relations or old enough to be her father. It might not have been quite proper if Peter had kissed Clair.

Only when the party was over and Anna asleep did they wish each other Happy New Year. This time Clair crept beneath the sheet. On purpose? By mistake? Peter helped her to do so.

"We shall have to get married," Peter whispered. "We should get married first." But it was too late for reasoning or conscience, or foretelling the future or remembering the past. There was only now. There was only touch, all the length of their bodies touching, kissing, caressing, a flooding warmth, nothing to be frightened of at all, it was all so natural. And Peter understood how Love could stride upon the mountains overhead and hide his face amid a crowd of stars. Much later when both of them were lying awake, their arms about each other, silently waiting for the dawn, he understood too what his mother had meant about that primitive creature needing two backbones to protect the soft, vulnerable inner parts of the body against a hostile world.

CHAPTER 29

It was a romance, a scandal, and all Assisi was talking about it.

"A special dispensation from the Bishop."

"Because he wasn't a Catholic."

"Because he was a foreigner."

"Because they couldn't wait."

"She must have been pregnant."

"And Fausto and Gina thought he was a Saint."

"And Anna not seeing anything wrong in having him in the house."

"And that fiancè down in Rome."

"All that talk about a wedding in the Basilica of San Francesco."

"Up at the Hermitage, at that time of the morning too, so nobody would know."

"Fausto and Peppe were there."

"As witnesses, that's all, and a few monks."

"Anna didn't go."

"They're up in some cottage in Armenzano now."

"Who-ever'd go there for a honeymoon?"

"If they spend all day as well as all night in bed what difference does it make where they go?"

"Isn't he supposed to be ill still?"

"For work maybe, not for the other thing."

"What would you do if you were that Paolo?"

"Maybe they haven't told him yet."

"Someone will count the months. If she wasn't before, she will be by now."

"What else can you do in Armenzano in the winter?"

Anna got over the shock more quickly than anybody expected. She went around saying of course she'd known Clair was in love with Peter, but she had never thought it possible that he would ask her to marry him, him being such a gentleman. Just to think, so modest, almost by mistake he had told her about the car he had when he was at university. And just to think, he even knew how to fly an aeroplane. He dressed in those awful old clothes because he was a true artist and did not need to go around showing off how important he was like an Italian would. The money he gave her each month was only a little part of all he had in England. But it was not because he was rich. She was happy because Clair was happy and Peter was such a dear boy, just like a son. There was nobody in Assisi who could boast of a son-in-law like hers. She had never liked the idea of Clair going down to live in Rome and Paolo was nothing compared to Peter.

CHAPTER 30

Barcelona was taken by General Franco's troops whilst Peter was up in Armenzano. He did not know until he returned down to Assisi with Clair.

There was a cablegramme for him at the post office. "Don't worry. Safe in England. Will write. Mummy."

When the letter arrived a week later he read it through quickly. "Peter dear, you've no idea what those last few days were like . . . And they gave us only forty eight hours to get out . . . Refugees ourselves now . . . Michael came to meet us off the boat. He wanted us to stay with him but the house is not large enough and the children are so noisy. We're with Aunt Sarah now in Shropshire . . . so damp and so cold . . . they don't seem to notice and so good of them to take us in. It would be so lovely if you came back. With that little investment of mine which is all we have left, that your allowance has been coming off, we could rent a small place for a few months perhaps. Then with your help, your father could start again. He's hardly spoken since we left Spain. It is as though he'd spent all his courage, all his energy not only his money and instead of giving him a medal they threw him out."

Peter pushed the letter into his pocket. His parents did not know he had had pneumonia and nearly died. He had not told them about Clair. All his life he had had money when he needed it and now his allowance would have to stop. He was down in the valley, never going to walk freely on Mount Subasio again. Only having Clair made it tolerable. But his time to be with her was running out too.

He went to the Basilica of San Francesco and to the hotels and the little shops around San Pietro and asked if they would accept some of his paintings and sketches. He got the same answer from all of them. One or two maybe, if they were faithful copies of Cimabue's St. Francis or Giotto's Francis with the birds, perhaps Lorenzetti's Madonna of the Sunset, but nothing original, for heaven's sake. In the summer, if the tourists liked them, he might be asked to do more, but now in winter, nobody wanted to pay much for work that might never sell.

Peter began immediately, copying, just copying faithfully, trying to use no imagination at all. One of the monks stopped to watch him, to talk for a little while.

"Did you know they're going to take the stained glass windows down shortly?"

"For restoration? All this work is being done now in preparation for the celebrations of Francis being made Patron Saint of Italy?"

"That's what we are supposed to believe."

"What do you mean?"

"There are a lot of German Franciscans."

"You mean they know something's going to happen, even here? It's a warning? They know more than is in the newspapers, on the radio?"

"I didn't say that. Restoring the frescoes is a sign of hope, isn't it?"

"And removing the glass from the windows a precaution?"

"Francis was a peace-maker."

"More than seven hundred years ago."

"There's been nobody as great as him since, has there?"

"Nobody."

The fortress walls of Assisi could not keep out the twentieth century any longer. In the bars of the Piazza there were radios, Peppe had one in his barber's shop. The little watch repairer twiddled and twiddled the knobs on his until he picked up an English programme for Peter to listen to.

Madrid was taken in March and that was the end of the war in Spain. But then it was Czechoslovakia's turn; Prague was invaded and England promised to go to the aid of Poland should the same happen there. And Peter knew that not only would his conscience make him go home to help his parents, who had never needed him before and were now asking for his help, he knew also that the next war was not going to be like Spain. The next was going to be his war.

He put off telling Anna and Clair as long as he could. Clair was so quietly happy, smiling to herself. She was not afraid of anybody or anything any longer. She could walk across the Piazza slowly with her head high and not care who was watching her or gossiping about her. Anna had forgotten all about her trials and tribulations. Peter and Clair were so obviously in love and they did not exclude her. They put their arms around each other and around her as well. Whilst she prepared lunch they went out into the patio yard outside the kitchen and coo-ed at the doves that Fausto had given them as a wedding present. The doves sat on the head and shoulders, sometimes on the tense outstretched hands of the statue of Peter's St. Francis and cooed back at them. Peter taught them to come and pick grain, that he held lightly between his own lips, a great fluttering of white wings against his face.

In the evenings, Peter and Clair went hand in hand up to the castle to look at the stars. They said they had to say goodnight to the world.

Peter's mother wrote again. "We're still waiting to hear from you. Perhaps you didn't get my last letter but the bank must have informed you by now that we've had to stop your allowance. Please come back to England. I'm not asking for myself but your father needs you. You wouldn't recognize him, he's grown so old in such a short time."

Peter gave the usual amount of money to Anna at the end of the month and she did not know it came from the sale of his paintings and sketches. Clair suddenly realized and she knew Peter was going to have to leave Assisi.

In bed that night she whispered, "You have not told your father and mother about me yet, have you? Then why have they stopped your money?"

"My father's ill."

"And you have to go to him?"

"Only for a little while. You do understand, don't you? And I have to tell them about you. I could not write and tell them something so important. Do you want to come with me?"

"You'll only be away a little while?"

"I promise. I'll come back as soon as I possibly can."

" Assisi is the only place in the world I can live in. We can be so happy together here."

"I know. You need never leave Assisi if you don't want to. You know I belong here with you now."

CHAPTER 31

The Etruscans used to claim that destiny could be postponed. Three times Peter postponed his departure. He stayed on in Assisi until after Easter.

He walked in the Good Friday procession, like the other men who did not want to be recognized, with a cowl over his head, carrying a huge wooden cross, barefoot, acccompanying the tall black statue of the Madonna, her heart pierced with swords. They went first from the Cathedral at the top of the city down to the Basilica of San Francesco to collect the statue of Christ, laid on a bier, covered with a black veil.

The streets were in darkness, except for the flickering wick candles high on the walls of the houses, when they returned slowly up Via San Francesco, through the centre of town to the Cathedral again where the two statues belonged. To begin with there was complete silence except for the Dum-dum, dum-dum, dum-dum of the death drum at the head of the procession. And then at intervals a chanting of prayers.The whole population of the city came out to watch, to cross themselves as it passed and for many to follow in at the tail end like mourners at one of their own family funerals. There was the Bishop carrying the consecrated Host, civic authorities, religious fraternities, and nuns,monks and priests from all the different churches. There were little boys with the symbols of the Passion of Christ in their hands, a bunch of nails and a crown of thorns. Giovanni, Gina's eldest son was holding a little ladder, symbolic of the one that had been used to climb up and take Christ down from the Cross. And spaced out amongst all these others, in the centre of the procession, came the cowled, barefoot men, each carrying his individual cross.

"That one there must be Peter," one of the local boys whispered.

"Sh."

"He's so much taller and broader than any of the others."

"It must be him."

"Carrying Fausto's cross for him, he can't any more since his accident."

"Why should he carry somebody else's cross? Doesn't he need to do penance for himself?"

"Because he seduced Clair, you mean?"

"Because he's leaving her."

"Haven't you heard?"

"Tired of her already?"

"Anna says his father's ill."

"He's never talked about his family."

"Didn't know he had one."

"Perhaps he's doing penance for what he hasn't done."

"That's ridiculous."

"He could have been a new St. Francis, couldn't he?"

"That's what some people tried to make out."

"Then he shouldn't have loved Clair."

"He should have abandoned his parents like all Saints are supposed to."

"Don't exaggerate. He's an ordinary man."

"An artist."

"But not a preacher or a prophet."

"What did he waste all that time up on Mount Subasio for then?"

While Peter was carrying his cross in the Good Friday procession, Italian soldiers were invading Albania.

He sold the last of his paintings, bought his train ticket and gave the little money he had left to Anna. She cried and cried.

"I'll come back, I promise. I'll send you money regularly whilst I'm away. You don't have anything to worry about."

That evening he picked up a British broadcast on the radio and heard that for the first time in history compulsory military service was being introduced in England in peace time. He did not tell Clair.

Anna prepared food for his journey and then went to bed. Peter and Clair climbed up to the castle hand in hand to look at the stars for the last time together. They did not talk, they had never talked very much. Back in bed they lay awake all night in each other's arms, all the length of their bodies touching.

In the morning only Fausto and Clair went to the station at Santa Maria degli Angeli with Peter.

Peter kissed Clair. Still holding her, he put one hand on Fausto's shoulder. "Take care of her, Fausto. I'll be back. I promise, as soon as I can, I'll be back."

As the train left the station, Peter could see only Clair and then he could see her no longer, but Assisi and behind Assisi, Mount Subasio.

When he closed his eyes, he saw all three superimposed upon each other, Clair, Assisi, Mount Subasio.

CHAPTER 32

Peter had known the limitations of his own destiny but he had no foreknowledge of Clair's.

In June Paolo took his annual leave from the post office and went to Assisi with his wedding clothes in his suitcase.

He was recognized the moment he reached San Pietro, the news spread up into the town ahead of him. Peppe was told and he went to the entrance of his barber's shop and saw Paolo at the bottom of the street. He sent one of the boys who had been waiting for a hair cut racing up through the back alleys to Via Santa Rosa to warn Anna and Clair.

Paolo did not stop at Peppe's. Those inside watched him pass, his neat little figure, slicked dark hair, shiny black shoes treading fastidiously, as though to avoid puddles, though the street was dry.

"Why has he come back?"

"Didn't Clair tell him the truth?"

"She returned his presents."

"He's a Southerner. Don't tell me he has to save his honour."

"Don't be dramatic."

"He wasn't married to her."

"But she was promised to him."

"He wouldn't have waited so long."

Aunt Agnes from behind her curtain saw him pass up Via Capobove. She finished eating the cold green beans soused in oil that were on her kitchen table. She wiped the oil off her fingers on her apron, then wiped her mouth and her fingers again on the curtain and went out, following Paolo up the street.

He was standing in the angle of the house opposite Anna's where he had waited for Clair that first morning when he had accompanied her down to the shop. Aunt Agnes went close to him and said, "If you're hoping to see Clair, it's no good you waiting here. She's gone with her mother to visit an uncle who's dying in Perugia. They won't come back tonight, maybe not for a week if he lasts that long."

Paolo looked at her. He neither smiled nor said anything. He just stared and then walked away.

Back in Capobove, Aunt Agnes said, "He was strange. He behaved as though he didn't recognize me."

"Clair should have told him about Peter from the beginning."

"What beginning?"

"Before ever she and Anna went to Rome."

Paolo booked himself into the little pensione where he had stayed before and he was told Clair was visiting relations in some village in the valley. The next morning in the bar where he went to get a cup of coffee he heard that Clair had left Italy with her rich foreign husband and Anna had gone with them because Clair was expecting a baby.

He believed none of the stories. He went back up to Via Santa Rosa and the street door of Anna's house was open and he climbed to the top of the inner stairs and heard Anna's voice and Clair answering. He knocked and there was silence and he knocked again and stood there all morning but nobody opened the door.

He returned to his pensione in the afternoon. He had not slept the night before and he could not now. In the evening he went back to stand in the angle of the street opposite Clair's house. The street door was locked. Everybody knew he remained standing there all night.

At dawn Fausto crept around to the back of the house and slithered and fell down into the patio yard outside the kitchen and Anna, who had just got up, screamed because she thought it was Paolo.

She let Fausto in when she recognized him. "Send him away! Send him away! We can't stay prisoners here! Why won't he go away?"

"Perhaps Clair should go out and talk to him."

"She daren't. She's frightened of him. She wants to go up to Armenzano. How can she in her condition?"

Clair came out of the bedroom. She had looked through the shutters and seen Paolo still standing below in the street. "Peter said Mamma and I should go up to Armenzano if there was any danger in Assisi. He said we'd be safe up there."

"Peter meant you would be safe up there if there was a war because Assisi is too close to the valley. He couldn't have known Paolo would come back."

"Madonna Mia, isn't this like a war? Prisoners in our own home."

"He'll have to go and get something to eat. He'll have to sleep somewhere soon."

In the middle of the afternoon they escaped. Aunt Agnes and Gina and her eldest children kept guard on the street corners. At Piazza Nuova, Fausto was waiting with a donkey and cart.

Clair was happy up at Armenzano, in the same cottage, in the same bed that she had slept in with Peter. He had written to her every week since he had left. He sent her money. He knew she was expecting his child. She only had to be patient a little longer.

Paolo spent all his leave in Assisi and nobody would tell him where Clair was hiding. But a little at a time he learnt the truth about her marriage. How she had given her virginity to a man who had been living in the house with her even before she had come down to visit him in Rome. Clair, her mother, all Assisi had deceived him. The saints had betrayed him too. He lighted no candles at the tomb of St. Francis and never entered the Basilica at all, nor that of Santa Chiara. There was no sense in praying. When he returned to Rome, he told his sister and his colleagues in the post office that the wedding had been postponed because Clair's mother was ill. They did not believe him. He knew they did not and there was only one way to save his honour. He spent the next three months planning for the day when he should do so.

The people of Assisi soon had something far more important to think and talk about than Paolo. Even before he had left, the long awaited announcement was made. From the Altar of the Cathedral, the Bishop read the Pope's Edict. St. Francis was the Patron Saint of Italy. The celebrations for the anniversary of his death, October the fourth, were going to be more important than any there had ever been before.

Poland was invaded. Half Europe was at war, but in Assisi, Cardinals, Bishops, Civil Authorities and Pilgrims began to arrive a week ahead of time to commemorate Francis, the peace maker. Amongst all the visitors was

Paolo, but this time nobody noticed him or sent any warning up to Via Santa Rosa.

It was late afternoon, not yet dark and the street door of Anna's house was open and the door at the top of the stairs was not locked.

Anna had gone up to Piazza Nuova to visit her sister.

Clair was out in the patio yard. Her baby daughter, Francesca, was sleeping in the bedroom.

Paolo went into the kitchen. He could see Clair feeding her doves. There was more than a pair of them now. They had hatched out young that had just learnt to fly. They were at her feet and on her shoulders. One was perched on her forearm and she was lifting it towards her face to peck grain from her lips. She had her back to him. He did not want to see her face. He took the knife out of his pocket. It was the knife he had been sharpening since June.

Clair neither heard him nor saw him.

He stabbed and stabbed and her blood was on his hands, on his clothes, on those tense, pleading, outstretched hands of the statue of St. Francis. Red drops of it splashed on the wildly fluttering white wings of her doves.

CHAPTER 33

In June 1944, the Germans evacuated their hospital centre in Assisi and retreated up into the mountains beyond Perugia.

There was fighting in the valley. The little airfield of Sant'Egidio and the railway line were bombed and every tiny footbridge crossing the tributaries of the Tiber river was blown up. But Assisi up on the side of Mount Subasio was saved from destruction.

The night the airfield was bombed, the people of the city climbed to the castle to watch the fireworks display down below as though it had been specially laid on for them; as though it were a Saint's Day.

That night, Gina was having another baby and Salvatore took the older children up to the castle out of earshot of her screams. He carried little Francesca, Clair's daughter on his shoulders. Since Anna's death, they had taken her into the family as one of their own. The sound of the aeroplanes, the explosions and the flashes of brilliant light were thrilling and when they went back home there was Gina, exhausted but no longer suffering, cooing, maternal and happy and her husband had another mouth to feed.

Because of his large family, Salvatore had been released early from the army and his children had, in fact, been better fed during the war than ever they had been before. It was he who organized most of the Black Market.

Not all the people of Assisi had been as lucky as Salvatore and Gina. Peppe and several of the younger boys were missing, believed killed. Nothing had been heard of Franco for over three years.

Shortly after the bombing of the airport and the German's retreat, the allies moved into Assisi and made it their own hospital city.

Less than a week later, a little before dawn, a single aeroplane flew over the Basilica of San Francesco. It circled the city two or three times and then headed towards Mount Subasio. The aeroplane was damaged or the pilot lost or looking for a place to land. Salvatore was up at the mill getting a sack of flour, there was no bread to be had in Assisi. He heard the aeroplane and he stood with the sack on his back looking up at the sky. He saw the outline of it in the semi-darkness. It might be Peter. But there was no reason to believe it should be, except that Peter had promised to return.

Salvatore saw the flames coming from one of the engines and the whole plane became visible. Why did the pilot not turn down towards the valley? He would have a better chance. Why didn't he bail out? The aeroplane headed towards the mountain, losing height.

Fausto was up at the Hermitage to receive early Mass. The door of the little chapel was open and he heard the aeroplane and he knew the pilot was Peter.

The priest held up the Sacrament and began to whisper. "And this is my body which shall be given for you . . ." The plane flew directly over the Hermitage, low, too low. it would never reach the top of the mountain; the engine was not normal; there was a stuttering and a roaring. Fausto gave an incoherent shout and rushed out of the chapel without receiving the Body of Christ and one of the monks genuflexed quickly and followed him.

It was just beginning to get light. The nightingales were still singing and the perfume of the yellow broom all pervading.

Fausto stumbled and scrambled over the rocks up the short cut, sometimes on his hands and knees and the monk, with his brown robe hitched above his shins impeding his movement, had difficulty in keeping him in sight. He could not catch up until they got above the tree line and there Fausto stopped, panting and whimpering like an animal and then rushed on again.

Miraculously the plane had gained the necessary height to reach a level spot on the mountain but the flames had spread from the engine and along the wing and were enveloping the whole body. The plane seemed to hang, suspended only a few feet above the dry sunbrowned grass, and then the grass beneath it began to catch fire. The plane seemed to give a great lurch forward until it was directly over a pattern of white stones like the markings of a landing strip. There it hit the ground and exploded.

Fausto wanted to throw himself in and pull Peter out but the monk's hand held him back. No human being could have survived that explosion.

The flames were already dying down and the remains of the aeroplane only smouldering when Salvatore and a few men and boys from Assisi arrived and then four British soldiers in a jeep.

Holding a small hand fire extinguisher, one of the soldiers approached the wreckage and wrenched the cockpit door open and pulled out the charred body of the pilot. What there was of it. The clothes and the flesh and the bone had melted into each other and become indistinguishable one from the other, and the surface was a blackened crust of ash. Only the metal studs of the flying boots and the buttons and a buckle remained intact.

The monk made the sign of the Cross and said a prayer and then the soldiers put "It" into an army blanket and took it down to the valley.

The sun was high in the sky now and larks had taken over singing where the nightingales had left off, soaring up and up and up out of sight above the wreckage. In the heat of the sun the perfume of the yellow broom became stronger than the acrid smell of burning.

* * *

In the flattest part of the valley, from which the whole panorama of Assisi and Mount Subasio can be seen, near the little church of Rivotorto, beside the road leading to Santa Maria degli Angeli, there is an allied war cemetery.

The cemetery is all smooth lawns and little head stones laid out in symetrical straight lines. The stones are engraved with the names and ranks and ages of those who died in the June fighting of 1944. One or two have a Star of David incised above the name instead of a Cross. Those who were killed were mostly British, Australian, Indian. One stone bears a Cross but no name. In the register there is only a number, for the spot where the remains of an unknown British airman were buried.

Until shortly before he died, Fausto helped to mow the lawns and keep the graves tidy.

One day, years and years after the end of the war, a girl came looking for her father's burial place. She walked all around the cemetery and could not find it, unless it was that grave with no name. She went into the little chapel and opened the visitors' book. People had been from all over the world. The comments were:

"Beautifully kept."

"Thank you so much."

"What a lovely place."

And someone had written, "So many died the day I was born."